HARDCASTLE'S SECRET AGENT

Also by Graham Ison from Severn House

Brock and Poole series

BREACH OF PRIVILEGE
ALL QUIET ON ARRIVAL
LOST OR FOUND
GUNRUNNER
MAKE THEM PAY
RECKLESS ENDANGERMENT
EXIT STAGE LEFT
SUDDENLY AT HOME
DEADLOCK
NAKED FLAMES

The Hardcastle series

HARDCASTLE'S BURGLAR
HARDCASTLE'S MANDARIN
HARDCASTLE'S SOLDIERS
HARDCASTLE'S OBSESSION
HARDCASTLE'S FRUSTRATION
HARDCASTLE'S TRAITORS
HARDCASTLE'S QUARTET
HARDCASTLE'S RUNAWAY
HARDCASTLE'S QUANDARY

HARDCASTLE'S
SECRET AGENT

Graham Ison

SEVERN
HOUSE

First world edition published in Great Britain and the USA in 2021
by Severn House, an imprint of Canongate Books Ltd,
14 High Street, Edinburgh EH1 1TE.

Trade paperback edition first published in Great Britain and the USA in 2022
by Severn House, an imprint of Canongate Books Ltd.

severnhouse.com

British Library Cataloguing-in-Publication Data
A CIP catalogue record for this title is available from the British Library.

ISBN-13: 978-0-7278-5034-8 (cased)
ISBN-13: 978-1-78029-778-1 (trade paper)
ISBN-13: 978-1-4483-0516-2 (e-book)

All Severn House titles are printed on acid-free paper.

Typeset by Palimpsest Book Production Ltd.,
Falkirk, Stirlingshire, Scotland.
Printed and bound in Great Britain by
TJ Books Limited, Padstow, Cornwall.

Graham Ison

25th October 1933 – 29th December 2020

'Writing a book is easy; you simply take a dictionary and rearrange the words'

ONE

The man was tall and slender and dressed in an immaculate dinner jacket, with a white silk scarf draped casually around his neck. His black homburg hat was similar in style to that worn by Anthony Eden and which ultimately became known by his name. A pair of unlined black leather gloves completed the picture of a man bent upon some pleasurable activity.

But that was the impression he intended to give, the better to disguise his criminal intentions and the fact that he was an agent of the Third Reich and a fanatical follower of its Führer, Adolf Hitler. He had received the honour of being commiserated by Hitler in person at the 1936 Olympic Games in Berlin. Leading the field in the 110 metres hurdles, he had broken his ankle after landing awkwardly at the penultimate hurdle and was forced to retire. Although the Führer had sympathized, there was a steely look in his eye that implied he personally, and indeed the Fatherland, had been let down by such failure.

The agent's training at the *Spionageschule* – the spy school – had taught him self-control. Consequently, he stood beneath a tree on the pavement opposite the house in which he was interested, watching patiently and unmoving for twenty minutes, not daring even to light a cigarette. His training had also included three years as a waiter at a prestigious London hotel in the late 1920s, where he perfected his English to the point where even the vernacular came easily to him. All trace of his native German accent had disappeared.

At last, satisfied that no lights had been switched on in the house upon which he had maintained a watch, and that there had been no signs of movement, he crossed the road, walked boldly up the path to the front door and rang the bell. There was no reply. Glancing around, he spent several seconds ensuring that he was not challenged by an inquisitive neighbour, before skirting the house until he reached the kitchen window at the rear.

Now that he was out of sight of the road, he took a Swiss-made officer's knife from his pocket and, working silently, used one of the blades to slide the window catch aside. Moments later he was in the kitchen. He pulled up his scarf and knotted it so that only his eyes were showing. If he was surprised by the occupier of the house, he would not hesitate to use violence to escape, but he did not wish to be identified later if misfortune should befall him in the shape of the house-holder surviving long enough to make a dying declaration.

This German agent was a vicious and unscrupulous survivor, which was why he had a Luger pistol in a shoulder holster. His entire evening suit had been specially tailored in Germany with particular attention being paid to the jacket so that the bulge of the pistol was disguised. Cut in the English style, the label showed that it had been created by a Savile Row tailor who had ceased trading two years previously following the owner's death. This agent's spymas-ters were thorough servants of the Nazi state, although they were occasionally responsible for an oversight and were aware that such oversights led to a death penalty sanctioned by an unforgiving Führer.

Next, the agent checked the front door and satisfied himself that it was not deadlocked. Fortunately, it was secured by a standard night latch and he would be able to effect an escape that way should it become necessary.

He then began a methodical search of the house, starting on the upper floor. He went through every room, hunting for a possible hiding place for the secret documents he was seeking. Descending to the ground floor, he opened a bureau, each of the drawers in a sideboard, and carried out a thorough examination of the kitchen, opening containers, a tea caddy and any other receptacle that might contain what he was looking for.

After at least twenty-five minutes, he concluded that the documents were not anywhere to be found. But even he recog-nized that the British could be very cunning and might have recorded such information on microdots. In which case, even a skilled espionage agent would have to be lucky to find them. In order to mask the real reason for the burglary, he pocketed a few easily portable items, mainly jewellery, before leaving by the front door and walking down the garden path, brazenly shouting a farewell to the absentee occupants of the house he had just burgled.

He pulled down the scarf before he reached the road and, uttering a cheery 'Good night, Constable' to a patrolling policeman, he disappeared into the night.

It was Saturday the second of September 1939.

For the whole of 1938 there had been a great deal of speculation about the international situation, the consensus being that there was really nothing to worry about, even though Adolf Hitler had annexed Austria in March of that year. Setting to one side that act of naked aggression, the wiseacres suggested that, when the appalling carnage of the Great War was taken into account, the human cost of the battles of the Somme and Passchendaele still fresh in older people's minds, the United Kingdom would not be so foolish as to go to war again.

In September of that year, the prime minister, Neville Chamberlain, returned from his talks with the prime minister of France, Édouard Daladier, and the two dictators Adolf Hitler and Benito Mussolini.

On his arrival at 10 Downing Street, Chamberlain appeared at a window and waved a piece of paper, declaring to the waiting crowd that it represented 'Peace for our time'. The cost had been the acceptance of Germany seizing control of the Sudetenland. Hitler had long wanted that part of Czechoslovakia, claiming that the majority of its population was German.

There was to be no war after all. The citizens of Great Britain and Northern Ireland rested easily in their beds. Except for one man whose name was Winston Churchill. But in many quarters, he was dismissed as a sabre-rattling scaremonger or, at best, a frustrated lone voice in the political wilderness of the back benches of the House of Commons.

Nevertheless, doubts began to creep in following Chamberlain's 'triumphant' return, and the issue of gas masks

began. Local authorities, saddled with making arrangements
for civil defence, began a programme of constructing air-raid
shelters in parks and other public areas. And secret plans were
drawn up for the evacuation of primary-school children and
their mothers.

Six months later, in March 1939, Detective Inspector Walter
Hardcastle of the Flying Squad was seated in his office at New
Scotland Yard.

'Well, that's that, I suppose, Sid,' he said to his sergeant,
Sidney Cross.

'What's that, guv'nor? Someone we know been nicked?'

'There are other things going on in this world apart from
crime, Sid. No, I'm talking about Hitler.' Hardcastle jabbed a
finger at his copy of the *Daily Express* that was spread out on
his desk. 'Despite the so-called agreement about the
Sudetenland, that bloody man Hitler's walked in and grabbed
the rest of Czechoslovakia.'

'Oh, that,' said Cross lamely. Knowledge of international
politics was not one of Cross's strengths. However, to offset
that lack, his expertise lay in his instinctive ability to spot a
villain.

But, fortunately for Cross, he and Hardcastle were interrupted by one of the Flying Squad's detective constables
knocking on the detective inspector's door.

'I've just had a phone call from upstairs, guv. The DAC
wants to see you immediately.'

It took Hardcastle only a few minutes to walk to the office
of the Deputy Assistant Commissioner in charge of the whole
of the CID of the Metropolitan Police.

Charles Marriott had been in his post for just over a year,
but he and Walter Hardcastle knew each other from the days
during the Great War when Walter's father, Ernest, had been
the divisional detective inspector of the A or Whitehall
Division, and Marriott had been his sergeant. Since Marriott's
promotion to inspector in 1927, his rise up the ranks had been
little short of meteoric. Despite his age – he was now fifty-
seven – he retained his chiselled good looks and women always
gave him a second glance. But he was happily married to

Lorna, a strikingly tall blonde who, in return, was devoted to her husband.

Marriott shook hands with the younger Hardcastle. 'Take a pew, Wally. How's your father keeping these days?'

'Same as ever, sir. Cantankerous and always telling me how I should be doing the job.'

'He hasn't changed, then.' Marriott laughed. 'And your mother?'

'She's fine, too, sir.'

'Are they still living in Kennington Road in Lambeth?'

'They are. I keep telling the old man that there's going to be another war and that he and Ma should get out of London, but he reckons it's all propaganda designed to raise taxes, apart from which he doesn't trust Chamberlain. I've even suggested that he should find himself a nice little bungalow somewhere in the country. You can guess what sort of reply I got to that idea. He just won't listen.'

'I'm afraid your father was never easily persuaded, Wally. Incidentally, how long's he been retired now?'

Hardcastle paused. 'Nine years, sir. He went a year before his sixtieth birthday. To be frank, I think he believes he'll be recalled.'

'I don't see that happening, Wally. However, it's the war I want to talk to you about. By the way, where are you living?'

'Brockley, south-east London, sir.'

'Well, it looks as though you're going to have to move again. I'm transferring you from the Flying Squad to V Division as divisional detective inspector with immediate effect. Your promotion and transfer will be published in *Police Orders* tomorrow.'

'Thank you very much, sir, but what does that have to do with the war?' Hardcastle was delighted by this sudden promotion, one he had not expected for at least another two or three years.

'The consensus is that we'll be at war before the year's out, Wally,' said Marriott. 'Between you and me, the DDI on V is close to the age limit and there are problems arising on V that I'll talk about in a moment. I'm transferring him up here to the Yard to do a wartime office job dealing with casualty identification or some such thing.

'I need a good man at Putney in charge of V Division's CID. It's a big area, as you know, with eleven police stations stretching from Wandsworth all the way down to Cobham. One of the reasons I need someone like you in charge of the CID is that the Alan Moore and Company factory is on your ground. There is also a suggestion that the river might be used for some arcane operations connected with the war. Thames Division have certainly been put on alert.'

'Are you suggesting that V Division could be a particular target for air raids, sir?'

'Exactly so. Moore's other factory at Windsor, in the Berkshire Constabulary area, is experimenting with a new type of small submarine. That's all I've been told. The doom and gloom merchants are suggesting that if we go to war with Germany again, it'll be an all-out war and much worse than the last one. The point is that part of the planning and production of this craft, or components of it, will be manufactured at the company's Windsor factory. But keep that under your hat. In fact, everything I'm telling you is top secret.'

'But the security of that factory is down to this Alan Moore and Company, surely, sir. And, of course, the Uniform Branch.'

'It's not that you have to worry about it, Wally. But it does throw up a number of possibilities. First, enemy agents will be taking an interest, if they haven't started already.' Marriott held up his hand as Hardcastle was about to speak. 'I know what you're going to say, Wally, that it's Special Branch's job, but if this war comes about, it'll be a case of all hands to the pump.'

'Yes, I suppose so, sir.' Hardcastle thought it a gloomy prospect.

'And as if that is not enough, the Hawker aircraft factory is in Kingston and they're beginning a heavy programme of building Hawker Hurricane fighters. And on another matter, there is a strong possibility of looting. If there are air raids and houses and shops are destroyed, there are always enough light-fingered villains to keep us occupied, and you've got a substantial amount of residential property on V Division's patch. Again, it's mainly Uniform's job but, as I said just now, we'll all be in this together. Finally, there's talk of building a barracks in Richmond Park to provide for an overflow of recruits from the East Surrey Regiment's depot in King's Road, Kingston, or even the ATS. And I don't have to tell you how the arrival of a whole load of single young women can affect the crime rate in an area.'

'When d'you want me to start on V Division, sir?'

'As soon as you can. Incidentally, what's the journey like from Brockley to Putney?'

'I haven't tried it, but I have no reason to believe it's easy, sir.'

'I can arrange for you to have a police quarter if you—'

'No, thanks all the same, sir. We spent too long in one as it is and Muriel would not be at all happy going back to one.'

'I know.' Marriott laughed. 'It took me a fair time to buy my own place, but Lorna finally put her foot down and said that she was thoroughly fed up with living in Regency Street. But as a newly promoted inspector, my pay only just enabled us to make ends meet, and the first mortgage repayments nearly bankrupted us.'

'Quite by coincidence, we've been looking around the Kingston area, sir, and Muriel's spotted a place that might do for the five of us.'

'Yes, I know, Wally. I am a detective, too, and I know what all my officers are up to.' Marriott chuckled. 'But, joking aside, if you want any help, let me know. You'll need to have a telephone installed as quickly as possible. Understandably, telephone lines are in great demand at the moment, so give me a call when you've got a date for moving in and I'll pull a few strings.' Marriott glanced at his desk diary. 'How about Monday the twenty-first of March to start at Putney? If the balloon goes up, I might have to send you there earlier.'

'I'd rather start today anyway, sir.'

'I was hoping you'd say that.' Marriott stood up and shook hands with the new DDI. 'If you make as good a fist of doing a DDI's job as your father did, you'll be all right, Wally.' But secretly, Marriott rather hoped that the younger Hardcastle would be considerably more flexible than his father had been.

* * *

Although the Flying Squad had a roving commission, it was some time since Walter Hardcastle had set foot in Putney police station in the Upper Richmond Road, which had recently been established as the divisional headquarters of the V or Wandsworth Division.

'Yes, sir? Can I help you?' The station sergeant stopped writing in the Occurrence Book, a record of everything that happened on the Putney sub-division, and glanced up, mildly irritated at being interrupted.

'Where's the DDI's office, Sergeant?'

'I'm afraid we don't have a DDI, sir, if that's who you was hoping to see. He's been transferred. But why are you so interested in him? D'you want to report a crime?' It suddenly occurred to the station sergeant that he had not enquired as to the identity of this inquisitive caller, but his unasked question was answered immediately.

'Because *I'm* the new DDI. My name's Hardcastle.'

'Oh, I beg your pardon, sir,' said the station sergeant, hurriedly scrambling to his feet. 'I didn't know.'

'Understandable. It won't be in *Orders* until tomorrow.'

'Allow me to show you to your office, sir.' The station sergeant suddenly became very helpful. 'At the moment Mr Simmons is occupying it.'

'Just tell me where it is. I'll find it.'

'Top of the stairs, sir, and it's the door facing you. There's a sign on the door that says "DDI".'

'That's useful.' Hardcastle sprinted up the stairs and pushed open the door of his new office to see a familiar face. 'Hello, Bob. What are you doing here?'

'Blimey! Wally Hardcastle as I live and breathe. More to the point, what are *you* doing here, Wally? The Squad getting too much for you?'

'I've just been posted here as DDI.'

'My congratulations, *sir*,' said a laughing Simmons, and stood up to shake hands.

'Are you acting DDI, then, Bob?'

'Not really. I was just using this office to catch up on a report I'm writing. It's a bit quieter in here, but I'll get my stuff shifted.'

'Don't hurry. I've got to go back to the Yard and pick up my gear, so just give me a quick rundown on what's happening.'

Simmons summarized the state of crime on the division and said that Hardcastle's predecessor had been particularly concerned about a spate of burglaries in the Kingston area, and to a lesser degree in Surbiton.

'Was anything done about that, Bob? Extra patrols or particular attention paid by beat-duty men?'

'Between you and me,' said Simmons, 'I think the last DDI was a bit overwhelmed by all the extra stuff that had been put on the police in case there's a war.'

Hardcastle nodded. It was the same everywhere. Not a panic, but the complete opposite as the population was disinclined to believe it would ever happen. After all, they had Neville Chamberlain's assurance of 'peace for our time'.

'I'd better make that one of my priorities, Bob, but right now I must report my arrival to the superintendent. What's his name, by the way?'

'Geoffrey Swain. He's all right,' said Simmons. 'For a Uniform Branch man,' he added, with a smile.

TWO

It had taken Walter and Muriel Hardcastle nearly six months to find a suitable house, but on Monday morning, the twenty-eighth of August 1939, they were moving to a detached property in Canbury Park Road, Kingston. And it was raining. Despite the best efforts of Pickfords removal men, it was inevitable that the Hardcastles' furniture would get wet as it was brought into the house.

But Muriel Hardcastle was undeterred by such a minor problem. The move from Brockley in south-east London to the far more prestigious Royal Borough of Kingston upon Thames in Surrey was very much to her liking.

There were drawbacks, of course. The children, Edward, Kate and Douglas, would all have to leave their friends behind and be placed in new schools. But having a police officer for a father had accustomed the three of them to his irregular hours and upheavals, particularly during his years on the Flying Squad. For Muriel, in her fifteen years of marriage to Walter, it had become a way of life.

'Wally,' said Muriel, 'there's a little green van pulled up behind the Pickfords lorry. What's that, d'you think?'

'I'm hoping it'll be an engineer from the Post Office come to connect a telephone.'

Minutes later a man appeared at the open front door. 'Mr Hardcastle?'

'That's me.'

'I've come to connect you, sir.' The engineer held up one of the new black telephones, and then stepped aside to admit two removal men carrying a table.

'Are you going to do it now?' asked Hardcastle.

'I am, sir. Fortunately, there was a connection here previously, so it won't take long. Even so, guv'nor, I reckon you've got a bit of clout, getting one of these phones and getting connected so quickly. You're very lucky.'

'That's a matter of opinion,' said Hardcastle who, like his father before him, knew that from now on he could be 'got at' whenever one of his officers felt inclined to dial his number. Ernest Hardcastle was always opposed to having 'one of those wretched machines' in his house, although he was eventually persuaded by his wife Alice to have one installed.

After a brief discussion, Muriel and Walter decided that the telephone should be placed in the kitchen-cum-dining room at the rear of the house.

'Good. That's that,' said Hardcastle, rubbing his hands together as the telephone engineer left the house an hour or so later, followed by the removal men. 'What's next, darling?'

'A cup of tea,' she said. 'I'm parched.'

'How are the children taking the move, Muriel?' When they had first met, Walter had once shortened his future wife's name to 'Moo', but her sharp reaction was such that he never did so again.

'There was a bit of an argument about bedrooms, love. But I explained that Kate must have her own room, now that she was twelve, and Edward and Douglas would have to share.'

'Are the boys happy about that?'

'No,' said Muriel, laughing, 'but I explained to them that it was a maternal order and carried with the full force of law. Your law.' She turned her head at a sudden noise. 'What was that, Wally?'

'Surprisingly enough, it was someone knocking at the front door,' said Hardcastle. 'I'll get it.'

'Probably one of our new neighbours come to say hello.'

Hardcastle opened the door to be confronted by a policeman.

'DDI Hardcastle, sir?' asked the PC.

'Yeah. What is it?'

'I'm PC Suttling from Kingston, sir.' The policeman raised a hand from beneath his glazed cape and sketched a salute before struggling to produce a piece of paper from a pocket. 'A message for you from Commissioner's Office, sir. You're to report to the Chief Constable CID as a matter of urgency, sir.'

'Thank you,' said Hardcastle, and glanced over the

policeman's shoulder. 'I suppose you didn't come in a car?' he asked, looking in vain for a police vehicle.

'No, sir.' Suttling grinned. 'On a bicycle.'

'What's the quickest way to get to London from here, Suttling? I've only just moved in.' Although Hardcastle had familiarized himself with much of the sprawling V Division, he had not thought to work out the quickest way to get to London from his new house.

'London, sir? Now let me see.' Suttling ran a hand round his chin as he considered the question of getting to somewhere that, as far as he was concerned, might as well have been on the other side of the world. 'I suppose the train would be your best bet, sir. Go to Waterloo from here and then get the Underground to Westminster.'

'Where is the railway station, then?'

'You go straight down this road as far as Richmond Road, sir, go under the bridge on your left, and you'll see the station on your right-hand side.'

Hardcastle shut the door and returned to the dining room. 'That was a PC at the door, darling. I've got to go up to the Yard.'

'Oh no! But there's an awful lot to do here to get organized.'

'Sorry, darling, but that's the job for you.'

'You don't have to tell me, not after all this time. Your mother told me I was making a terrible mistake marrying a policeman,' said Muriel, but she was smiling as she said it. 'I hope to God they're not going to transfer you again.'

'I don't think there's any chance of that.' Hardcastle put on his raincoat and grabbed his trilby before kissing his wife. 'I'll be back as soon as I can, darling.'

'Why don't you telephone me and let me know what's happening,' said Muriel.

'Good idea. I'll write down the number because I'll never remember it. Not immediately, anyway.' Hardcastle walked to the front door and paused to shout up the stairs. 'Got to go to the Yard, kids. See you later. Mum needs a hand, so see what you can do for her.'

*   *   *

When Hardcastle reached the east end of the large Hawker factory, at the bottom of Canbury Park Road, he was confronted by a policeman manning a barrier.

'D'you have business down here, sir?'

'No, I'm on my way to the railway station.'

'I'm afraid you'll have to go round by way of Cromwell Road, sir. This road's closed to the general public.'

'My name's Hardcastle. I'm the DDI on this Division.'

'Oh, I see, sir,' said the PC as he examined Hardcastle's warrant card. 'I'm sorry, sir, I didn't recognize you.'

'What's this all about?' asked Hardcastle, pocketing his warrant card and waving at the barrier.

'New orders, sir, said to have come from the Air Ministry. Anyone who hasn't got business with the Hawker factory won't be allowed to come down this road any further than here. I don't know what these clever chaps in Whitehall think'll happen if we let them walk past it. Blow it up, perhaps. Mind you, they're quite happy to let the ice-cream barrow stay at the other end, and the bloke who owns it is an Italian. The rumour is that if we go to war, that clown Mussolini will join his mate Hitler.'

'The DAC is down the road at the War Office, Wally, and I'm acting for him,' said Chief Constable Henry Catto. Even at forty-eight years of age, there was still a trace of the dandy about Catto, for which Ernest Hardcastle blamed William Sullivan, the DDI of C Division where Catto had been a sergeant. Ernest Hardcastle detested Sullivan, who always wore a curly brimmed bowler hat and a monocle. Local villains called him 'Posh' Bill with the Piccadilly window, but it was now five years since Sullivan's death, and in a forgiving mood, Ernest Hardcastle had actually gone to his old adversary's funeral. 'Take a pew and I'll tell you what's worrying us.' He donned a pair of black-rimmed spectacles. 'Incidentally, how's your father these days?'

'Still telling me what to do, sir.' Hardcastle hoped that one day people would stop asking him about his father, but Mr Catto had been one of the officers under Ernest Hardcastle's command during the Great War and for a few years as a sergeant after the Armistice.

'Sounds familiar,' said Catto. 'I suppose your brother-in-law has got some high-powered job.' He paused. 'Sorry, I shouldn't have asked that.'

'It's not a secret, sir. He's got a post at the War Office at the moment, but now that he's a major general, he'll probably be given command of a division if war does break out.' Hardcastle's brother-in-law was Charles Spencer, a regular army officer, who had married Walter's sister Maud in 1919. In the latter months of the Great War, Spencer had been wounded in Flanders and Maud had nursed him back to health. It had been a fairytale romance and they had been married shortly after Charles had been discharged from hospital.

'I don't think there's any doubt about that, Wally. Now, the reason I sent for you concerns a number of burglaries on your patch. Mainly the Kingston area.'

'I know, sir.' Hardcastle felt like telling Catto that he had been told of this and its possible reasons by DAC Marriott. In any case, now that he was the DDI, he had very quickly familiarized himself with what was happening in his new bailiwick.

'Several of the senior management of the Alan Moore facility at Kingston have had their houses broken into, but oddly enough very little was taken and the thief or thieves have, in quite a few cases, left valuable stuff untouched.'

'I did know that, too, sir.'

'I imagine you did, Wally, but just hear me out. Special Branch are concerned that this is a concerted effort by German espionage agents searching for vital information about the new project that the Moore factory is working on. Personally, I think it unlikely that people working on such a project would take important paperwork or plans home. And even if they did, I doubt that they'd leave them lying about.'

'But that's a Special Branch job, surely, sir.'

'As far as SB is concerned, it's straightforward crime at the moment, but with the underlying suspicion of spying. If your people can catch the burglar or burglars, Special Branch will take it over from there.'

'Typical,' said Hardcastle. 'My old man warned me about

that lot. Once the dirty work's been done, they step in and grab all the glory.'

'Yes, I know. Your father had a bee in his bonnet about SB. But this is serious, Wally.'

'We're not at war,' said Hardcastle.

'Perhaps not, but I reckon we will be by the end of the week. That's the informed opinion of the Whitehall warriors, anyway.'

'I'll get on to it straight away, sir.'

'You can tell your men why you're intensifying the search for these housebreakers, obviously, but tell them not to talk to anyone about it. Everything these days is on a need-to-know basis.' Catto tapped the side of his nose. 'But anyone you think ought to know must be informed.'

'Of course, sir.' Hardcastle had every intention of telling his detectives why the operation to find the mysterious burglar or burglars was being stepped up, even if he'd been told not to.

'Well, that's it, gentlemen,' said Hardcastle, when he'd finished briefing the CID officers of the Surbiton, Kingston, and Richmond sub-divisions. The addition of the last two was because some burglaries had taken place at properties in those areas occupied by members of staff of Alan Moore and Company Ltd. 'I need hardly say,' the DDI continued, 'that what we've discussed in this room must go no further. Anyone found talking out of turn will face strong sanctions, the very least of which is likely to be dismissal. On the other hand, any disclosure could be a contravention of the Official Secrets Act. I hope that brings home to you the seriousness of the situation.'

There were a few mumbled acknowledgments before the detectives dispersed.

'Come up to my office, Bob,' said Hardcastle, as Detective Inspector Simmons was about to leave the subterranean parade room at Putney police station where the briefing had been held.

The two detectives mounted the stairs and Simmons followed Hardcastle into the latter's office.

'Take a seat.' For a few moments, Hardcastle stood at the window, hands in pockets, staring down at the traffic in the Upper Richmond Road. 'From time to time, Bob, I'll need a skipper to act as a bag carrier,' he said, turning to face Simmons. 'Who can you recommend?' Crossing the room, he seated himself behind his desk.

'If I was looking for someone to help me out, I would pick Jack Bradley without hesitation, guv'nor.' Simmons had quickly adapted to Hardcastle being his superior officer. 'He's thirty years of age, a sergeant first-class and he's been here at Putney for a year. He was a second-class at Vine Street on C Division before his promotion.'

'If he's in the nick at the moment, ask him to come and see me, Bob.'

The tall, slim, well-dressed man who appeared in the DDI's office possessed a full head of brown, wavy hair, and a neat moustache that did not seem to suit his smooth features. His necktie looked as though it ought to represent a regiment or a school.

'DS Bradley, sir. Mr Simmons said you wanted to see me.' The voice was an educated one that some people erroneously referred to as an Oxford accent.

'Sit down, Jack. Smoke if you want to.'

'Thank you, sir.' Bradley pulled out a chrome cigarette case, opened it and offered it to Hardcastle.

The DDI shook his head. 'I'm a pipe man, thanks. One of the bad habits I picked up from my father.' As if to confirm what he had just said, he took out his pipe and slowly filled it with Player's Navy Cut tobacco. 'It's one of life's inevitabilities, Jack, that sooner or later a murder will occur on this division and, when it does, I'll need a good bag carrier.' He lit his pipe and waved the smoke away. 'I'll also need a skipper who's close at hand – like in the next office – so that he can assist me with any other important enquiries,' he added with a smile. 'D'you think you're up to it?'

'Yes, sir,' Bradley replied without pausing to consider the request. 'Have we got one?'

'Got one what?' Hardcastle was briefly nonplussed by the question.

'A murder, sir. I thought that's why you'd sent for me.'

'Not yet.' Hardcastle laughed. 'I was just making sure that if and when we have a murder to deal with, I know who to shout for. Are you married?'

'No, sir. I've been going out – on and off – with a girl called Blanche since last year, as a matter of fact.'

'She obviously knows you're in the job, then, or do you intend keeping that a secret until after you've proposed to the girl?'

For the first time since arriving in Hardcastle's office, Bradley smiled. 'Oh, she knows, sir, but I'm not too sure she knows what she's in for if we should get spliced.'

'Incidentally, I noticed that you had some sort of crest on your cigarette case. Is that something to do with your girlfriend?'

'Oh, that.' Bradley took out the case again and laid it on the desk. Attached to the centre of it was a shilling dated 1938. 'When I asked Blanche out for the first time, this mate of mine on the Fraud Squad bet me a shilling that she'd turn me down flat.' He laughed. 'I won and just to make sure I'd never lose it, I had it soldered on to my cigarette case.'

'And if she finishes up marrying someone else, will you take it off?'

'I haven't thought that far ahead, sir.'

'Where are you living at the moment, Jack?'

'I've got a flat in Richmond, sir. It's rather small, but it will be all right for the two of us if we do marry. However, if a baby comes along, I think we'd have to look for something bigger. But that's all in the future at the moment – assuming we have a future, particularly with war looming.'

'If you want some advice, Jack, steer clear of police married quarters.'

'Right, sir.' Bradley laughed again. 'I don't think I could sell that idea to Blanche anyway.'

Hardcastle's next task was to brief the officer commanding V Division. He walked along the corridor to Superintendent Geoffrey Swain's office.

'D'you have a minute, sir?'

'Yes, of course, Mr Hardcastle. Take a seat and tell me

what's on your mind.' Swain, a product of Trenchard's Police
College, was a tall, rather portly man with prematurely greying
hair. A graduate of Oxford University, he wore his uniform in
such a way that it gave the appearance of having been made
to measure. He had a rather disdainful air about him, giving
the impression that he was wondering what on earth he was
doing in the Metropolitan Police Force. Whether it was his
upbringing or his education that gave him that slightly aloof
air, he certainly behaved in the way he thought a senior officer
should behave. And that included addressing all his subordinates as 'Mister'. At least, those of inspector rank and above.

'I've been strictly cautioned by Chief Constable Catto not
to mention this to anyone who doesn't need to know, sir, but
clearly I must put you in the picture.'

'Sounds mysterious, Mr Hardcastle. Do go on.'

The DDI outlined the concerns that Henry Catto had
expressed about senior executives at the Alan Moore factory
being targeted by burglars who may be enemy agents.

'I could arrange for extra patrols in the vicinity of those
properties,' said Swain, 'if you think that would help.'

'The problem is that we don't have the addresses of the
people who might become victims of that particular burglar's
interest, sir,' said Hardcastle. 'Although I said burglar, in the
singular, there may be more than one. I had considered asking
the managing director of the company for them, but that might
create unnecessary concern. It could even result in action being
taken by the occupiers to safeguard their property. As I understand the situation, that might frighten off these suspect spies
when, in fact, Special Branch would very much like to lay
hands on them. Apart from which, we'd look rather foolish if
it turned out that there *wasn't* a war.'

'Frankly, Mr Hardcastle, I don't think there's any doubt that
there will be one. God help us if there is, because I don't think
Chamberlain's the man to steer this country through a crisis
of that sort. However, I'm not sure that we should allow
householders to be used as bait. The job of the police is, after
all, the prevention of crime, but I suppose the circumstances
justify the means.'

THREE

DAC Marriott, Chief Constable Catto and Superintendent Swain had been right in their predictions. By the end of the week, world events began to move with giddying swiftness.

On Friday the first of September 1939, Hardcastle arrived home at half past seven in the evening. He had remembered to telephone Muriel so that she was able to time the preparation of supper.

'Have you heard the news, Wally?'

'I've been a bit busy. Why, what's happened?'

'I've had the wireless on nearly all day. Hitler's air force has bombed Warsaw and his troops have crossed the border into Poland. They've occupied the whole country. Apparently, Parliament is going to sit tomorrow. Would you believe it, sitting on a Saturday?' Muriel paused. 'D'you know, the BBC is still calling that wretched man *Herr* Hitler.'

On Sunday morning, the third of September, in common with most people in the country, the Hardcastle family was seated around the wireless set in the front living room. They listened in to the BBC's frequent news bulletins in the hope that, even at this late hour, a way to avoid conflict could be found.

But it was to no avail.

Finally, at eleven fifteen, the doleful, grating voice of the prime minister, speaking from the Cabinet Room at 10 Downing Street, announced the news that no one wanted to hear.

'This morning,' he began, 'the British Ambassador in Berlin handed a final note to the German government stating that, unless we heard from them by eleven o'clock that they were prepared at once to withdraw their troops from Poland, a state of war would exist between us.

'I have to tell you now that no such undertaking has been

received, and that consequently this country is at war with
Germany.'

'Well, that's it, then,' said Hardcastle. 'So much for
Chamberlain's bit of paper that he waved so triumphantly.'

Twenty-seven minutes after the end of the broadcast, the
ominous sound of an air-raid siren filled the air. It was a sound
that would soon become all too familiar, and which the
irrepressible British christened 'Moaning Minnie'.

Muriel and the three Hardcastle children looked at Walter
as if seeking his leadership in this dark hour. As a policeman,
they expected him to know about such things as air-raid warn-
ings and what to do when one sounded.

'That'll be a false alarm,' said Hardcastle. 'The Germans
can't possibly have got here in that short space of time.' He
sounded more confident than he felt; he really did not know
how fast a German bomber could travel, and in any case, it
had been revealed that the German bombing of Warsaw had
taken place without any prior warning. 'I'll tell you what we'll
do, Ted,' he said to his eldest son, Edward, now fourteen years
of age. 'We'll take a turn round to the Fairfield and have a
look at the air-raid shelters the council has built.' He glanced
at his wife. 'Are you coming with us, love?'

Muriel scoffed. 'Someone has to stay here and make Sunday
lunch, Wally, war or no war,' she said. 'It won't cook itself.
You be careful,' she added, after a moment's pause, as if taking
care would be sufficient to avoid the effects of an incoming
bomb.

'What's that smell, Dad?' asked Edward as he and his father
descended the steps and made their way along the tunnel-like
structure of the air-raid shelter. It was lined on either side by
a continuous row of wooden benches.

'That smell is the concrete they use, son.'

It was an odour that was to remain with Edward Hardcastle
for the rest of his life, and he would be winged back to that
first day of the war every time he smelled it.

'Where are the toilets, Dad?'

'There aren't any, son.'

'I've decided that I want to join the Royal Air Force, Dad,' announced Edward.

'This lot will be over before you're old enough, Ted. The last lot only lasted four years and a bit.'

But in that, Walter Hardcastle was wrong. The war lasted until August 1945, when the Japanese surrendered.

On the Monday, the day following the declaration of war, Hardcastle and Detective Sergeant Bradley made their way to the establishment of Alan Moore and Company Ltd in Portsmouth Road, Kingston. It did not look much like a factory and turned out to be two three-storey houses converted into one and enclosed by a newly built high-brick wall topped with barbed wire surrounding the entire building.

The gatekeeper who confronted them was a squat, red-faced man with a bushy moustache. His blue tunic bore the ribbons of the three Great War medals known jokingly as Pip, Squeak and Wilfred.

'Yes?' The gatekeeper, thumbs tucked beneath the buttons of his tunic top pockets, seemed to puff himself up, as if to emphasize the importance of his job now that there was a war on.

'We have an appointment to see the managing director,' said Hardcastle.

'Have we now? And when was this here appointment made, might I ask?' The gatekeeper peered closely at Hardcastle and Bradley, both of whom were, in his view, quite clearly spies attempting to gain admittance to this secret building with some spurious story about having an appointment.

'This morning.' Realizing that he was dealing with a rather dim individual, Hardcastle clarified his statement. 'It was made this morning *for* this morning.'

'Really? In that case, it's very likely been cancelled now there's a war on.' The gatekeeper failed to see the illogicality of that statement as the war had been on since yesterday. 'But wait here while I look in my book.' He nodded at the sentry standing next to the gate, armed with a rifle and fixed bayonet. 'Keep an eye on 'em, Charlie.'

'He's taking the war very seriously, guv'nor,' said the sentry, and eased the chinstrap of his steel helmet with his free hand. 'Probably worried he'll get called up again for a second go at Fritz if the management think he's surplus to requirements.'

The gatekeeper returned. 'I've just had a word with the MD's secretary and there's only one appointment booked for today. What's your name?'

'Hardcastle,' said the DDI.

'Oh! That's the name what the young lady give me. Have you got any identification on you?'

'Divisional Detective Inspector Hardcastle.' The DDI held up his warrant card so that the gatekeeper could inspect it. 'And this is Detective Sergeant Bradley.'

'Oh, you never said as how you was police officers, sir,' said the gatekeeper, suddenly becoming very respectful. 'You should have said, sir. I mean we're all on the same side now, ain't we?'

'I sincerely hope so,' said Hardcastle, wondering what the man's odd cliché actually meant. 'How do I get to the managing director's office?'

'Oh, well, I . . .' It was a quandary. The gatekeeper could not leave his post, but was uncertain where the MD had his office. But he was saved by the appearance of a middle-aged woman.

'Mr Hardcastle?'

'Yes.'

'I'm Grace Lovell, Mr Austin's secretary, Mr Hardcastle. If you'd like to come with me, I'll show you to his office.' The secretary was dressed in a tweed suit with flat shoes and a white blouse. She wore a minimal amount of make-up and her hair was dragged back into a severe bun.

'Thank you. This is my colleague Detective Sergeant Bradley.'

'Pleased to meet you both,' said the secretary. 'Thank you, Baldwin,' she said to the gatekeeper. Baldwin responded by raising a single finger to the peak of his cap, to the woman he had earlier described as a young lady.

After a journey up a carpeted flight of stairs near the centre of the building, the two detectives were shown into the managing director's office. Sticky tape criss-crossed the windows as a protection against flying glass in the event of a bomb, and a stirrup pump stood in one corner alongside a fire bucket full of water and another containing sand. Against the wall alongside the window was a wooden frame covered in black cotton material, which would fit into the window aperture to comply with blackout regulations.

'Howard Austin, gentlemen.' A tall, dark-haired man, probably in his fifties, Austin sported a carnation in the buttonhole of his well-cut suit. A sober tie and a white shirt completed the picture of a well-dressed, confident executive. Noting Hardcastle's apparent interest, he said, 'Pick one of these up every morning from my greengrocer on my walk into work.' As if to emphasize its freshness, he raised his lapel and sniffed at the bloom. Almost as an afterthought, he crossed the room and shook hands with the two police officers.

'Very nice.' In fact, Hardcastle was not much interested in flowers. 'I'm Divisional Detective Inspector Hardcastle and this is Detective Sergeant Bradley, Mr Austin.'

'Do take a seat, gentlemen, please.' Austin took a hunter watch from his waistcoat pocket, glanced at it and returned it. 'I daresay Miss Lovell will appear with some coffee shortly. In the meantime, perhaps you would begin by telling me how I can be of assistance to the police.'

Hardcastle explained about the burglaries that had taken place in the Kingston, Surbiton and Richmond areas, and the police belief that some senior members of Alan Moore and Company's staff might have been the targets.

'We believe it possible that German secret agents are seeking information about what goes on here, Mr Austin.'

'This is a very serious matter, Inspector,' said Austin. 'Very serious indeed. However, I think it's safe to say that it's unlikely that any of my people would take sensitive material home with them, if that's what you were suggesting. But, now that the war has actually begun, I think it would be a sensible precaution for me to remind all the staff about security.'

'I've brought coffee, sir,' said Miss Lovell, appearing in the MD's office.

'Thank you, Grace. If you'd like to put it on that table, I'll deal with it.'

'The main reason for our coming to see you this morning,

Mr Austin,' continued Hardcastle, 'is to ask for the addresses of the senior people here who might be suspected by German agents of possessing useful information. In that way, I could arrange for police to keep special observation on their property.'

'That's very good of you, Inspector.'

'There's actually more to it than that, sir,' said Jack Bradley. 'It may give us the opportunity to lay hands on a German agent.'

Austin, a thoughtful expression on his face, handed coffee to the two CID officers. 'You think it's that serious, do you?' he asked, as he sat down again.

'To be perfectly candid, Mr Austin, I don't really know,' said Hardcastle. 'All we can do is to act on the information passed to us by people who claim to know about such things.'

Austin smiled. 'There are so many component parts in what we do that most of the people here don't even know what the company is making. However, I'll give you the addresses of those three people.' He paused for a second or two. 'And I suppose I'd better give you my address as well.'

'That's probably a good idea, sir,' said Hardcastle.

Austin pressed a key on his intercom system and asked Miss Lovell to come in. 'Would you get me the addresses of these three people, please, Grace?' he asked, handing her a slip of paper.

The efficient Miss Lovell was back within a few minutes and handed the managing director a list.

'Thank you, Grace. Incidentally, there's no need for these people to know I'm giving their addresses to the police, should they ask.'

'Of course not, sir.' Grace Lovell managed to look slightly affronted that the thought should even have occurred to the managing director.

Austin took out a fountain pen and added his own Kingston address to the list before handing it to Hardcastle. 'There we are, Inspector. I hope you catch this fellow.'

'We'll do our best, sir, but I probably won't be able to let you know if we've succeeded, secrecy being what it is now that war's been declared.' Hardcastle paused. 'As a matter of interest, I was wondering why this company is named Alan Moore.'

Austin chuckled. 'There is no such person as Alan Moore, Inspector. He's a figment of our imagination, a non-person. But we have an elderly clerk here who we can wheel out in the unlikely event that someone wants to see Alan Moore.' He stood up and shook hands with the two officers. 'Well, I'd better get on with what we're doing here,' he said. 'If that old doomster Churchill's to be believed, the Royal Navy is going to need these seagoing vessels, but he is First Lord of the Admiralty, so I imagine he knows what he's talking about.' He stopped suddenly. 'I shouldn't have said that. However, as you're police officers, it's all right, I suppose. Having gone that far, it probably won't hurt to tell you that among the things we're developing here is a very small submarine. Hence our close proximity to the river.'

'Your secret's safe with us, sir,' said Bradley.

'Just proves I'll have to be more careful. As I was about to say, Churchill's the chap we need in Number Ten if we're to get out of this mess in one piece.'

In fact, that is exactly what happened some eight months later when Winston Churchill became prime minister.

Bradley opened the crime book on Hardcastle's desk and turned to the relevant pages.

'Do any of Austin's addresses tally with any of the burglaries that have been reported, Jack?'

Bradley looked up. 'No, sir. But they might be the addresses of Moore's employees nevertheless. Our burglar won't have had the benefit of knowing which were the sensitive workers.'

'Are you sure about that, Jack? He might have acquired details from somewhere.'

'I suppose it's possible that he got alongside someone who works there and tapped them for a few addresses. I mean, he might have seduced a female clerk from the personnel office, for example. Bit of pillow talk and Bob's your uncle.'

'You could be right, Jack.' Hardcastle laughed. 'But whether that's the case or not, it won't have been Miss Grace Lovell who spilled the beans. I don't somehow see her as vulnerable to pillow talk.'

'Do we arrange for extra patrols, sir, or do you want CID officers to do it?'

'I've no intention of tying up detectives for that sort of job, Jack. Apart from anything else, it's really down to Special Branch. If they're that interested, perhaps they should get a few of their chaps out from behind their desks. However, what we will do for a start is to reinvestigate some of these burglaries and check whether the householders work for Moore's.'

'Why don't I make a list of the break-ins so far, sir, and ask Austin if they work at the Kingston establishment?'

'Good idea, Jack. I was just going to suggest that.'

'Shouldn't take me long, guv'nor,' said Bradley, as he picked up the crime book and returned to his desk in the general CID office.

After Jack Bradley had made a list of the seven burglaries that had taken place over the past three months on V Division, he arranged a follow-up meeting with Howard Austin at the offices of Alan Moore and Company Ltd.

'We have examined burglaries in the area, Mr Austin, and we would be interested to know if any of these addresses were of your employees.'

Austin took the list and ran his eye down the seven addresses. He sent for Grace Lovell, his secretary, and handed the list to her. 'Miss Lovell, would you be so good as to go down to personnel, please, and see if any of these are our people.'

It took Grace Lovell only a matter of minutes before she returned to the managing director's office. 'Three of these addresses are recorded as being occupied by company employees, sir,' she said, handing over the annotated list.

Austin glanced at it briefly before handing it to Bradley. 'I've no wish to teach you your job, Sergeant Bradley, but I fear that you're rather barking up the wrong tree. It would be regarded as a serious offence if any of these people were to take any sensitive information out of these offices.'

'But does the Abwehr know that, sir?' asked Bradley.

'The *what*?'

'The German intelligence service, sir.'

'One address is halfway between Kingston and Richmond, sir; another is in Surbiton and the third is in the centre of Kingston.' Bradley placed the list on Hardcastle's desk.

'I think we'll pay these people a visit, Jack,' said Hardcastle, tapping the paper with his pencil, 'and see if we can find out a bit more about the burglaries. As for those that seem to have no connection with the Moore establishment, they're of no interest to us in the present situation.'

'When d'you want to start, sir?'

'It'd better be this evening, I suppose,' said Hardcastle. 'These people are probably working until at least six o'clock and it won't be any good going earlier. First of all, we'll tackle the one that's halfway between Kingston and Richmond.'

'It's in Albany Park Road, sir, a turning off the Richmond Road. Mr and Mrs Charles Cavanaugh are registered as being the only residents.'

'Do we know anything about them, Jack?'

'No, sir. I did a search of records, but there's nothing at all. But I wouldn't have expected to find anything adverse, given where he works.'

FOUR

The Cavanaughs' double-fronted house lay sufficiently far back from the tree-lined street to allow for quite a large front garden. It was eight o'clock in the evening and not yet blackout time, although the windows were blacked-out in accordance with the defence regulations. The sound of music coming from inside the house indicated that the occupants were at home.

Hardcastle rapped loudly on the brass knocker several times. Eventually, the music stopped – apart from a pianist softly playing a Chopin nocturne – and a man came to the door.

'Yes, what is it?' The man peered searchingly into the gloom of an autumn evening made worse by the absence of street lighting.

'Mr Charles Cavanaugh?'

'Yes.'

'We're police officers, Mr Cavanaugh. I'm Divisional Detective Inspector Hardcastle of V Division, and this is Detective Sergeant Bradley. It's about the burglary that took place here on Friday the eighteenth of August.'

'Oh, I see. Have you caught him, then?'

'Not yet, sir, but we will,' said Hardcastle, although he had no idea how he was to achieve his aim. At the moment there was no evidence pointing to a particular housebreaker and Hardcastle had considered the possibility that it was an experienced burglar from afar who had decided to try his luck in this neighbourhood. But he then dismissed that thought; it was more than coincidence that the burglar had broken into at least three homes of Moore's employees, and there may be more to discover.

'You'd better come in, Inspector.' Cavanaugh was wearing a cardigan over a check shirt, corduroy trousers, and held a violin and a bow in his left hand. He conducted the two officers into the spacious front room. There were seven or eight people there, most with glasses in their hands, although a couple were holding stringed instruments and one young woman was caressing a lyre. The woman seated at the piano stopped playing when Cavanaugh and the police entered, and turned on her stool to face them.

'As you can see, Inspector, we're having a little musical soirée. Hitler will have to do more than he's doing to stop the British enjoying themselves. Oh, I should have introduced you to my wife, Eve. She's the one tickling the ivories.' Cavanaugh turned to his wife. 'This is Detective Inspector Hardwick, my dear,' he said.

'The name's Hardcastle, sir,' corrected the DDI.

'Oh, I do apologize, Inspector.'

'Are we making too much noise?' The slender Mrs Cavanaugh had yet to celebrate her thirtieth birthday. Her long, black velvet dress was cut daringly low and her blonde hair fell freely around her shoulders.

'No, madam,' said Hardcastle.

There were one or two silly remarks from the guests asking what 'Charlie' had done to attract the attention of the police. This was followed, predictably, by a cackle of laughter.

'Perhaps there is somewhere private we could go, sir,' said Hardcastle, 'rather than disturbing your guests.' He had no intention of carrying on his conversation against a background of childish badinage.

'Oh, yes, of course. Careless talk and all that.' With that pointless comment, Cavanaugh led the two detectives into another sitting room at the rear of the house and invited them to take a seat.

'Can I offer you a drink, Inspector?'

'No, thank you, sir.'

'Well, what can I tell you about this burglary that the police don't already know?'

'I understand that you work at Alan Moore and Company's offices in Portsmouth Road, Mr Cavanaugh.'

'How on earth did you know that?' Cavanaugh frowned as he posed the question. It sounded like an accusation. But in reality, he was somewhat alarmed that the police should know that's where he worked.

'Since the outbreak of war, the police have compiled lists
of all persons in sensitive employment. The plan is that they
should be given priority assistance should anything occur that
prevents them from getting to work.' That was not the case at
all, but Hardcastle thought it unwise to alarm Cavanaugh by
telling him his house may have been targeted by German
intelligence agents because of his employment. 'If you've no
objection, I'll send an officer to see you who can advise on
making your house more secure.'

'Oh, I see. I must say that's all very commendable.'

'Now, sir.' Bradley took out his pocketbook. 'Can you
remind me exactly what was stolen.'

'It was really rather silly, Sergeant. Hardly worth the effort
of breaking in.'

'As a matter of interest, how *did* the burglar break in?'
Bradley knew the answers to all the questions he was asking,
but was checking to make sure that the detective constable
who had carried out the initial investigation had not omitted
anything that could be important.

'The officer who came the next day had a good look round
and said he thought the burglar had probably come in through
the kitchen and had used a blade of some sort – probably a
penknife – to slide the window catch open. All this audacious
thief took were a few items of Eve's jewellery – nothing of real
value at all – and a few knick-knacks from the mantelshelf in
the other room. Oh, and he took the brass table bell we use for
summoning the maid. That was more of a nuisance than anything
else because we couldn't get a new one for love nor money. A
bell, I mean, not a maid.' Cavanaugh laughed. 'And that's probably the fault of firms like Alan Moore's who want all the metal
they can lay hands on,' he said, and laughed again.

'Were you in the house at the time, Mr Cavanaugh?' asked
Bradley.

'No. My wife and I were at the Kingston Empire. We saw
a rather risqué play called *While Parents Sleep*. I can't
remember who wrote it, though.' He frowned, as though
remembering the playwright was important.

'Anthony Kimmins,' said Bradley quietly. 'I've seen it
myself.'

'That's right. It was very good and apparently had been running in the West End for some time. I have to say, though, that I rather wish we'd gone the week before, because that comedian Tommy Handley was on.'

'How long were you out of the house altogether, sir?'

It took Cavanaugh a few seconds of recollection before he replied. 'It must have been three hours or so,' he said. 'We were at the theatre's second house – that's at ten to nine – and would have left here at about eight o'clock. Time to have a drink at the Kingston Hotel before the show, you see, because the crush bar at the theatre is always so crowded. The hotel's almost next door which makes it very convenient for a drink. And we got back at, oh, almost eleven o'clock, I suppose. That's when I found the kitchen window open.'

'One last question, Mr Cavanaugh, before I let you get back to your guests,' said Hardcastle. 'What exactly do you do at Moore's?'

'I'm a draughtsman. I draw up plans for various components. Half the time I don't know what it is I'm drawing. I wouldn't be allowed to tell you what we're doing even if I knew, but it's pretty complex, and I've no idea where my bits fit in. Was there a reason for asking me that question, Inspector?'

'Not really, sir, but my chief is very insistent on me getting all the details, whether they're relevant or not.'

Cavanaugh laughed. 'I've got a boss like that. Are you sure I can't press you to a drink before you go?'

'Quite sure, sir, thank you.'

'What's the address of the man you said lives in the centre of Kingston, Jack?' Hardcastle asked, as they drove away from the Cavanaugh residence.

'Hardman Road, sir. It's a Mr Roy Bridger and his wife, Dorothy.'

'We may as well see if they're at home, I suppose.'

Insofar as Hardcastle could see in the gloom of an autumn evening, the Hardman Road house was a residence similar to his own in nearby Canbury Park Road, except that this one was semi-detached.

Bradley knocked and the door was answered promptly by a man.

'Yes, who is it?' It was a common enough question. Since the war had started all manner of rumours had been flying about. One of Bridger's friend's neighbours claimed that a German pilot, who had been shot down, knocked at his door, surrendered and asked for a cup of tea.

'Police,' said Hardcastle. 'Mr Roy Bridger, is it?'

'Yes, that's me. What's it about?'

'I'm Divisional Detective Inspector Hardcastle and this is Detective Sergeant Bradley. It's about the burglary here on . . .' The DDI paused. 'What date was it, Jack?'

'Friday the twenty-fifth of August, sir.'

'You'd better come in.' Once the two detectives were inside, Bridger switched on a light. 'Before we go any further, may I see some sort of identification?'

'Indeed, you may.' Hardcastle and Bradley each produced his warrant card. Bridger donned a pair of heavy horn-rimmed spectacles and examined the documents carefully.

'Thank you, gentlemen.' Roy Bridger was a middle-aged man of medium height and build. He was wearing a collar and tie, but had substituted a green cardigan for his jacket. 'One can't be too careful these days. There are even rumours circulating of German spies being dropped by parachute all over the place,' he added with a smile. 'I don't know what I can tell you that I didn't tell the detective who came immediately after the break-in. But please come in and take a seat.' Bridger led the two into the sitting room at the front of the house. 'This is my wife, Dorothy,' he said. 'The police have come to see us, my dear.'

'Oh, no! Is it bad news?' Bridger's wife dropped her knitting into her lap and put a hand to her mouth, a concerned expression on her face. 'Our son Ian is in the army, you see, and I'm knitting him a balaclava as the winter will be on us soon,' she explained. 'He was in the Territorial Army but was called up immediately. We've no idea where he is. It's such a worry with all that's going on in France.'

'Yes, it must be, Mrs Bridger, but we're not here about your son. If anything had happened to your son, I'm sure the War

Office would let you know immediately. I'm Divisional Detective Inspector Hardcastle and this is Detective Sergeant Bradley. We're actually making further enquiries about your recent burglary.'

'I understand that you are employed at the offices of Alan Moore and Company, Mr Bridger,' said Bradley, as he and Hardcastle sat down.

'How did you know that?' There was an element of suspicion in Bridger's voice, similar to that of Charles Cavanaugh's when the same question was posed to him earlier in the evening.

'We are keeping a list of people living in the area who have jobs important to the war effort, Mr Bridger, so that if anything should happen to them or their property, we'll treat it as a priority. And you are one of those people.'

'That's very good of you, but I'm only a manager in the personnel department, and I'm on the roster for doing fire-watching at the office. Neither of those tasks can be described as essential war work. D'you think this burglary is connected with my work, then?'

'I shouldn't think so,' said Hardcastle, in an attempt at reassurance, 'but I'll send an officer to see you who can tell you about securing your property more effectively. It's something we're doing for everyone who's been burgled. Now, Mr Bridger, would you remind me how the thief gained entry?'

The story that Bridger told was akin to the one Cavanaugh had related, and the items that had been stolen very similar in terms of portability and value.

'Were you in the house when the burglary occurred, sir?' asked Bradley.

Bridger laughed. 'No, I wasn't. It would have been a different outcome if I had been here, I can tell you that, Inspector. I did a bit of boxing in my youth and I haven't forgotten the basics. Actually, my wife and I walked through to London Road and had a drink at the pub there. It's called the Magnet, if you need to check.'

'Thank you, Mr Bridger, but we have no reason to doubt your word,' said Hardcastle, when Bridger had finished, 'and I apologize for interrupting your evening.'

'Not at all, Inspector. I'm most grateful to you for taking the trouble.'

'What's next, sir?' asked Bradley, as he and Hardcastle left the Bridgers' house.

'I think that'll do for tonight, Jack. We'll make our way back to Putney and try the Surbiton address tomorrow evening.'

'We don't seem to have learned much so far,' said Bradley. 'Cavanaugh is a draughtsman and Bridger works in the personnel department. From what Cavanaugh told us, even he didn't know what he was drawing, and it's highly doubtful that Bridger's work in the personnel department would involve military secrets. But as I said to Austin, perhaps the Abwehr doesn't know that.'

'You're right, of course, Jack, but we've got to keep trying. It might be that the personnel manager is more important than we give him credit for. Where better to find the names and addresses of all of Moore's Kingston employees?'

'Are you suspecting Bridger, then, guv'nor?'

'Not necessarily, but someone on Moore's payroll might have gained entry to Bridger's office. Mind you, this is the sort of stuff that Special Branch should be looking into.'

'They're too busy arresting spies, sir,' said Bradley cynically.

'You sound as though you've been speaking to my father, Jack.'

Keith Shaw, the third Moore and Company's employee on the list of burglary victims, occupied a detached house in Pine Walk, Surbiton.

'There's one common factor, Jack,' said Hardcastle, as he knocked on the door. 'This is the third house we've visited and each of them has easy access to the rear of the property.'

'Yes, what is it?' asked the man who answered the door.

'It's the police, sir. Mr Shaw, is it?'

'Yes. What seems to be the problem?' It was still daylight and the householder had no reason to mention the blackout. In any event, and in common with much of the population,

Shaw took the view that it was an unnecessary regulation and would soon be abandoned.

'We'd like to talk to you about when you were burgled on the first of September, Mr Shaw.'

'Oh, I see. You'd better come in.' Shaw was a stocky man with a shock of auburn hair. The DDI reckoned him to be about forty, even though he appeared to be younger.

Once Hardcastle had introduced himself and Bradley, Shaw invited them into the sitting room.

'This is my wife, Elizabeth, Inspector. We were just listening to the wireless. Nothing important.'

'Good evening, Mrs Shaw,' said Hardcastle and then turned to the woman's husband. 'Were you at home when your house was broken into, Mr Shaw?'

'No, we'd walked down to the Berrylands – it's the pub on the corner. You probably passed it on the way here. The St John's Ambulance people have hired an upstairs room there so that they can hold first-aid classes every Friday evening. It seems to be a good idea. If the threatened bombing begins in earnest, we'll need to know these things. The lecture lasted an hour and after we'd learned how to splint up broken legs and arms, stop bleeding and start breathing and all that sort of business, Liz and I went downstairs to the bar and had a couple of drinks.'

'The officer who reported the break-in said that the burglar entered through the kitchen window.' Bradley was reading from his pocketbook.

'Apparently so. He said that the burglar had used a penknife or some similar sort of implement to slide the window catch aside and he got into the house via the kitchen.'

'I understand that he didn't take very much,' said Bradley.

'No, that was the strange thing about it. We've got some reasonably valuable stuff in the house and it's not hidden away, and yet he ignored that and just took one or two pieces of Liz's jewellery.'

'It was only cheap stuff anyway, comparatively speaking,' said Elizabeth Shaw candidly. She was a good-looking blonde who appeared to be in her early thirties, although Hardcastle suspected that she may have been a little older. 'I've never seen the point of having diamonds when you can have something that looks the same. Some of my friends have got diamond necklaces and things like that and they're constantly worrying about having them stolen, or fretting about the cost of insuring them. It's too much trouble for my liking. And there's one woman I know who keeps her jewellery in a bank deposit box and wears paste copies. Well, what's the point in that?'

'Why are the police taking a renewed interest in a tuppenny-ha'penny burglary when we've got a war to worry about?' asked Shaw.

'It's because of your employment, sir,' said Bradley. 'I understand that you work for Alan Moore and Company.'

'How the hell did you know that?' In common with the other two burglary victims, Shaw posed the question suspiciously.

'We've been liaising with companies that are engaged in war work, Mr Shaw,' said Hardcastle, and went on to give Shaw a similar excuse for his interest as he had given Cavanaugh and Bridger.

'Oh, I see,' said Shaw. 'That's very comforting.'

'As a matter of interest, what do you do at Moore's, Mr Shaw?'

'Procurement. Arranging for the supply of the metal and Perspex, and all the other sort of stuff we use in our work, which I can't tell you about, of course.'

'Must be difficult trying to obtain this stuff,' said Hardcastle.

'It's a nightmare,' said Shaw. 'A great deal of the raw materials came from abroad before the war started. Much of it came from Germany, but ironically there's now a risk to shipping from German submarines. We're now forced to shop around in the United Kingdom, although we still can't get everything we need in-house, so to speak. There's even been some suggestion that everyone's garden railings are to be taken and melted down for the war effort. We're hoping for some help from the United States, even though they're not in the war.'

'I don't envy you your task,' said Hardcastle. 'However, I'll arrange for an officer to call on you to give you advice about security.'

'Thank you, Inspector,' said Shaw. 'That's very good of you. I'll show you out.'

'I don't understand it, sir,' said Bradley, when he and Hardcastle were back at Putney police station. 'This burglar, whoever he is, must be interested in these employees for security reasons. In each case, he only took worthless items when he could have taken more valuable stuff. D'you think it's worthwhile following up some of the other break-ins to see what was taken then?'

'Good idea, Jack, but there's no need to do it physically. The crime book will tell us the method of entry and what was stolen – assuming, of course, that it's the same burglar who's responsible for this spate of break-ins. Mind you, of the three we've interviewed, the only Moore employee of interest is Shaw. The procurement of material for military submarines would be of vital interest to the enemy.'

'I thought that was a very expensive house that the Shaws lived in, guv'nor. It doesn't exactly tally with the pay he must be getting.'

'Worth bearing in mind, Jack.'

However, when Bradley checked, he found that the other properties had been broken into by a burglar using similar methods of entry to those on the Moore employees. The only difference was that the others had lost quite valuable items. Either there were two burglars at work or one, an enemy agent, was acting differently. But why?

FIVE

A chill in the September air had persuaded the man to don a black overcoat over his dinner jacket. In addition, he wore his customary white silk scarf, unlined leather gloves and the Anthony Eden homburg hat he always chose in order to give the impression of a dashing man-about-town, rather than his true persona of a German national and agent of the Abwehr. This evening, he had picked one of the houses in a turning off Kingston Hill for his next burglary. It was not a random decision. As was his custom, he had carefully reconnoitred that particular house and researched the occupations and habits of its residents. He had sensed that there was now a greater wariness among people since the declaration of war, probably engendered by the scaremongering rumours that German parachutists were arriving unheralded. Everywhere there were posters advising the population that 'Careless Talk Costs Lives', accompanied by the brilliant cartoons of Kenneth Bird, better known as Fougasse.

Now that the autumn evenings were made even darker by the blackout, it was easy for the man to become invisible simply by standing behind one of the few trees in the road. Fortunately, the one he had selected was opposite the house that interested him.

He was a patient man for the very simple reason that he had no desire to be caught. In his view, that would mean that he had failed in his chosen profession. He stood, silent and immobile, for a whole hour until he saw the man of the house and his wife emerge, turn on to Kingston Hill and walk in the direction of Kingston town centre.

The watcher knew from previous observations that on Friday evenings Frank and Helen Roper always visited the George and Dragon public house, further down Kingston Hill, where they would remain for at least two hours, sometimes longer.

Waiting until the pair were out of sight, the man in black

crossed the road to the house and walked swiftly across the lawn to avoid the noise that would be made by treading on the gravel of the driveway, even though he assumed the house was empty. Skirting the property, he reached the French doors at the rear of the property and with practised ease and the use of a skeleton key, gained entry in a matter of seconds. Once inside, he closed the French doors again, but did not lock them. The way in which he had entered might have to serve as an escape route in the event of some sudden emergency. As was his custom, and to make doubly sure, he checked that the front door was not deadlocked, thus ensuring that there was an escape route that way as well, should it be required. Only then did he ascend the staircase to begin his search of the upper floor, starting with the master bedroom.

This, too, was a carefully thought-out stratagem. Were someone to enter the house, he would have sufficient warning either to hide or resist.

One of the advantages of the blackout was that he was able to use his torch quite freely, secure in the knowledge that it could not be seen from outside by a vigilant policeman, an inquisitive neighbour or one of the officious ARP wardens of the newly formed Civil Defence.

A matter of seven minutes after he had entered the master bedroom, he heard the front door opening and the sound of voices. He froze, not from fear but from prudence. Provided whoever had entered the house did not come up to the first floor, the man in black would be safe for the time being. Nevertheless, he switched off his torch, took off the glove that was on his right hand and withdrew the pistol from its holster that he wore beneath his left armpit.

A man ascended the stairs at a run, at the same time shouting to his wife that he was sure he had left his wallet in their bedroom.

Flinging open the door, and switching on the light, he was confronted by the man in black, who had just had time to adjust his white silk scarf so that it obscured the lower part of his face.

'Who the hell—?' The householder made a brave lunge towards the intruder, but that was as far as he got.

The man in black unhesitatingly fired two rounds into the householder's chest at point-blank range.

'Frank, what on earth's happened?' Hearing the sound of shots, Helen Roper, Frank's wife, came running up the stairs. As she reached the top, she was struck by two rounds, again fired at point-blank range. Vainly, she tried to grab the banister rail, but her threshing body tumbled back down the stairs, dead before it reached the bottom.

Calmly, the killer picked up the four spent bullet cases, put them in his pocket and briefly considered the situation. Deciding it would be too dangerous to remain any longer, he made for the ground floor, stepping over Helen Roper's body, and left the house, shouting a convincing 'good night' to the dead occupants as he closed the front door.

As he disappeared into the blackness of the night, he realized that he had left his leather glove on the bedroom floor, but he dare not go back to recover it. He was furious that he had done so. Not that he was concerned that it might lead to his identity, but that it was a personal failing. Personal failings, he had been taught, would not be countenanced by the Führer.

There was quite a crowd in the George and Dragon public house on Kingston Hill on Saturday evening, the evening following the murder of the Ropers. Most of the drinkers seemed to know each other and the atmosphere of bonhomie was more like that of an intimate club than a public house. Among them was Detective Constable Iain Campbell, known by his colleagues as Jock, although none of the assembled drinkers knew him to be a policeman. Campbell, a mature, dour Scot, was not a great one for small talk, but he was a good listener and he knew that much information could be picked up in pubs about criminal activity. As a result, he frequented those hostelries that were likely to yield the most information. The George and Dragon was one such inn. The houses in its immediate area were occupied by the well-off and were attractive targets for burglars.

This evening, however, the conversation took on a slightly different theme.

'Anyone seen Frank and Helen tonight?' boomed a

moustached man in a sports jacket and cavalry twills who was nursing a large Scotch and soda.

'No,' said the landlord, briefly wiping the top of the bar, more out of habit than necessity. 'I haven't. They weren't in last night, either. And I've never known them miss a Saturday evening before.' For a moment or two, he paused in thought. 'Or a Friday night, come to that.'

'Perhaps he's working late,' said another. 'I imagine Alan Moore's outfit is going all out now the war's started.'

'Careless talk costs lives,' cautioned the moustached drinker who had served in the last war, as the Great War was now being called. 'Shouldn't talk about that sort of thing in pubs, old boy.' He adjusted his regimental tie and asked the landlord for another large Scotch.

'Make the most of it, Colonel,' said the landlord. 'They tell me that it'll soon be as rare as gold dust.'

'You mean that gold dust will soon be as rare as Scotch, eh what?' The 'colonel' chortled at his own lame joke.

Turning to his neighbour at the bar, Campbell broke his customary silence. 'Who are they talking about?'

'Frank and Helen Roper,' said the man. 'Nice couple. Live just up Kingston Hill. Well, one of the turnings off the hill. But they're always in here Friday and Saturday evenings. I've never known them miss one. Perhaps they're on holiday.'

'That's not very likely,' said Campbell. 'No one would go on holiday at this time of year, surely? And certainly not now there's a war on.' He finished his beer, nodded to one or two people and left.

There was a police box just a few yards down the hill from the pub. Taking out his box key, Campbell unlocked the door and stepped inside. Lifting the telephone receiver, he was immediately connected to Kingston police station.

'It's Jock Campbell here. Put me through to the CID at Putney, will you, pal?' When his call was answered, Campbell asked if the DI was there. Seconds later, Bob Simmons was on the phone.

'What is it, Jock?'

'You remember the briefing we had from the DDI, guv'nor?'

'Yeah. What about it?'

Campbell repeated what he had heard in the George and Dragon and offered the suggestion that Roper's employment might have something to do with his absence.

'Stay there, Jock, while I ring the DDI. Fortunately, he lives on your manor. I'll ask him what he wants done about it.'

It was less than five minutes before the light on the telephone lit up and Campbell answered it.

'Stay where you are, Jock,' said Simmons. 'The DDI will meet you there very shortly.'

Ten minutes later, the Kingston area wireless car drew into the kerb by the police box, and Hardcastle flung open the rear door.

'Get in, Jock.'

'I don't know the Ropers' address, sir,' said Campbell, as the police car sped away.

'I've got it,' said Hardcastle. 'This civil defence register's a very useful source of information.'

The area car stopped on the drive of the Ropers' house and Hardcastle and Campbell got out.

Hardcastle rang the doorbell several times, but received no response. He stooped and peered through the letterbox.

'There's a woman's body lying at the foot of the stairs, Jock, and she's wearing a topcoat. Looks as though she was getting ready to go out. The question now is how do we get in?'

'I'll have a walk around the house, sir.' A few moments later, Campbell returned. 'The French doors are unlocked, sir. If there was an intruder, I reckon that's the way he gained entry. On the other hand, of course, Roper might have murdered his wife and then cleared off somewhere.' It was a detective's wont always to look for the sinister side of an incident.

Hardcastle followed Campbell to the back of the house; the two detectives entered and made their way to the front.

Hardcastle stooped to examine the body. 'This one's dead all right, Jock. Judging by the bloodstains on her coat, I reckon she was shot.'

Campbell stared down at the body. 'A tragedy that, sir,' he said. 'She was a bonny lass, by the looks of her.'

Hardcastle and Campbell went upstairs where they found the dead body of a man.

'I reckon these are the Ropers, who the people in the pub were talking about, Jock. But it's odd that Austin, the managing director of Alan Moore's establishment, didn't mention Roper when he gave us the addresses of his senior people.'

'Perhaps Roper's only just arrived at the firm, sir.' Campbell knelt down and began to go through the dead man's pockets.

'Maybe,' said Hardcastle. 'If he and his wife didn't turn up at the pub last night, it's possible that they were murdered some time yesterday,' he continued thoughtfully. 'However, we'd better get a team down here a bit quickly. We'll need a pathologist, a team of technicians from the forensic science laboratory at Hendon, and a few more detectives. But, above all, we need someone from the fingerprint department and, if we're lucky, we'll get Mr Cherrill. This is the sort of case that would interest him. There's a telephone downstairs in the hall, Jock. Start phoning round and get it organized. You know the drill. Oh, and one other thing: I want DS Bradley from Putney to meet me at my home address not later than ten o'clock tomorrow morning.'

'Aye, sir, I'll get on to it straight away. By the way, the dead man is Frank Roper; he had his identity card in his pocket.' Campbell returned to the ground floor. Using his handkerchief in order not to compromise any fingerprints, he picked up the receiver of the telephone and used a pencil to dial the number of Kingston police station.

It was gone ten o'clock that evening before the full investigation team was at the Ropers' house. Detective Superintendent Frederick Cherrill was intrigued by a double murder and made his way to Kingston Hill as quickly as possible, bringing with him a case containing all the equipment he would need and which he always kept at home. Sir Bernard Spilsbury, the Home Office pathologist, was the last to arrive. In Hardcastle's father's day, Spilsbury would more often than not be attired in morning dress and arrive in a chauffeur-driven Rolls-Royce. Later in the day it was not unusual to see the eminent pathologist in white tie and tails or a dinner jacket. But times had changed and there was a war on. Now, albeit halfway through the night, Sir Bernard was wearing a superbly cut lounge suit.

'My dear Hardcastle,' said Spilsbury. 'I don't think we've met before, but I knew your father very well. How is he?'

'Very fit for his age, Sir Bernard, and resisting all my attempts to get him to move to the country out of harm's way.'

Spilsbury laughed. 'Your father was never one for moving out of harm's way, my dear Hardcastle.' He rubbed his hands together. 'Now, tell me, what have we got here?'

As briefly as possible – because Spilsbury disliked anything but the bare facts – Hardcastle explained the circumstances leading up to the finding of the Ropers' bodies. Without further ado, Spilsbury took off his jacket and began his examination of the deceased. After twenty minutes or so, he stood up and scribbled a few notes on the back of an envelope.

'That's the most I can do here, Hardcastle. I tend to go along with your assessment that they were probably killed sometime yesterday evening. I'd be grateful if you could arrange for the cadavers to be taken up to St Mary's where I'll conduct the post-mortem examination.' Taking his jacket from DC Campbell with a murmur of thanks, he bade farewell to Hardcastle.

'I've found a number of fingermarks, Mr Hardcastle.' Detective Superintendent Cherrill appeared in the sitting room. 'But I suspect that you're dealing with a professional who made sure he kept leather gloves on all the time. However, I think you're right that he probably took off a glove in order to fire his weapon and left it in the rush to escape. It may prove to be his undoing. I'll arrange for a search of those prints I have lifted and compare them with those in the system. I've taken prints from the two deceased, but I suspect that most of those I've lifted will match them or friends who have visited at some time.'

'Thank you, sir,' said Hardcastle, as Cherrill was leaving. 'I'll wait to hear from you.'

The forensic scientists who had been called in from Hendon spent another hour, photographing and searching, and eventually the senior man reported to Hardcastle.

'So far, the only thing we've found, sir, is a black unlined leather glove. It's right-handed and was on the floor of the main bedroom.'

'So I understood from Mr Cherrill,' said Hardcastle. 'Any label inside it?'

'No, sir, and it may belong to the male deceased, although we've not found a left-handed glove of similar pattern anywhere in the house.' The scientist looked down at his notes. 'There's just a trace of mud inside the French doors, which I suspect was the result of the killer having crossed the lawn rather than the noisy gravel path. But there's precious little else that we found that will help your investigation. I reckon you're dealing with a consummate professional. Nevertheless, we'll keep looking.'

'Mr Cherrill made the same suggestion: that this killer was a professional, and I'm inclined to agree with him,' replied Hardcastle gloomily. 'Thanks anyway. Just my luck to get a couple of murders like these.'

Despite it being almost three o'clock in the morning of Sunday before Hardcastle got home, he was ready and waiting for Detective Sergeant Bradley when he arrived at the DDI's house at ten o'clock.

'What was Howard Austin's address, Jack?'

'Birkenhead Avenue, sir,' said Bradley, opening his pocketbook. 'I've got a note of the number here.'

'Good. That's walking distance from here.'

The two detectives set off down Canbury Park Road, turned left under the railway bridge and finally into Birkenhead Avenue.

'Inspector Hardcastle!' Austin could not conceal his surprise at finding the DDI on his doorstep on a Sunday morning. 'What brings you here? Has something happened? Oh, I'm sorry, do come in.'

Hardcastle and Bradley followed Austin into the large sitting room. A few moments later, they were joined by a woman.

'This is my wife, Eunice, Inspector,' said Austin, and turned to his wife. 'This is Detective Inspector Hardcastle, my dear.'

'How d'you do?' Eunice Austin was dressed in navy-blue slacks and a polo-necked jumper, and her brunette hair was tied back into a ponytail. 'It's my air-raid shelter outfit,' she said. 'Not that we've had any air raids yet, but it pays to be prepared.' She gave a gay laugh. 'Would you gentlemen care for a cup of coffee? Howard and I usually have one about now.'

'Thank you, Mrs Austin, that would be most welcome.' As Eunice Austin left the room, Hardcastle added, 'We were up until three this morning, Mr Austin, which is the reason we're here.'

'Oh dear! A policeman's lot and all that sort of thing, eh?' Austin seemed to find it rather amusing. 'You'd better take the weight off your feet, Inspector. You too, Sergeant Bradley.'

The two policemen sat down and Hardcastle went on to tell Austin about the murder of Frank Roper and his wife Helen.

'Good God!' Austin was visibly shocked by the news and sat down suddenly. 'This is a terrible blow. Eunice and I knew Frank and Helen Roper extremely well. We were good friends.'

'How long has he been with the company, Mr Austin?'

'Oh, not that long. I think he came from abroad somewhere. America maybe.' Austin paused in thought. 'Yes, I'm sure he said America.'

'His name wasn't on the list of employees that you gave us,' said Hardcastle. 'Was it that his job was not a particularly sensitive one? Or too sensitive, perhaps?'

'On the contrary. He was a design engineer. It's a very important job, but the reason I didn't give you his address is that he doesn't work at Kingston. He's one of the chaps who's based at Windsor. Their personnel department would usually deal with any such request. He drives there every day and has one of those gas bags fitted to his car. You've probably seen them on some of the buses and taxis. The gas is produced from anthracite and we've got a unit at our place in Portsmouth Road to produce the stuff.' The scientist in Austin demanded that he explain about the gas bags, even though Hardcastle was fully conversant with how they worked. 'Have you any idea who was responsible for this awful crime, Inspector?'

'Not at this stage, sir,' said Bradley, 'but I think it's fair to say that we are dealing with a professional killer.'

'D'you think the murderer might've been a member of this . . . What did you call it the other day, Sergeant Bradley?'

'The Abwehr. The German Intelligence Service,' said Bradley. 'Not necessarily. There's nothing at this point to suggest that's the case.'

Eunice Austin entered the room carrying a tray of coffee and set it down on an occasional table.

'Mr Hardcastle has just brought some terrible news, darling,' said Austin. 'Frank and Helen Roper have been murdered.'

For a moment or two, Eunice stood absolutely still, her face white with shock. 'Both of them?' she eventually managed to ask.

'I'm afraid so, Mrs Austin.' Hardcastle turned back to Howard Austin. 'I wonder if I could rely on you to tell the people at Windsor what's happened, Mr Austin. I shall be in touch with them in due course, but our immediate concern is to find the Ropers' killer.'

'Yes, of course, Inspector. And I hope you do.'

'I'm sure we shall.' Hardcastle was not all that confident, but he could hardly say that he had no idea where to start looking. 'There is one other thing, Mr Austin: do you know if the Ropers had any relatives? If there is a family, then they must be informed.'

'I believe Frank had a married sister who lived in Weybridge, Inspector.' Austin turned to his wife. 'Can you remember the name of Frank's sister, darling? I mean her married name, of course.'

'I've got it written down in my address book. I'll go and get it.' Eunice Austin left the room, returning only minutes later holding a small notebook. 'Daphne Shepherd is Frank's sister, Inspector. She and her husband, Basil, live in Weybridge, in a road very close to the Brooklands racing circuit which, of course, is closed now.' She handed the book to Sergeant Bradley so that he could make a note of the exact address.

'Thank you,' said Hardcastle. 'I'll arrange for her to be notified today.' He paused briefly. 'On second thoughts, I think I'll go myself.'

SIX

Following their visit to see Howard Austin on Sunday morning, Hardcastle and Bradley settled down in the DDI's office that afternoon to consider what should be done next.

Before leaving the scene of the murder earlier that day, Hardcastle had directed Ken Black, the detective inspector at Kingston, to deploy as many of his CID officers as he could spare to carry out house-to-house enquiries in the area where the Ropers had lived. Because of the blackout and the lack of street lighting, he was not very hopeful that anything would be discovered, but there was always an outside chance that somebody might have spotted something, however minor, that would assist the police. He also suggested the possibility that a neighbour may have heard four shots being fired. That would at least fix the time of the murder, but not much else. Hardcastle also tasked Black to put a couple of detectives – preferably a man and a woman – into the George and Dragon public house for an evening or two, to listen to the local gossip. Hardcastle also said that if nothing was forthcoming, they should identify themselves and start asking questions.

Detective Superintendent Cherrill had telephoned Hardcastle to confirm that the only fingerprints found in the house were those of the dead couple and a number of others that, subject to elimination prints being taken, probably belonged to a cleaner; they were certainly small enough to have been those of a woman or even a child and were not in places that the killer was likely to have touched. The implication was that the Ropers rarely received visitors or that the cleaner was very good at her job. However, a cleaner could not remove all fingerprints, no matter how efficient she was.

The first reports of the scientific search of the Ropers' house also came to Hardcastle on the Sunday afternoon. Although the forensic science people had told the DDI that they had found a man's glove, they now reported in writing that a search of the wardrobes in the house had not discovered its companion. The provisional deduction confirmed Hardcastle's view that it had been left by the murderer. There was, however, an interesting discovery in Helen Roper's wardrobe: a green tweed costume with the labels inside the jacket and the skirt of a German supplier with an address in Dusseldorf.

'There's not much chance of following that up, guv'nor,' said Bradley.

'You could try, Jack,' said Hardcastle. 'You'd probably get a Commissioner's Commendation.'

'Or a spy's funeral,' said Bradley. 'In Berlin.'

'Seriously though,' said Hardcastle, 'it puts an entirely different slant on this enquiry. Were the Ropers agents of the Abwehr? Leaving those labels in the woman's costume is the sort of stupid mistake the Germans did sometimes make.'

Overall, though, nothing else of importance had been found that would lead the DDI to the immediate arrest of the murderer. If, however, the Ropers had been identified as spies, and had been 'taken out' by an operative of MI5, the chances of an arrest became extremely remote. That said, Hardcastle thought it extremely unlikely that MI5 would resort to murder, even in time of war, particularly when arrest by Special Branch officers, on behalf of MI5, was a much safer option.

The scientists had collected soil samples from the front lawn of the house that matched the small deposit inside the French windows. They had also found footprints on the lawn and had taken plaster casts of them in the hope that one day the killer might be identified by the shoes he wore that night. They had already checked those footprints against the shoes found in the Roper residence and were satisfied that they did not match.

There had also been a few, almost indiscernible, strands of fibre on the edge of one of the two doors that comprised the French windows. They were preserved in the hope that the killer, when he was found, had matching traces on some piece of his clothing. It was possible, of course, that one of the Ropers had brushed against the edge of the door and that the fibres had nothing to do with the killer, but that would be decided once the scientist had examined the contents of the Ropers' wardrobes in greater depth than the cursory glance that they had been afforded so far.

There was, however, a piece of hard evidence from the ballistics section of the Hendon laboratory. The senior ballistics scientist, a man called Gordon Strutt, regarded it as of sufficient importance for him to appear in person in Hardcastle's office at Putney police station that afternoon.

'It is Sir Bernard Spilsbury's opinion, Mr Hardcastle, that these are the two rounds that killed Frank Roper,' said Strutt, donning protective gloves to remove two rounds of ammunition from the thick paper envelope in which they had been transported. 'And the other two killed Helen Roper. It was a bit of luck,' he continued, in a matter-of-fact sort of way, 'that in both cases the rounds went straight through the bodies of the deceased and we were able to extract them from the fabric of the property. As you can see, they're nine-millimetre parabellum and that gives them a very high muzzle velocity, which is why they passed straight through the bodies of the victims.'

'That helps us, does it?' asked Hardcastle, already having some difficulty in keeping up with Strutt's technical explanation.

'Of the two that killed Frank Roper,' continued Strutt, clearly intending to go at his own pace regardless of Hardcastle's question, 'one lodged itself in the door jamb and the other in the wall just to the left of it. The two that killed Mrs Roper were both embedded in the front door on the ground floor after passing through her body. Presuming that Mrs Roper was on her way upstairs at the time the shots were discharged, the killer would probably have fired downwards rather than aiming a level shot, if you see what I mean. Fortunately, the rounds were relatively undamaged and that will enable us to make a comparison with the weapon that fired them.' He paused. 'When you find it, of course, Mr Hardcastle,' he added with a smile.

'Can you suggest the sort of weapon that might have been used, Mr Strutt? I mean, what are we looking for?'

Strutt made a wry face as he pondered the problem. 'I'm somewhat reluctant to suggest a particular weapon, Mr Hardcastle. However, there is no doubt that it was an automatic pistol because, as I said, the cartridge rounds are parabellum, and the killer probably fired the four rounds in pretty quick succession: two and then another two a matter of seconds later. Secondly, the striations on the four rounds that were recovered led me to think in terms of the Luger Parabellum PO8 pistol as the possible murder weapon. But I hasten to add that it could have been one of several other weapons.' The cautionary note in Strutt's voice implied that he was unhappy at committing himself to a specific firearm.

'I gather that the weapon you're talking about is German, Mr Strutt. Lugers *are* German, aren't they?'

'Yes. That model was developed by Georg Luger in 1900 and adopted by the German Army in 1908.'

'If that's the case, it could be that I'm looking for a German murderer,' Hardcastle mused aloud as he considered the original possibility of a German agent seeking information about the research being conducted by Alan Moore and Company's two factories.

'Not necessarily. These pistols were in widespread use in the last war. It's quite possible that a British soldier could have picked one up on a battlefield and kept it as a souvenir. We have received dozens of weapons that were surrendered by soldiers who had found them, but when they got home found that their wives wouldn't tolerate having them in the house.'

'Thanks very much, Mr Strutt,' said Hardcastle. 'You've cheered me up no end.' He laughed and then shook hands with the ballistics expert.

'If you're lucky enough to find the pistol, Mr Hardcastle, I should be able to confirm that it was the murder weapon almost immediately. Or that it was not,' he added, after a short pause, and laughed.

'We'll have to find out whether the Ropers had a cleaner, Jack,' said Hardcastle, once Strutt had departed. He glanced at his watch. 'I suppose we'd better get down to Weybridge and talk to the Shepherds today.'

'Couldn't we get the Surrey Constabulary to do that, guv'nor?'

'No, Jack. The Shepherds might know something that will

point us in the right direction. After all, we may not be dealing with a random murder. The Ropers might have been targeted for a particular reason, a reason not necessarily connected to Roper's work as a design engineer for Alan Moore and Company. It could be a gambling debt, a jilted woman with whom he'd had an affair and had lost her mind as a result – in fact, there are dozens of reasons for committing murder. Or perhaps the Ropers *were* German agents, if Mrs Roper's Dusseldorf clothing is anything to go by.'

'Mr Basil Shepherd?' The man who answered the door of the Weybridge house where, according to Eunice Austin, Frank Roper's sister lived, was probably in his mid-thirties. He was holding a copy of the *Sunday Express* and his frown gave the impression that he was annoyed at having his Sunday afternoon disturbed.

'Yes. I'm Basil Shepherd.' He tugged briefly at his right ear lobe, a habit that he was to repeat often during their conversation.

'Divisional Detective Inspector Hardcastle, Mr Shepherd, and this is Detective Sergeant Bradley. We're from the Wandsworth Division of the Metropolitan Police.'

'What's happened?' Shepherd's frowning countenance immediately changed to one of concern.

'If we may come in, Mr Shepherd, I'd like to talk to you about your brother-in-law, Frank Roper.'

Shepherd led the way into a comfortable sitting room. 'These gentlemen are from the police, my dear,' he said, addressing an attractive young woman who was listening to a programme on the wireless. 'This is my wife, Daphne, Inspector.'

Daphne Shepherd swung her feet on to the floor and turned off the wireless. 'I was only listening to a repeat of ITMA,' she said. She touched her long blonde hair that was dressed in victory rolls.

Hardcastle had learned over the years that there was no easy way to break news of the death of a relative, other than to come straight out with it. 'I'm sorry to say that I have some bad news, Mrs Shepherd,' he began. 'It's about your brother and his wife. They've been killed.'

Daphne Shepherd stared at Hardcastle with a stunned look on her face, as though her brain was attempting to absorb what he had just told her. 'But how? Was it a car accident? Not an air raid, surely? The raids have only been on the east coast, according to the *Daily Mail.*'

'They were murdered, Mrs Shepherd. Friday just gone, we believe. The matter is still being investigated, of course.'

'Murdered! Oh God! How awful.' Daphne Shepherd put a hand to her mouth. 'Who would have done such a thing?' It was apparent that she was only just managing to hold back the tears.

'That's what we're attempting to find out, Mrs Shepherd,' said Bradley.

Daphne's husband, seeing his wife's distress at the loss of her brother, quickly crossed the room to a cocktail cabinet and poured her a glass of brandy. 'Drink this, darling.' After a pause, he said, 'Can I offer you gentlemen a drink?'

'No, thank you, Mr Shepherd. From what we've learned at this stage of the investigation, Mrs Shepherd,' said Hardcastle, 'it would appear that your brother and his wife left their house and were on their way to a local pub. Apparently, it was their custom to do so every Friday and Saturday evenings. The fact that they didn't show up at the pub this weekend resulted in the customers' concern being brought to the notice of the police. We are guessing at the moment, but the most likely sequence of events is that minutes after setting off to walk to the pub, they returned to the house for some reason. In fact, Mr Roper's wallet was found on one of the bedside tables, so I think it's possible that he and his wife went back to the house to collect it. At the moment, we are assuming that Frank must have gone upstairs and disturbed a burglar who shot him and then shot his wife.'

'Good God!' exclaimed Shepherd. 'The war's only been on for a week, but suddenly everybody has become belligerent, or so it seems.'

'Do you happen to know, Mrs Shepherd,' asked Bradley, 'if your sister-in-law employed a cleaner or someone who would have gone to the house fairly regularly?'

'Yes. It was a Mrs Timms, Violet Timms. I met her once when I dropped in on Helen after I'd been shopping in Kingston. She was a birdlike little woman, nearly sixty, I should think, and didn't seem to have the physique to do all that Helen said she did. She'd not been with them for very long, Helen told me. In fact, only since they'd moved in.'

'How long had the Ropers lived at their Kingston Hill address, then?' asked Bradley.

'Not very long,' said Daphne. 'Frank had been working abroad for years in, I think, South Africa. They probably returned to this country about six months ago or thereabouts, although I'm not sure about that.' Daphne Shepherd paused as a sudden thought occurred to her. 'But surely you can't possibly think that Mrs Timms might have had something to do with this terrible business?' she said, a look of disbelief on her face.

'Good heavens, no! It's just that our fingerprint people found marks about the house that were neither your brother's nor his wife's. We need to eliminate all the innocent people, you see – including yourself. Did you often visit the house?'

'Apart from that one occasion I mentioned, Basil and I hadn't been to see them, so far, but from what Helen told me, the way Mrs Timms cleaned the place, I shouldn't think she left any fingerprints anywhere,' said Daphne Shepherd, a statement that confirmed what little the public knew about the science of fingerprints.

After obtaining Daphne's fingerprints, Bradley turned his attention to Timms once more. 'You wouldn't happen to know where this Mrs Timms lives, would you?'

'No, I'm sorry. Although, I should think it was probably quite local.'

'One other thing, Mrs Shepherd,' said Bradley. 'D'you know how often Mrs Timms went in to clean for the Ropers?'

'I think it was Monday, Wednesday and Friday.' Daphne Shepherd paused. 'Or it may have been Saturday rather than Friday. I don't honestly remember.' She frowned as a thought occurred to her. 'I suppose it'll be up to us to arrange the funeral,' she added pensively.

'I'll advise you when the coroner releases the bodies for

burial, Mrs Shepherd,' said Hardcastle. 'Incidentally, are your parents still living?'

'No, they're not. There's no one else who needs to be told. Frank and I don't have any other relatives.'

'Thank you for your help, Mrs Shepherd, and you too, Mr Shepherd. I'll leave you my telephone number in case you think of anything that might be of assistance to us.' Hardcastle paused. 'I'd be grateful if you didn't mention this tragedy to the press, should they get in touch.'

Hardcastle and Bradley walked out to their car and set off for Putney. 'I've made sure that nothing's been released to the press about these murders, Jack. Consequently, it's unlikely that Mrs Timms knows about them. In fact, I think I'll ask for a D-notice to be applied to this investigation.'

'With any luck, this Mrs Timms will turn up for work tomorrow morning, sir,' said Bradley.

'Exactly, Jack, and we'll be there to meet her.'

Detective Inspector Kenneth Black had assigned Detective Constable Douglas Dyer to duty at the George and Dragon that evening. There were no women detectives on V Division, but Black was a resourceful officer and called in a favour from Detective Inspector Duncan Fraser, an old friend of his at Vine Street police station on C Division.

When the Metropolitan Police finally decided that women detectives could be of some value, it was C Division that had first call on their services.

For members of the general public who were looking for a good time on an evening out, Soho and the West End were regarded as the places to go, affording them a daring glance at what they believed was a more risqué side of life. The police, however, had a different view. To them the area was a hotbed of vice, decadence and gambling. But, above all, it was those three pursuits that attracted the villains who made a profit out of preying on the smaller minnows of the underworld. The innocent and honest traders, too, were easy marks for those who used the payment of 'protection' money as a euphemism for extortion.

'Well, it's good to talk to you, Kenneth,' said Fraser, once the niceties were exhausted, 'but I'm sure you didn't ring me just to pass the time of day. What d'you want?'

'I'll say this for you, Duncan,' said Black, 'you always cut to the chase. I want a woman.'

'Don't we all, Kenneth, dear boy. Well, you've come to the right place. What age, colour and size d'you want? Long hair, blonde hair? And will it be by the hour or all night?'

Black roared with laughter. 'You don't change, Duncan,' he said, and went on to explain about the double murder that had occurred on the Kingston sub-division. 'Have you got a woman detective constable you can lend me just for this evening?' he continued, and told Fraser why he needed her services.

There was only the briefest of pauses before Fraser said, 'Aye. You can borrow WDC Marion Lewis. She's a bright lassie and she runs rings round half the male detective constables I've come across. I'll get the area car to run her down to Kingston police station on the bell, Kenneth. In that way, she'll be with you in a matter of about twenty minutes. I'll leave it to you to take it from there, rather than her trying to make a meet at the venue.'

'Thanks very much, Duncan. I owe you one. Incidentally, what does this lady detective look like?'

Having received a brief description of WDC Lewis, Black deputed Douglas Dyer to take the CID car, collect her from Kingston police station and go straight to the George and Dragon on Kingston Hill.

'You can brief her on the way, Douglas, but despite what the guv'nor said about being discreet, I don't see the point. Start asking questions as soon as you get there.'

Douglas Dyer was taken aback by WDC Marion Lewis's appearance. She was a bottle blonde, wore an excess of make-up, a clinging woollen dress and fishnet stockings. In short, that and her seductive figure made her seem to be the epitome of a Soho tart.

'Don't look so worried, Jock,' said Lewis, using Dyer's nickname, once introductions had been effected. 'I was helping a couple of the lads to track down a particularly nasty ponce operating in Shepherd Market when I got the call from the DI.

But the ponce will keep. If you can find me somewhere to change, I've got a much more respectable dress here.' She held up a holdall. 'And I'll get rid of some of this make-up.'

By the time that Dyer and Lewis arrived at the George and Dragon, it was getting on for eight o'clock. Bearing in mind what DI Black had said, Dyer made a point of approaching the licensee the moment they entered the pub.

'Can I have a word, guv'nor?' said Dyer, discreetly displaying his warrant card.

'There's never any problems here, Officer,' said the landlord, believing that the arrival of the police usually brought trouble with them. 'This is a law-abiding tavern, I can assure you.'

'I've no doubt about that,' said Dyer, 'but I'm involved in the enquiry into the murder of Frank and Helen Roper.'

'Terrible business, that. Always in here Friday and Saturday evenings without fail, were the Ropers. Never known them miss, not until this weekend. So, what can I do for you?'

'We want to learn as much as we can about their background,' continued Dyer. 'Is there anyone in here tonight who might know something of them, apart from just passing the time of day?'

The landlord ran a hand around his chin as he considered Dyer's request. 'Yes,' he said eventually, 'the colonel.' He pointed to a man at the far end of the bar. 'I think he knew them quite well.'

'What's his name?'

'No idea. He's always been known to us as the colonel.'

'Thanks.' Dyer and Lewis moved along the bar to join the man that the landlord had indicated. 'Good evening, Colonel.'

'Do I know you?' The colonel's sharp response was a combination of irritation and suspicion.

'No. I'm Detective Constable Dyer and I understand from the landlord that you knew the Ropers – Frank and Helen – quite well.' Once again, he displayed his warrant card discreetly.

'Quite right, old boy,' said the colonel, his attitude softening immediately. He glanced at Marion Lewis. 'I see you've brought your wife with you. Pretty clever that, using your good lady as cover. Attractive, too, if you don't mind my saying so, my dear.' He smiled at Marion Lewis.

'She's not my wife, Colonel. May I introduce Detective Constable Lewis.'

The colonel bent low, pretending to kiss Marion Lewis's outstretched hand. He then stood up to survey her. She was, indeed, a good-looking woman, now attired in a summery dress, her shining blonde hair decently arranged and her make-up skilfully applied. No longer did she resemble the prostitute that had so alarmed DC Dyer. But it would be a foolish man who attempted to take advantage of her, and she had already assessed the character of the red-faced army officer. She'd met a few like him in the past.

'By Jove! Well, I must say that the old police force is looking up, eh? By the by, my name's Curtis – Peter Curtis – and I'm not a colonel, I'm actually a major, a serving major.'

'I see,' said Dyer. 'You must be stationed locally, then.'

'Indeed, and I'm not telling you where, or what I do. Secret and all that, don't you know.'

'Of course. Can I buy you a drink, Major Curtis?'

'Damned decent of you. A large Scotch and soda, please.'

Dyer ordered the drinks, including one for DC Lewis and a small Scotch for himself, secure in the knowledge that he could claim the cost as a legitimate expense incurred in the garnering of valuable information.

'Good health,' said Curtis, raising his glass in salute. 'Now then, what can I tell you?'

'For a start, what sort of people were they?'

'Very hospitable.' Curtis paused. 'This conversation is entirely *entre nous*, I trust.'

'Of course,' said Dyer, not meaning a word of it.

'When you say hospitable, Major Curtis, what exactly d'you mean by that?' asked Marion Lewis, tiring of what she saw as 'pussyfooting around'.

'Ah! Cutting to the chase, I see.' Curtis faced the WDC. 'They invited me to dinner on two or three occasions. My wife is in Cornwall, you see, and one gets a bit tired of eating in the mess night after night. Damned decent of the Ropers.' He brushed at his moustache, something he did frequently during the course of their conversation.

'Was she a good hostess?' asked Lewis.

'A very good hostess. Why? What have you heard?' Curtis suddenly seemed very wary of the question.

'D'you mean about the affair?' suggested Lewis casually. As a WDC serving at Vine Street in the heart of London's West End, she was accustomed to dealing with women of questionable morals, and realized immediately what was behind Curtis's question. But her own fictitious allegation, although failing to confirm it, led to an admission of sorts.

'There wasn't an affair,' said Curtis sharply, and took a sip of his whisky. 'But it was a damned close-run thing, as the Duke of Wellington's supposed to have said after the Battle of Waterloo, don't you know? She invited me to dinner one night and it wasn't until I got there that I found that Frank was absent. She gave me some story about him having been called away to Windsor suddenly, but quite frankly, I think she'd set it up knowing he was going to be away. However, I misread the whole thing. She was as straight as a die. Consequently, I didn't finish up spending the night with her as I'd hoped, begging your pardon, miss.' He coughed affectedly. 'Another drink?'

'Was that the only occasion?' asked Dyer, once Curtis had bought a round of drinks.

'No, it wasn't. I'm sorry to have to say that she felt sorry for me, nothing more. In fact, I think that half the time she wanted the company. Whatever the reason, she invited me to dinner on several future occasions, but the lady was not into playing games.' Curtis chuckled and brushed at his moustache again, but Marion Lewis deduced that, despite his bluster and his overt ladies' man attitude, his ego had taken a knock at having failed to seduce Helen Roper on those occasions.

SEVEN

Hardcastle and Bradley arrived at the house of the murdered Ropers at eight thirty on Monday morning.

'All correct, sir.' The police constable on duty at the house saluted.

'Good morning. PC Suttling, isn't it? Am I right?' Hardcastle had not had time to do more than glance at the constable when he had called at his house the day he had moved in, but now that he studied him, he could see that he was one of the old-school policemen. His belt strained to contain his rotund belly, and he was a man clearly content to remain a PC until the day of his retirement.

'Yes, sir.' Suttling grinned, pleased that the DDI had remembered him. In his experience, PCs were usually addressed by their divisional number, if they were spoken to at all. It was unusual for a senior officer to recall a name, and particularly if that senior officer was a detective.

'Has Mrs Timms arrived yet, Suttling?'

'Nobody's arrived until you turned up, sir. Anyway, I don't know a Mrs Timms.'

'She's the Ropers' charlady. When she does arrive let her in, but don't tell her why you're here. If she asks, you can tell her it's about a burglary, but don't mention the murders.'

'Very good, sir,' said Suttling, and saluted again as Hardcastle and Bradley entered the house.

Ten minutes later, Mrs Timms arrived and marched into the kitchen where Hardcastle and Bradley were sitting. 'Why is there a policeman outside?' she demanded to know, hands on hips. 'And who are you?'

Daphne Shepherd, Frank Roper's sister, had described Violet Timms as birdlike and it was a good description. She was no more than five foot four or five in height and appeared almost frail of stature, as though a puff of wind would blow her away. She was wearing a black dress and flat, no-nonsense shoes.

Nevertheless, there was an air of determination about her that implied she would not stand for any nonsense, even from policemen, no matter how important they thought they were.

'I'm Divisional Detective Inspector Hardcastle of V Division, and this is Detective Sergeant Bradley, Mrs Timms.'

'Well, that's as maybe, but what's going on, I'd like to know?' Mrs Timms planted her large bag on the table and took out an overall that she donned while continuing to talk to the detectives. She also took out a paper packet of five Woodbine cigarettes that she slipped into her pocket.

'I'm sorry to have to tell you that Mr and Mrs Roper are dead, Mrs Timms. They were murdered on Friday evening, here in their own home.'

'Glory be to God!' exclaimed Violet Timms, and crossed herself. Her spontaneous adulation of the Almighty revealed the trace of an Irish accent. 'Who would have done such a thing?'

'Do sit down, Mrs Timms,' said Hardcastle, pulling out a chair from beneath the kitchen table. 'Perhaps you'd like a cup of tea. Sergeant Bradley has just made a pot.' Without waiting for a reply, Bradley poured the tea and handed it to the charlady.

'Have you caught whoever did this dreadful deed?' asked Violet Timms, once she had taken a mouthful of tea. She took out the packet of cigarettes and extracted one without offering any to the policemen. She did, however, accept a light from Bradley.

'No, we haven't. Not yet,' said Hardcastle, 'but perhaps you can help us, Mrs Timms. What sort of couple were the Ropers?'

Mrs Timms carefully replaced her cup in the saucer and looked searchingly at Hardcastle and then at Bradley, as though gauging whether to trust them. It was as if she was emulating the confidentiality observed by clergymen and doctors. 'They were always arguing, Inspector,' she said eventually, as she rolled the ash carefully from her cigarette into her saucer. 'I'd be upstairs cleaning the bedrooms and they'd be down here in the drawing room, going at it hammer and tongs. I'm surprised they didn't start throwing things. That Mrs Roper had a temper on her, I can tell you that. And her language wasn't what I'd have expected of a lady. But then, perhaps she wasn't a lady – a real lady, I mean. Mind you, she had her fair share of airs and graces, had Mrs Roper, as if she'd been one of them memsahibs in India with a houseful of servants. A bit of a madam, but like I said she had a tongue on her when she was up to full steam.'

'Have you any idea what the arguments were about?' asked Bradley.

'I'm not one for tittle-tattle, Sergeant Bradley, but they were shouting so loud, I couldn't help overhearing. On the one hand it seemed to have something to do with Mr Roper's work, although I've no idea what he did for a living. Mind you, they didn't seem short of money. But on the other it was about herself wanting to have children, so it was. It seemed that Mr Roper was dead against it. I felt sorry for the mistress in a way. It's only natural that a woman should want children.' After a moment or two, she said, 'Mind you, I sometimes wonder how we managed to bring up our three, seeing as how my Reg only gets a railway fireman's pay. Of course, he'll get a bit more if he can get upgraded to driver.'

'And you've no idea where Mr Roper worked, Mrs Timms?' asked Hardcastle, loath though he was to interrupt the char-lady's flow in case a gem of information was missed. 'And was that the real cause of their arguments, that and his wife's desire to have children?'

'It was that. Mind you, she hadn't got any room to talk. She wasn't above entertaining gentlemen friends when her husband was at work.'

'Did you ever see any of these people, Mrs Timms?'

'No, but you can always tell. Cigar butts in the ashtrays. Brandy glasses, but herself didn't drink brandy.'

'Well, thank you, Mrs Timms,' said Hardcastle. He had seen the report that DC Dyer had submitted before going off duty the previous evening, a copy of which DS Bradley had brought with him, and which Hardcastle had scanned before he and Bradley had left for the Ropers' house. Included in that report was Major Curtis's account of his failure to seduce Helen Roper. It was clear from Timms that she had indeed had male guests visiting the house in her husband's absence, but the true nature of their visits remained unclear. Were they totally innocent? On the other hand, it was possible that the major was lying. 'You've certainly given us something to think about. We also found some prints at the house that don't belong to the Ropers, so we must eliminate all innocent visitors to the house from our enquiries. May we take yours now, and your address, in case we need to talk to you again?'

'You may. And I hope you catch the devil incarnate who did this. I never held the Ropers in any high respect, but they didn't deserve that. I live in Hudson Road, Inspector. Number six, it is.'

Taking their leave of the informative charlady, Hardcastle and Bradley walked out to Kingston Hill just in time to catch a bus.

'We'll call in at the nick and see if DI Black has anything to report from the house-to-house enquiries, Jack.'

'There's a Mrs Wright, who lives opposite the Ropers' place,' said DI Kenneth Black. 'She seems to have known them quite well. Jock Campbell spoke to her and she said Campbell ought to talk to her husband who wasn't there at the time. He'll be home this evening, though. I could have a word with them unless you'd like to talk to them yourself, guv'nor? It's Trevor and Catherine Wright.'

'I've learned quite a bit about the Ropers already, Ken, and it'd be a good idea if I spoke to the Wrights. It would help to verify – or not – what I've learned already. In the meantime, Jack and I will have a run down to Windsor and find out what the management there can tell me about the Ropers.'

It was midday when Hardcastle and Bradley arrived at Alan Moore and Company's factory at Windsor. The DDI had telephoned in advance of their visit and they were greeted at the main entrance by the managing director's secretary, a vivacious young woman who introduced herself as Sheila Maskell.

'If you come this way, Inspector, I'll show you to Mr Hughes' office.'

They followed her up a flight of stairs, which gave them the opportunity to admire her shapely legs. She knew they would, and turned at the top and smiled at them. 'This way, gentlemen.'

The managing director looked up from his desk upon which there was a large blueprint that he carefully rolled up. 'Sorry,' he said. 'For some unknown reason things seem to be happening faster since the outbreak of the war.' He chuckled at his attempt to make a joke and handed the blueprint to his secretary. It was noticeable that he had a strong North Country accent. 'Perhaps you'd take that back downstairs, Sheila, lass, and tell 'em it's OK as far as I'm concerned.' Skirting his desk, he shook hands, first with Hardcastle and then with Bradley. 'Tom Hughes, gentlemen. Do take a seat and tell me how I can help you? Oh, Sheila, love,' he said, as his secretary reached the door. 'See if you can rustle up some tea when you've delivered that blueprint.'

'Has Howard Austin been in touch with you, Mr Hughes?' asked Hardcastle.

'No, I can't say he has. At least, not lately. Is there a reason why he should have done?'

Less than ten minutes later, Sheila Maskell returned to the office with tea on a tray.

'By heck! That were quick,' said Hughes. 'She's a magician, this girl, Inspector. Produces tea at the drop of a hat. You haven't taken any calls from Howard Austin, have you, Sheila?'

'Yes, first thing this morning, but you were on the shop floor and he said he'd ring back. I did leave a note on your desk.'

'Aye, happen you did, lass. I really must sort this lot out.' Hughes shuffled through the dozens of pieces of paper that littered his desk and picked up one or two that were on the floor, but then gave up.

'I'd clear all that up for you, Mr Hughes, if only you'd let me,' said Sheila, an element of criticism in her voice. It was not the first time she had made the offer.

'All right, lass. Received and understood.' Hughes held up both his hands in a demonstration of surrender.

Once Sheila had poured the tea and handed it round, she left the men to their discussion.

'She keeps me in order, does that girl,' commented Hughes. 'Now then, you obviously haven't come here to listen to me.'

'It's about Frank Roper—'

'Who's Frank Roper, Inspector?' Hughes was immediately attentive, and a frown creased his forehead.

'I understand from Howard Austin that he is a designer here,' said Hardcastle.

'I'm sorry, but I think you've been misinformed, Inspector. Not only is there no designer called Frank Roper, but as far as I know there's no one in the company by that name. But just to make absolutely certain, I'll have it checked.' Hughes walked to the door. 'Sheila, come in a moment, lass.'

'Yes, Mr Hughes.' Sheila Maskell appeared, holding a short-hand notebook as if expecting a letter to be dictated to her.

'Sheila, would you slip along to the personnel department and check if there's anyone on the payroll by the name of . . .' Hughes turned to Hardcastle. 'What was the name again, Inspector?'

'Frank Roper,' said Hardcastle, and spelled out the surname.

'That's it. Just making sure I got the name right. Do that as quickly as possible, Sheila, there's a good lass. By the way, there's no need for 'em to know it's a police enquiry.' Turning back to Hardcastle, Hughes asked, 'As a matter of interest, why are you making enquiries about this individual anyway?'

'He's been murdered, along with his wife, Helen,' said Hardcastle.

'Good God! And you say that Howard Austin told you he worked here?'

'Not only did Howard Austin say that Roper worked here at Windsor, but that he and Helen Roper were among the Austins' close friends,' said Bradley. 'And Mrs Austin was genuinely shocked when we told her of the murders.'

There was a knock at the door, followed immediately by the entry of Sheila Maskell. 'There is no one on the staff with the name Roper, Mr Hughes. I asked the head of personnel himself to check it.'

'Thank you, Sheila. Well, I don't know what to make of it, Inspector,' said Hughes, once Sheila had departed. 'Both branches of Moore's have their own personnel department. I think I'd better have a word with Howard Austin and ask him where he got the idea that this fellow Roper worked here.'

'I'd rather you didn't do that, Mr Hughes,' said Hardcastle. 'There may be more to this business than meets the eye, and other departments might become involved in the matter.'

'Ah, like MI5, you mean.'

Hardcastle just smiled. 'Thank you for your time, Mr Hughes. We'd better try and get to the bottom of this story.'

'Oh, for a nice, simple murder,' said Hardcastle, as he and Bradley arrived at the Wrights' house situated opposite where the Ropers had lived.

'Is there such a thing, guv'nor? asked Bradley, as he rang the doorbell.

'Mr Wright, we're police officers,' said Hardcastle, when the door was opened. 'I'm Divisional Detective Inspector Hardcastle and this is Detective Sergeant Bradley,' he continued, once they were in the hall with the front door closed and the hall light turned on again. 'We'd like to talk to you about the Ropers.'

'Of course. Catherine told me someone would be calling here this evening. Do come into the sitting room.'

A blazing fire was keeping the room warm and comfortable, and the two detectives were invited to take a seat.

'Would you like coffee?' asked Catherine Wright, a woman of about forty. She was dressed in a skirt and jumper and had allowed her long brown hair to follow the peek-a-boo style adopted by Veronica Lake, the American cinema and stage actress.

'Or something stronger?' asked Wright, whose tweed suit had obviously been made to measure.

'No, coffee would be most welcome,' said Hardcastle.

During the ten minutes it took Catherine Wright to prepare the coffee, Trevor Wright and the two CID officers discussed the war, a topic that was becoming more common than the English people's usual opening discussion about the weather.

Once they were all settled, each with a cup of coffee, Hardcastle said, 'I understand from the officer who came to see you yesterday that you have something to tell us about the Ropers.'

'He was a charming Scotsman, Inspector, that detective who called here,' began Catherine Wright. 'But there wasn't a great deal I could tell him about the Ropers.'

'You'd be surprised, Mrs Wright,' said Bradley. 'Our job is to discover who murdered the Ropers and anything you and your husband can tell us, however unimportant it might seem to you, could well be useful in achieving that object when put with other information.'

'Yes, I suppose so.' Catherine glanced at her husband.

'What Catherine is trying to say, Inspector,' said Trevor Wright, 'is that she formed entirely the wrong opinion of Frank Roper.'

'In what way?' asked Hardcastle.

'He came over one morning,' began Catherine, 'just before lunchtime, it was, and started by saying that he knew Trevor was away and if there was anything I needed or anything he could do for me, just to shout. They'd only moved in a few weeks previously and this was the first time I'd met him face-to-face. I have to admit that I assumed he'd timed his visit for when Trevor wasn't here. He looked the sort who would make a pass at any woman he met. I'm sure you know the sort of thing: excessively polite, always rushing to open a door. The desire to be seen as a gentleman. But I have to admit I was completely wrong. His visit was nothing more than a neighbourly gesture, like being prepared to mend a fuse or something of that sort. Naturally, I invited him in and offered him a cup of tea, which he accepted. We sat here, in this room, and had a long conversation. But the strange thing about it, when I think back, was that he never said anything about himself. We talked about the war, obviously everyone does, but when I thought about it afterwards, I knew no more about him when he left than when he'd arrived.'

'So, you've no idea what he did for a living, for example?'

'No. I asked him if he worked locally, but he avoided the question very neatly. It was only afterwards that I realized that I'd asked a few quite natural questions but never got a straight answer. It was almost as if he'd been trained to avoid telling anyone anything. But it didn't stop him asking me questions, again without giving the impression of prying, if you know

what I mean. For instance, he asked about that.' Catherine
Wright pointed at a curved ceremonial sword that was above
the mantelshelf, held in place by two brass hooks.

'It's a talwar, Inspector, a sword used mainly by the military
in India,' volunteered Wright. 'We brought it back from India
when we finally decided to come home to the old country in
1937.

'I told him it was Indian and, straight away, Frank asked
if Trevor and I had ever worked in India, and we had quite
a long chat about the sub-continent. On looking back, I'm
sure he knew what the talwar was and used it as a convenient
means to ask another question. I got the impression that he'd
worked there himself at some time, but I never really learned
much about him. It was all done so cleverly and I didn't
realize until later that, like I said just now, I didn't learn
anything about him or his wife, but he must've learned a lot
about Trevor and me.'

'*Were* you working in India, Mr Wright?' asked Bradley.

'Yes, I was the editor of a newspaper in Bombay, but then
they decided they wanted a native Indian to do the job.
Reasonable enough, I suppose, and if you know anything about
India, Inspector, you'll know they've been agitating for self-
rule for some time. That fellow Gandhi is one of the agitators.
Anyway, we decided it was time to come home to England,
just to be on the safe side. There was talk before we left that
the Japanese might have their eye on India.'

'Are you still in the newspaper business?' asked Hardcastle,
ever wary of saying too much to the press.

'No. I'd had enough anyway, so I got myself a job as a
whisky salesman. Very convivial, travelling from pub to pub,
and it's not awfully demanding. I also try to drum up business
by visiting gentlemen's clubs and doing what I can to sell
them our particular brand of Scotch. Not sure whether I'll be
able to keep it up, mind you. If there's a crackdown on petrol,
I might have to give up travelling my bit of the country. And
there's a rumour that Scotch will be in short supply very soon.
I'll probably finish up in the fire brigade or something to do
with the war effort, I suppose. Might even get conscripted
unless they think that forty-five is too old.'

'To sum up, then,' said Hardcastle. 'Frank Roper learned quite a bit about you two, but you learned very little about him.'

'That's about it,' said Wright, 'but oddly, I saw him a week or so later when I went to London to have lunch with a client, and it seemed completely out of character. I'd taken my client to Kettner's in Romilly Street and, lo and behold, there was Frank Roper sitting in a booth with some brassy tart who looked as though he'd just picked her up in Piccadilly.'

'Did you speak to him?'

'No. I gave him the benefit of the doubt. Having learned from Catherine what an unrevealing chap he was, I wondered whether he was on some sort of war work and the woman he was with was perhaps an informant.' Wright shrugged. 'On the other hand, perhaps I've read too many spy novels.'

Bradley asked whether they'd ever set foot inside the Ropers' house and, receiving a negative response, he and Hardcastle left feeling none the wiser about the couple.

EIGHT

Rather than waiting until the evening to speak to Howard Austin at home, Walter Hardcastle decided that he would instead call on him at the Kingston offices. He had not made an appointment, but in view of the urgency he hoped that Austin would be able to see him. Unlike the first time he had visited the company's offices, he received a respectful salute from Baldwin, the gatekeeper.

Miss Lovell, Austin's secretary, served Hardcastle and Bradley with coffee and explained that Austin was engaged on a lengthy telephone call, but would see the detectives the moment he was free.

Ten minutes later, Austin emerged from his office. 'I'm so sorry to have kept you waiting,' he said, 'but the Admiralty is getting a bit twitchy. They always want something yesterday. It must be something to do with Winston Churchill becoming First Lord of the Admiralty. However, enough of my complaining, do come in.'

'I'm sorry to trouble you again so soon,' began Hardcastle, 'but we spoke to Tom Hughes, the managing director at Windsor.' The three of them sat down: the two CID officers in armchairs and Austin behind his desk. Miss Lovell appeared with fresh coffee.

'Oh, yes, and what did Tom have to say about Frank Roper?' Austin asked, once Miss Lovell had departed and closed the door.

'He said he'd never heard of him,' said Jack Bradley.

Austin froze, his coffee cup halfway to his mouth. 'What on earth does that mean?'

'We can't put it any plainer than that, Mr Austin.' Bradley took a sip of his coffee. 'We told him that we were investigating the murder of the Ropers and that you had told us that Frank Roper was a close friend of yours and that he worked at the Windsor plant.'

'But when I telephoned Tom Hughes this morning to let him know you'd enquired about Frank—'

'When you telephoned this morning, you were unable to speak to Mr Hughes because he was out of the office.' Hardcastle was beginning to get a little suspicious of the whole story and particularly Austin's part in it.

'Yes, that's quite right. His secretary, Sheila Maskell, said he was on the shop floor and suggested I rang back later, but unfortunately I was sidetracked and when I rang again, Tom was off somewhere else. But I don't understand why he'd never heard of him.'

'He had Sheila Maskell check with the head of personnel and there is no one at the Windsor plant by the name of Roper. No one at all. What made you believe that he was employed there?'

'Frank told me that's where he worked, and he seemed to know the principals there, people like Tom Hughes and the location. All the things I'd expected someone who worked there to know about.'

'How did you meet him, Mr Austin, if it wasn't at one or other of the Alan Moore and Company locations?' asked Bradley.

'At my golf club. He was a member.'

'When was this?'

Austin stared at the ceiling as if seeking the answer there. Eventually, he looked down again. 'It must have been about ten or twelve weeks ago, I suppose. I bumped into him one Sunday morning. Eunice, my wife, was supposed to play a round of golf with me, but cried off at the last minute with an awful headache. I wandered up there on the off chance of finding someone who fancied eighteen holes before lunch. It seemed that Frank Roper was in a similar situation and was delighted to join me. We got talking and I was astonished to hear that he worked for the same firm as me, albeit at Windsor.'

'What a coincidence,' said Bradley, his tone of voice verging on the sarcastic. Together with the DDI, he was beginning to find this entire tale a little unlikely, to say the least.

As Austin's account unfolded, Hardcastle's doubts grew even stronger. He was not a Special Branch officer, but any detective would have found Austin's chance meeting almost unbelievable. That Austin had not found the encounter remarkable either demonstrated his naivety or indicated that his background needed a very close examination. Furthermore, that Roper had told a complete stranger that he worked at the same establishment engaged in top-secret war work as the stranger seemed extremely unlikely.

'Presumably, you met often at the golf club after that,' said Hardcastle.

'Yes. As a matter of fact, Frank's wife, Helen, was a golfer too, and it soon became the norm for us to play a foursome every Sunday. Of course, one thing led to another and Frank and Helen invited us to dinner at their house, and we returned the compliment by inviting them to our house.'

'And at no time during this, ten to twelve weeks, I think you said, did you question his claim that he worked for your company?'

'No, I took his word for it. After all, we tended not to talk shop, and as for the war, well, I think everyone was sick of the speculation, and we never discussed it.'

'Did he say where he'd been before suddenly turning up at your golf club three months ago, Mr Austin?' asked Bradley.

'No. I presumed that he'd been with the Alan Moore set-up for some time, but that we'd never met before.' Austin paused. 'Well, we don't often meet the chaps from Windsor. The plants are separate; our work is kept separate. Most of the time, contact is made by telephone.'

'Which golf club do you belong to, Mr Austin?' Hardcastle asked.

Austin took out his wallet and produced his membership card. 'You're not going to make enquiries there, are you?' he asked, somewhat apprehensively.

'Mr Austin, the Ropers have been murdered in cold blood,' said Hardcastle. 'They suddenly turn up out of the blue a few weeks before the war starts, and Frank Roper pretends to work for Alan Moore and Company. No one knows anything about him or his wife, including you, and I'm beginning to think that they're not all that they led people to believe. I shall certainly make enquiries at this club, if for no better reason

than to discover what sort of tale Roper told them.' Having
made a note of the golf club's address and telephone number,
the DDI returned the membership card.

'We'll get over to this golf club before Austin has a chance
to get at them,' said Hardcastle, once he and Bradley were
back in their car.

'Mr Dudley Carfax?' enquired Hardcastle, as he and Bradley
entered the club secretary's office.

'It's Captain Carfax actually.' The blazer-clad secretary rose
from behind his desk, brushed at his guardee moustache and
fingered his regimental tie. Now that he was standing up, he
proved to be rather short and somewhat overweight, and did
not seem like the figure of a man Hardcastle had always
visualized as an army officer. He was certainly unlike his
brother-in-law, Major General Spencer.

'I'm Divisional Detective Inspector Hardcastle and this is
Detective Sergeant Bradley.'

'Oh! Can't say I've seen you before. Local chaps, are you?'
Carfax waved a hand, indicating that the two officers should
sit down, but remained standing himself, presumably to give
himself some physical advantage over the two tall police
officers who were now seated.

'In a manner of speaking,' said Hardcastle. 'We're investigating
the murders of Frank Roper and his wife.'

'Good God!' Carfax did now sit down, rather heavily.
'Murdered? When did this happen?'

'Last Friday evening, at their home. How well did you know
the Ropers, Captain Carfax?'

'No more than to pass the time of day, you know. We do
have quite a few members, although I daresay a lot of them
will disappear once conscription gets under way.' Carfax
looked past Hardcastle, out of the window. 'Probably get
recalled myself, come to that, seeing I'm still on the reserve
of officers.'

'Presumably you dealt with the Ropers' application for
membership personally,' suggested Bradley.

'Yes, yes, I did.'

'Does that include an enquiry about profession?'

'Usually, yes. Is that important? I mean to say, he seemed of the right sort of class, if you know what I mean.'

Hardcastle did know what he meant; he'd met self-important characters like Carfax before, desperately trying to enhance their status with their airs and graces. 'What did Frank Roper tell you about his profession?'

Standing up and crossing the room, Carfax pulled a key-chain out of his pocket, selected a key and unlocked the filing cabinet. Riffling through the files, he eventually withdrew a slim manila folder and returned to his desk.

'I'm not sure I should reveal this information. It is given to the club in confidence.' Carfax kept his hand on the folder as if defying the police officers any attempt to see what it contained.

'They're both dead, Captain Carfax,' said Bradley sharply, 'and I would warn you against obstructing police, especially in time of war. The Defence Regulations are quite draconian, you know.'

'We could obtain a warrant if that would help to placate your members, Captain,' said Hardcastle quietly. 'Of course, it would have to be applied for in open court.' That was untrue, of course, but he was certain that Carfax did not know much about obtaining search warrants. 'And it would cover the entire premises.'

'Yes, well, quite,' said Carfax, hurriedly opening the folder and running a forefinger down the only sheet of paper it contained. 'Under "profession" it says "of independent means." And that's all the form contains, apart from giving his address, which, presumably, you already know.'

'And Mrs Roper?' asked Bradley.

'The word "none" was written against profession in her case. Then there is the signature of the club captain granting the Ropers membership.' Carfax closed the folder and handed it to Hardcastle, the prospect of a search warrant and all it entailed still playing on his mind.

'Did you ever have a conversation with either of the Ropers?' asked Hardcastle.

'No, I'm afraid not, apart from when I processed their application to join the club. If I happened to see them in the bar, I'd nod to them, or pass the time of day just to be sociable, but I never got to know them as well as I know some of the other longer-serving members, so to speak. Frank Roper favoured gin and tonic, if that's any help. I know that inconsequential snippets of information can sometimes be useful. That was certainly my view when I was briefly in Intelligence.'

'I see. Thank you. I'll make a note of it,' said Bradley. He was not overly impressed by officers who claimed to have been 'in Intelligence'. It was usually an attempt to imply that they quite understood the way in which the CID operated, and Bradley knew there was absolutely no similarity.

Hardcastle and Bradley were back at divisional headquarters at Putney by half past four, to be met by the DDI's clerk, hovering in the corridor outside Hardcastle's office.

'What is it, Winters?'

'Mr Canning wants to see you as a matter of urgency, sir. He's the chief constable of Special Branch, sir.'

'Yes, thank you, Winters,' said Hardcastle rather curtly. 'I do know who Mr Canning is. Tell my driver to get the car ready.'

'Now, sir?'

'Yes, man, now.'

After a thirty-minute journey, Hardcastle arrived at the foot of the steps leading to the main entrance to New Scotland Yard.

Due to the heightened security since the outbreak of war, he was obliged to produce his warrant card to the police constable at the door, before being allowed to make his way along the corridor to Canning's office.

'DDI Hardcastle of V, sir. You wanted to see me.'

'Yes, I do, Mr Hardcastle. Sit down.' Chief Constable Albert Canning was six feet tall and immaculately dressed in a three-piece pin-striped suit and a white shirt with a starched collar. His moustache was neatly trimmed. Now fifty-four years of age, he had been head of Special Branch for three years, but his experience of the branch's duties went back much further to when he'd joined as a detective constable before the Great

War. During that war, when he was a detective sergeant, he had been seconded to the army's Intelligence Corps and served in the Field Security Police in France until the end of the conflict. 'You're investigating the murders of Frank and Helen Roper.' It was a statement not a question.

'Yes, sir.'

'Why did you not report the matter to this branch the moment you knew of it, Mr Hardcastle?' Canning's twinkling blue eyes were proving to be deceptive; there was a sharpness behind the question.

'I saw no reason to report it to Special Branch, sir.' Hardcastle was wondering what this interrogation was all about. 'They were two murders apparently committed on the spur of the moment by an opportunist burglar.'

'But you were informed by a sergeant of this branch that Frank Roper had been placed at Windsor specifically to trace or attempt to trace anyone who was passing information to an enemy agent.'

'I was not informed of that by anyone, sir, or that I was required to inform your branch.'

Canning studied Hardcastle's face for a moment or two, as if seeking signs of mendacity, and then pressed a bell push on his desk. A detective constable appeared.

'Sir?'

'Ask Superintendent Aubrey Drew to see me.'

A few moments later a smartly dressed, middle-aged man entered the chief's office.

'Ah, Mr Drew. This is DDI Hardcastle of V. He's handling the Roper murders. Find out who was supposed to tell him about Roper's involvement at Windsor and find out what the hell went wrong. And I want a written report.'

'Very good, sir.' Drew turned to go, but stopped. 'Hardcastle, eh?' he said thoughtfully. 'Was your father in the job?'

'Yes, sir. He was the DDI on A Division when he retired.'

'How is he?'

'Same as ever, sir. Argumentative and always telling me how to do the job.'

Drew laughed. '*Plus ça change*. We worked together on an espionage case during the last war. I don't think he liked me very much . . . or the branch for that matter. Nevertheless, give him my regards when you see him.' With that forgiving comment, Drew departed.

'I suppose I'd better tell you what you should have been told, Mr Hardcastle.' Canning was clearly very annoyed at having to admit that there had been a breakdown in communications. 'Frank Roper was not a police officer; he was an agent of MI5, although he'd been recruited by them only recently and for a specific job. He was a design engineer who had been working in Germany until about nine months before the war started, but he decided that things were getting a little too unpleasant for an Englishman and his wife. Consequently, they decided to come home.'

'And that's when he settled in Kingston, was it, sir?'

'Yes, at a meeting between this branch and MI5 it was decided that Roper would be ideally qualified to infiltrate the factory at Windsor because we – that is to say Special Branch and MI5 – were pretty sure that there was a traitor in the workforce who was passing information to the Abwehr about the work that Alan Moore and Company were doing. Roper, of course, knew Germany and the Germans and also had the advantage of speaking their language fluently. Helen Roper was also involved in trying to extract information from local people with links to Moore's, as well as keeping an eye out for other potential MI5 recruits who might be able to help with the war effort.'

'I presume that Tom Hughes, the managing director of the Windsor plant, was not informed about this arrangement, sir.'

'No.' Albert Canning let out a sigh of frustration. 'We had given Roper a false identity as Frederick Ringham to work at Windsor, but we didn't expect him to be murdered, Mr Hardcastle. The truth of the matter is that he was given time to settle in and he was only very recently activated, in the sense that he allowed it to be known that he was working for Alan Moore and Company. The idea was that we would inform Hughes at Windsor – in confidence, of course – once Roper, alias Ringham, had begun working at Windsor and had settled in. Unfortunately, the best laid plans, and all that, were overtaken by this unfortunate event. At the time he was murdered, he'd only been at Windsor for a matter of weeks – as Ringham, of course.' The chief constable shook his head. 'Are there any indications at all who the killer was?'

'Not at this stage, sir, no.' Hardcastle got the impression that Roper's murder was nothing more than an inconvenience to Canning. 'I have to admit that I have no promising lines of enquiry at the moment.' He went on to tell the Special Branch chief about Timms' suspicions about Mrs Roper, the reason for her being nothing more than an excellent hostess now understood – although exactly how far her hostess skills went no doubt depended on the extent of her devotion to obtaining information – and the stories he had heard from Trevor and Catherine Wright, who lived opposite the Ropers, and Major Peter Curtis, that painted the picture of a perfectly ordinary couple.

'Yes, well, he was merely following instructions there about how much he could say and to whom. Together with MI5, we briefed the Ropers to give the impression that they were a perfectly ordinary middle-class couple that would attract no interest from their neighbours in order to disguise what Frank Roper was really being tasked to do '

'I've spoken to Frank Roper's sister, Daphne Shepherd, sir, but she had nothing to tell me, other than to say that her brother had been working in South Africa for some years. That was, presumably, a deliberate deception.'

Canning said nothing.

Hardcastle, presuming Canning's silence was also deliberate and that he intended to give nothing away, went on to outline the possibility of an enemy agent, posing as a burglar, deliberately targeting houses occupied by Moore's workers. 'It's possible, in my view, sir, that the Ropers' house was picked on for that very reason. One of my Kingston-based officers overheard mention in a pub frequented by the Ropers that Frank Roper worked for Alan Moore's. It seemed to be an open secret.'

'You've got a job on your hands, Mr Hardcastle, and that's a fact,' said Canning. 'If there's anything that the branch can do to assist, let me know. In fact, I'll assign Mr Drew to liaise with you.'

'Thank you, sir. It's evident that we're dealing with a very professional murderer here. It's possible that he is an agent of the Abwehr tasked to kill Roper because the Nazi regime saw him as a threat to their agent in the factory. Mr Cherrill visited the scene himself. He could find no trace of strange fingerprints on surfaces the killer was likely to have touched, but there were other prints that don't belong to the Ropers. We're in the process of checking these against those we've taken from their cleaner and a family member. Our scientific team only found an abandoned glove that we're in the process of trying to identify. Furthermore, there was nothing taken, but that may be accounted for by our belief that the killer was disturbed.' And Hardcastle finished by telling Canning about the other burglaries where only small items of little value had been taken.

'Keep Mr Drew fully informed about any further burglaries that appear to be targeting Alan Moore employees, Mr Hardcastle, and he will apprise me of any details that affect this branch. However, I suggest that you now deal with this double murder as if it were an ordinary murder and don't get distracted by what I've told you.'

'Very good, sir,' said Hardcastle, but he was unsure what the chief constable meant by 'an ordinary murder'. He had never come across an *ordinary* murder, and the Ropers' seemed to be anything but. As he walked back to his car, parked in the road between Cannon Row police station and New Scotland Yard, he wondered why Special Branch and MI5 had to make things so damned complicated. Why, for instance, were the murdered couple known in Kingston as Roper, but Frank Roper was known in Windsor as Fred Ringham?

But then, his father claimed always to be having problems with Special Branch.

NINE

When he returned to Putney police station from his interview with Chief Constable Canning at New Scotland Yard, Hardcastle sent for Detective Sergeant Bradley.

'Take a seat, Jack.' Hardcastle pulled out his pipe and filled it with tobacco.

'All right if I smoke, guv'nor?' asked Bradley.

'Of course. Carry on.' Once Hardcastle's pipe was alight to his satisfaction, he leaned back in his chair. 'I think we're faced with what Sherlock Holmes would've called a three-pipe problem, Jack,' he said, and went on to tell him what he had learned from the head of Special Branch.

Bradley laughed. 'Sounds like SB has made a bugger's muddle of it, guv'nor,' he said, lighting a cigarette.

'It's that all right, Jack, but I don't think they're entirely to blame. As Mr Canning said, they didn't anticipate that Roper alias Ringham would be murdered. However, despite all that, it doesn't alter the fact that we've still got two murders to solve.'

'Is it possible that Helen Roper was the target, if she was also working for MI5?'

'But Frank Roper was shot first, Jack. Whether he was the actual target and Helen was in the wrong place at the wrong time, I don't know. It is possible, of course, that Frank went upstairs and was shot simply because he disturbed a burglar. But you could be right that she was the target and Roper would have been a witness, so he had to die as well. On the other hand, I think my original theory still holds good.'

'What, that they were the victims of a burglar who thought they'd gone out?'

'Exactly. The unusual aspect to this burglar, though, is that he went about his business armed. And that leads me to believe that maybe he *is* an enemy agent searching for something the Ropers had – this wasn't a burlarly gone wrong.'

'Why should him being armed make a difference, guv?'

'Because there's a war on now, Jack, and spies are shot at dawn at the Tower of London. Just like they were in the last war. The fact that this burglar shot the Ropers without hesitation leads me to believe that he was a spy.'

'And murderers are hanged. Not a great deal of difference, is there, sir?' observed Bradley drily.

'That's true, and that's why burglars don't usually carry a gun, in case they're tempted to use it. A German agent, on the other hand, wants to avoid the death penalty at all costs and, it would appear, would rather shoot his way out of a confrontation.'

'D'you think that the other burglaries – those on the homes of Alan Moore and Company's employees – were carried out by the same man, sir?'

'I'm beginning to think it more than likely, Jack. The modus operandi is very similar. A clean break-in and no evidence of his identity. No fingerprints, nothing, and no one saw him. In addition to which, only a few worthless items were taken, if anything was taken at all. That's the strangest bit: why take useless items? It makes no sense, unless he was searching for sensitive documents. This time, though, he left a glove and that might turn out to be a mistake that gets him shot at the Tower if we can identify where it was bought.'

'Do we know it was his glove, sir?'

'Well, put it this way: there is no single left-hand glove in the Ropers' house, and that seems to indicate that the right-hand glove we found didn't belong to Frank Roper. The only thing it tells us is that if it's the murderer's, he was right-handed.' Hardcastle cynically added, 'And that should make him easy to find.'

'Might it be a good idea to have the fingerprint people carry out a closer examination of the other properties concerned in case there's a stray fingerprint that might help us, sir? One that was missed the first time around.'

'That would be a pointless exercise, given the time lapse,' said Hardcastle. 'And I doubt that Mr Cherrill would be prepared to come down here to examine the Ropers' place again or, for that matter, send one of his people. He's probably the best fingerprint officer in the world and I wouldn't like to be the one to suggest he might've missed a mark. Apart from anything else, it's quite on the cards that our murderer has no previous convictions, which means his prints won't be on record anyway.'

'And if he's an Abwehr agent, his prints wouldn't be anyway, sir,' said Bradley. 'At least, not here.'

In the weeks that followed the murders of Frank and Helen Roper, little progress was made in finding their killer despite Hardcastle's best efforts. The fingerprints that weren't the Ropers' were confirmed as being Mrs Timms, and the glove was taking a while to pin down. Progress was not helped by a plethora of new Defence Regulations that the police were obliged to enforce, much of which had to be undertaken by the CID.

Christmas 1939 came, but it was not the sober and austere celebration for which the government had hoped. It was as if the population realized that conditions were going to get worse and that this was their last chance to have a 'good' Christmas. Some doomsters even suggested that it might be the last Christmas before the jack-booted, goose-stepping Germans invaded.

Rationing had yet to be introduced, although curbs on bacon and butter had been promised for January. The blackout prevented any sort of display that contravened the regulations and, in some cases, family get-togethers were more sober than usual because the head of the household was absent. Quite a few men had been reservists, and had been recalled to active service together with those elements of the Territorial Army that had been mobilized, and were spending their Christmas in France as part of the British Expeditionary Force. Regrettably, some men had already been killed in action in France and the Middle East. Furthermore, some of the children who had been evacuated to the countryside had come home for the Christmas holiday, and the authorities feared that they might be tempted to stay.

In common with other detectives, one of the increases in crime that Hardcastle had noticed was that the blackout had brought about a rise in the number of burglaries as criminals took advantage of the lack of street lighting to carry out more audacious housebreakings. Shortages of food and luxuries had caused black marketeers to become active, too. All of which increased pressure on the police.

Although there were further burglaries on V Division, there was none that Hardcastle could liken to the one that had ended with the murder of the Ropers, and none involving Moore employees. He wondered if the murderer had been called up and was now serving with one of the armed forces, or even if he had been killed in the opening stages of the war on the Continent. Maybe he had found what he was looking for and fled the country; in which case, they had no chance of ever catching him.

Despite the problems of shortages, and the difficulties of travelling, Walter and Muriel Hardcastle and their three children managed to get to Kennington Road on Boxing Day.

It was some time since Walter had spent any part of the Christmas holiday with his parents, but the house seemed exactly the same. Even the Christmas decorations were as he remembered them. There were paper chains from each corner of the sitting room to the central light pendant. In one corner stood a Christmas tree of a similar size to the one the elder Hardcastles always had and decorated in much the same way. But now there was the addition of Christmas presents beneath it for the younger Hardcastle family.

Walter's father, Ernest, now sixty-eight years of age, looked no different from the day he had retired from the police some nine years previously. He had, however, mellowed during those days to the extent that he would make a fuss of his grandchildren. But then he turned to his son and displayed some of the old familiar sharpness that Walter remembered so well.

'Have you solved that double murder in Kingston yet, Wally?'

'Not yet, Pa.'

'Why not? What's keeping you?' Ernest then launched into a rambling lecture about how to solve murders, and recalled some of the cases he had investigated and how he had gone about the investigation. 'And then there was the woman's body that was found under Palace Pier in Brighton a couple of days after the Armistice . . .'

Walter listened in patient silence. It would be futile to try to explain that since his father's days in the job, great advances had been made in the various forensic sciences that supported and assisted detectives. He held back because he knew his father would make some acerbic comment, pointing out that it had not helped his son on this occasion.

'By the way, Pa, Mr Marriott sends you his regards.' Walter Hardcastle decided to change the subject.

'Ah! Young Marriott. What's he now? Must be a detective chief inspector, I suppose.'

'He's a deputy assistant commissioner, Pa.'

For some time, Ernest Hardcastle stared at his son, astonishment clear on his face. 'Of course, he was properly trained as a sergeant, Wally,' he said eventually. 'Assisting a good DDI is where you learn the art of the thief-taker.'

'And Mr Catto is chief constable CID now.'

'Good God!' After a few moments of silent introspection, Ernest Hardcastle added, 'Of course, he was trained at Vine Street. Like me.'

'It sounds to me as though you miss the job, Pa, even though it's nine years since you put your papers in.'

Ernest took out his pipe and polished the bowl on his trouser leg. He accepted Walter's tobacco pouch without a word of thanks. 'You really ought to try St Bruno, Wally,' he said, but still filled his pipe with his son's offering. 'You never lose it, you know,' he commented reflectively. 'Locking up villains is in the blood, and if they asked me to go back tomorrow, I'd go like a shot. Now is when they need experienced detectives, good thief-takers.'

'Well, you might get called back, Pa.'

'D'you think so, Wally? Have you heard anything?'

'For goodness' sake, stop talking shop, you two,' said Alice, Walter's mother, ever the peacemaker. 'It's about time you poured us all a drink, Ernest, while Muriel and I put the finishing touches to the Boxing Day dinner. It's hot work in the kitchen and we're dying of thirst before we even start.'

'Yes, dear,' said Ernest, recognizing that his wife was using his full name, instead of Ernie. Always a warning sign that her temper was shortening.

Ernest however, was not to be silenced completely. 'I'm beginning to wonder when this war's going to start,' he proclaimed. 'Nothing much seems to be happening in France and there's certainly been none of the raids the government told us to expect. I don't wonder it's being called the phoney war.'

'Drinks, Ernest!'

'Yes, dear.'

The dinner went well and by three o'clock the men expressed their satisfaction and raised their glasses to toast the two Hardcastle women for their efforts, made no easier by the food shortages.

Ernest Hardcastle, now in a quite jovial mood, led the grandchildren back to the sitting room and handed them their Christmas presents. The two sets of Hardcastles exchanged gifts and by the time they left the house everyone declared it had been a most enjoyable day.

Ernest Hardcastle could not resist a parting shot at his son. 'You make sure you get those murders cleared up, Wally. The reputation of the Hardcastles depends on it. If you want any advice, you can always ring me up and I'll do my best to help you out.'

'Thanks, Pa.' Wally kissed his mother and shook hands with his father. 'By the way, Detective Superintendent Aubrey Drew sends you his regards.'

'D'you mean that Special Branch chap?'

'That's him, Pa.'

'How do you know him anyway, Wally?'

'Can't say, Pa.' Wally smiled. 'But there's something big going on. The army are talking about setting up a special investigation branch and seconding detectives from the Metroplitan Police for deployment in France. I may just be one of them.'

'A superintendent, eh?' muttered Ernest, ignoring his son's news. 'I can see this war has done some people some good. Perhaps I should've stayed on a bit longer.'

'Ernest!' Alice spoke sharply. 'They've got a train to catch.'

TEN

In the last days of May 1940 came the devastating news of the Dunkirk evacuation. On the June day it was completed, Walter Hardcastle, now back on V Division after his secondment to France, was in the Lower Richmond Road in Putney where a body had been recovered from the river.

'Hello, Wally. How are you?'

'I'm all right, Ted. How about you?' Edward Hunter, an inspector in Thames Division, had joined the Metropolitan Police on the same day in 1918 as Walter Hardcastle. 'What are you doing down here, anyway? I thought inspectors in the river police stayed in the warm at Wapping.'

Hunter laughed. 'I was inspecting the station books down at Barnes and cadged a lift on the despatch boat to Waterloo when we got this shout about a floater near Putney Bridge. This is your manor now, isn't it?'

'Yes, it is, and I'm dying to know why you sent for me. Has the body been identified?'

'It's all a bit bloody mysterious, Wally,' said Hunter. 'The PC on the beat spotted this parachute floating in the river. He called us and to no one's surprise, there was a dead body attached to the parachute. According to the papers on the body, he's Hauptmann Konrad Fischer, but the odd thing is that he's dressed in plain clothes, and the parachute is definitely German. And as if that's not enough, he has a leather despatch case chained to his left wrist. The other thing is that he was wounded, but it appears likely that he shot himself. I don't know if it's relevant, Wally,' continued Hunter, 'but we had a report of a downed two-seater Messerschmitt beyond Wapping at about the time that this guy Fischer was seen floating down to Father Thames. The aircraft contained only the dead pilot.'

'Where are you taking him?' asked Hardcastle, turning to one of the ambulance attendants.

'Putney hospital mortuary, guv'nor.'

'Right. I'll meet you there and once I've made a few phone calls, I'll know what to do next.'

'What d'you reckon, Wally?' asked Hunter when the ambulance had departed complete with a police escort, the constable having been told to stay with the body until relieved.

'Another unsuccessful attempt at landing a spy?' suggested Hardcastle. 'We'll have to wait and see what Special Branch has to say about it.' He spent a few moments lighting his pipe. 'Has this business at Dunkirk affected your outfit, Ted?' he asked.

Hunter scoffed. 'Don't talk to me about Dunkirk, Wally. We asked the guv'nor if we could take the boats across to pick up some of our troops, but he turned us down flat. He said that the boats were far too valuable to risk losing them.' Hunter paused, reflecting. 'I suppose he had a point, really, but all the same, the lads were bloody annoyed by his decision.'

'According to the news, about three hundred and forty thousand of our boys have been saved and brought back to England. I heard that the arrivals hall at Dover was awash with blood.'

'Yes, so I heard.'

'I just hope to God that the German army doesn't follow our troops across, Ted. If they do, we've had it. We just haven't got the resources to resist.'

'If they come up the Thames,' said Hunter, 'they'll have the river police to contend with.'

'Mind you don't damage the boats, then,' said Hardcastle, 'or your guv'nor will be cross.'

Hardcastle returned to Putney police station to find that Jack Bradley was waiting for him with some news.

'Since you've been out looking into that floater, sir, some progress has been made regarding the Roper murders. I think I've found someone who can give us a lead on the glove. I spoke to an official at the Worshipful Company of Glovers yesterday. He said that if we showed him the glove, he might be able to tell us where it came from. He did, however, warn me that it's more likely to be one made for the mass market.'

'Good work, Jack. When can this man see us?'

'Any time during office hours, sir.'

Hardcastle glanced at his wristwatch. 'Half past three. No time like the present, then. These two murders have been on the books far too long, and I don't want Mr Marriott breathing down my neck. Or my father, come to that.' He was also acutely aware that this was his first double murder case since gaining his promotion, and he desperately needed a good result.

'Christopher Waring, gentlemen. 'Delighted to meet you both.' He was probably somewhere between forty and fifty years of age. He shook hands with his left hand – his right arm was missing – and a severe limp impeded his progress. 'The other bits of me are somewhere in Beaumont-Hamel,' he explained with a laugh.

'I'm Divisional Detective Inspector Hardcastle of V Division, Mr Waring. I understand that you've already met Detective Sergeant Bradley.'

'Only on the telephone. He explained that you have a glove to show me.'

'Yes, indeed. Sergeant Bradley probably told you that we're investigating a double murder. This glove was found at the scene and I was hoping that you might be able to give us some idea about its origins in the hope that we would be able to trace the owner. I appreciate that it's something of a long shot.' Hardcastle took the glove from an evidence bag and placed it on Waring's desk.

Waring took out a pair of spectacles and opened its arms with an adroit flick of his remaining wrist. Putting them on, he looked closely at the glove. Apparently dissatisfied, he opened a drawer of his desk and took out a magnifying glass with which he examined the glove more closely than before.

'Interesting,' said Waring, as he straightened up. 'Have a look at this pattern.' Selecting a pencil from a pot of them, he slowly traced the stitching on the back of the glove. 'Normally, the stitching is in three rows radiating from the wrist up to the points where the fingers begin. It is usually a very simple design, but in this case, the pattern is far more elaborate with loops and figures of eight.'

'Have you any idea where it might have originated, Mr Waring?'

'Yes, but let me check.' Waring turned to his bookcase and, with some difficulty, took down a heavy volume. Riffling through the pages, he eventually looked up. 'I thought so,' he said. 'Unless I'm sadly mistaken, that glove was manufactured by a firm called Otto Krause of Cologne. The stitching is unique.'

'Unfortunately, there's no chance of going over there to find out who they sold this glove to,' said Hardcastle gloomily. 'However, Mr Waring, I'm much obliged to you. It certainly gives us a lead of sorts that might help us to track down the murderer.' What he did not say was that it lent credence to his suspicion that the killer was a German agent who had somehow learned that Frank Roper was looking for a spy on the Alan Moore and Company payroll. But the DDI had not lost sight of the fact that Frank Roper had worked in Germany prior to returning to England. It was possible, therefore, that the glove belonged to him, but if that were the case, where was the matching glove for the left hand? He knew it wasn't at the Ropers' house.

'A German agent wouldn't wear a pair of German gloves, surely, guv'nor?'

'You'd be surprised at the compromising things that have been found on German spies, Jack.'

'Perhaps it's a double bluff,' muttered Bradley.

Hardcastle decided that while he was in central London, he would call in at the Yard and bring Detective Superintendent Aubrey Drew up to date.

The Special Branch reserve sergeant, having carefully examined the warrant cards produced by Hardcastle and Bradley, eventually conducted them to Drew's office.

'Take a seat, Wally. You too, Sergeant Bradley.'

'I'm afraid we've not made much progress with the glove in the Roper murders, sir,' said Hardcastle, and repeated what Waring had told him.

'I'm sorry if your time has been wasted and progress hampered by not knowing about the deception involving the

Ropers. As I told Canning in my report, unfortunately the sergeant who was told to give you this information was posted abroad before he was able to see you. Entirely my fault, I'm afraid. I should have checked.'

'I see, sir.' Despite being curious, Hardcastle did not bother to ask why a Special Branch officer had been sent abroad during the war; he knew he would not get an answer.

'The Ropers had both done a bit of amateur dramatics with the British community, Wally, and it was simplicity itself for them to play the part of a couple of innocents.'

'Unfortunately, sir, that doesn't help much with finding the murderer.' Hardcastle then told Drew about Thames Division finding the dead body of Hauptmann Konrad Fischer, and that there was a despatch case chained to his wrist.

'Thank you, Wally,' said Drew. 'You can leave the matter entirely to us. Where is the body at the moment?'

'In the mortuary in Putney hospital, sir, under police guard.'

ELEVEN

The time was eleven fifteen on the evening of Friday the seventh of June 1940. Police Constable 133V Gordon Tomlin, patrolling Kingston Hill not far from where the murdered Ropers had lived, stopped a man attired in evening dress. The late-evening burglar who, it was believed, was responsible for the Ropers' murders, was still uppermost in policemen's minds despite the lack of leads and their growing focus on other, more recent cases, and they were reminded of it daily by the inspector who paraded them for duty.

'Excuse me, sir, but where are you going?'

'Home, Officer.'

'And where is your home?'

'Why d'you want to know? I'm not doing anything wrong.'

'I'll ask you again, sir: where do you live?'

The man remained silent.

'Show me your identity card,' said Tomlin.

Again, the man remained silent and made no move to comply with the police officer's demand.

'Very well, I'm arresting you for failing to produce your identity card and for being a suspicious person loitering with intent to commit a felony.' Conscious of the fact that the Ropers had been murdered with a firearm, Tomlin quickly searched the man, but found no weapon. Walking the arrested man the few yards down the road to the police box near the George and Dragon public house, Tomlin telephoned Kingston police station and asked for assistance. Minutes later, a police van arrived and conveyed Tomlin and his prisoner to the police station.

'Well, what've you got, one-three-three?' asked the station officer, as he entered the charge room with a bundle of books and papers which he set down on the charge desk.

Tomlin outlined the reasons for having arrested the man

who now stood in front of the station officer. 'When I searched him, I didn't find any weapons or an identity card, Sergeant.'

The sergeant directed his gaze at the prisoner. 'Are you going to give me your name and address?'

The prisoner remained silent.

'Name and address refused. Put him down, one-three-three,' said the frustrated sergeant. 'Number two cell, and we'll see if the gentleman's more co-operative in the morning. Or perhaps he's mute of malice,' he added sarcastically.

Having done as the sergeant ordered, Tomlin returned. 'He spoke, Sergeant.'

'Oh, he did, did he? How very obliging of him. What did he say?'

'He said that he'd talk to Inspector Hardcastle, but no one else.'

'Well, if he thinks I'm calling the DDI out this late, he's got another think coming. He can wait till the early turn comes on.'

'He also asked to be allowed to phone his solicitor.'

'Well, if he said he'll only talk to Mr Hardcastle and no one else, he's not talking to his solicitor until the DDI says so.'

Walter Hardcastle arrived at Kingston police station at just after eight o'clock in response to the early turn station officer's telephone call.

'Put this silent prisoner in the interview room, Skip, and I'll talk to him there. And you've no idea of his identity?'

'None at all, sir,' said the station officer. 'I even had a look inside his jacket to see if there was a name, but nothing.'

Hardcastle entered the interview room and closed the door.

'Good morning, Mr Hardcastle.'

'What are you doing here, Mr Shaw?'

'Perhaps you should ask the officer who arrested me.'

'What were you doing on Kingston Hill when you told the officer that you were going home? You live in Pine Walk in Berrylands. Or have you moved?'

'It's a bit complicated, Mr Hardcastle.'

'We're very good at sorting out complicated things,' said Hardcastle. 'Try me.'

Shaw paused before replying. 'I was on my way home from a masonic meeting,' he said haltingly.

Hardcastle shook his head. 'There is no masonic lodge anywhere near Kingston Hill. Would you like to try again?'

Shaw hung his head. 'I was seeing another woman,' he said. 'My wife thinks I go to a masonic meeting, but I'm not a freemason.'

'How often d'you meet this woman?'

'Once a week.'

'Do you own a firearm, Mr Shaw?'

'Good heavens, no.'

'The one thing I don't understand,' said Hardcastle, taking out his pipe and slowly filling it with his favourite Player's Navy Cut tobacco, 'is why you didn't explain all this to the police officer who stopped you last night.'

'I thought he might check the story with my wife,' answered Shaw lamely. A sudden thought occurred to him. 'My employers won't have to be told, will they, Mr Hardcastle?'

'Yes, they will. For one thing, you are engaged on secret government work, and you didn't turn up for work this morning. Doubtless, someone from Alan Moore's will have telephoned your home to ask your wife where you were. She won't have known and is now probably worried sick. Apart from anything else, you have wasted a great deal of police time as a result of your hare-brained decision not to answer the officer's questions. I would have you charged, but you've wasted enough of our time. However, we will take your fingerprints and I'll admit you to bail to report here again in one month's time. If we do not require you to return to this station, we will let you know.'

'By what right can you possibly . . .?' Shaw began to protest, but then realized it was pointless.

'There is just one other thing,' said Hardcastle. 'What is the name and address of this woman you've been seeing?'

'Oh God! You're not going to speak to her, are you?'

'I most certainly am.'

'But she'll wonder what's going on.'

'Does she know you're married, Mr Shaw?'

'No, she doesn't, but *she* is. Her husband is a naval officer stationed at Portsmouth.'

Hardcastle shook his head. 'Once I have her details and your fingerprints have been taken, you're free to go, Mr Shaw.'

'Is there any chance of a lift?' asked Shaw, unwisely.

'No, there isn't.'

Seconds after Shaw had left the interview room, Jack Bradley arrived. 'Have I missed all the fun, guv'nor? I saw Keith Shaw leaving just as I arrived.'

Hardcastle explained briefly. 'I think we'll have a talk with Mrs Gillian Flint straight away.'

'Who's Gillian Flint, guv'nor?

'I'll explain on the way, Jack.'

Gillian Flint's house was in Crescent Road, off Kingston Hill, a substantial property that lay beyond a lengthy front garden.

'We're police officers, Mrs Flint.'

'Please come in.' She was probably in her forties and, oddly, bore a striking similarity to Elizabeth Shaw. But it wasn't the first time Hardcastle had come across this quirk of adulterous behaviour. It surprised him how often men leave one woman in order to start an affair with another who was similar to the woman he'd just left. 'Is it the commander?' she asked breathlessly.

'Who is the commander, ma'am?' asked Bradley.

'My husband, Commander Rollo Flint. Is he all right? He's stationed at Portsmouth, you see, and Portsmouth gets a real plastering from the Luftwaffe.' The words tumbled out as if hurrying would make what she was convinced would be awful news easier to bear.

'As far as we are aware,' said Hardcastle, 'he's perfectly all right.'

'Oh, I'm frighfully sorry, keeping you standing in the hall. Do come in.' Gillian Flint led the way into a cosy sitting room.

Hardcastle introduced himself and Bradley, and advised Mrs Flint that she should never admit anyone to her house without seeing some evidence of identity.

'Sorry!' Gillian Flint contrived to look like a naughty schoolgirl who had been caught out. 'Do sit down. If it's not about Rollo, what is it about?'

'Keith Shaw,' said Hardcastle.

'Who?' she said, initially attempting complete denial.

'He was arrested in this area last night for refusing to tell a constable where he had been or where he was going. This morning, I interviewed him at Kingston police station and he eventually admitted spending a few hours with you last evening.'

'Quite right, he did, Mr Hardcastle.' Gillian laughed. 'Don't tell me that adultery is against the Defence Regulations now. There are so many new laws being introduced since the war started that it's difficult to keep up with it all. But why are you checking up on him?'

'Mrs Flint, there is a war on, and when individuals are stopped late at night and refuse to tell the police what they've been up to, it naturally arouses suspicions. We are duty bound to verify his claim.'

'Well, it's me taking the risk. I'm the married one.' Gillian paused thoughtfully. 'Mind you, I wouldn't mind betting that my husband, Rollo, has a Wren in his bed from time to time down in Portsmouth.'

'I've no doubt that Keith Shaw's wife was worried sick last night when he didn't go home. There had been an air raid that lasted for two hours.'

'Wife!' Gillian Flint almost spat the word. 'Well, the double-dealing little—' She broke off. 'I'm sorry, but I was about to launch into some very nautical language. It's what comes of being married to a sailor, I suppose.'

Hardcastle and Bradley left the commander's wife gently fuming.

'I imagine the next conversation between Gillian Flint and Keith Shaw will be quite colourful, guv'nor,' said Bradley.

Outside, another air-raid warning began its wailing alert. It was not long before the familiar crumps were heard as bomb after bomb sought a target.

On the Monday morning following his visit to Gillian Flint, Hardcastle decided it was time to report to Detective Superintendent Aubrey Drew and bring him up to date. But before he could dial the Special Branch officer's number, a sergeant from Special Branch telephoned and asked Hardcastle to see Mr Drew at the Yard. Twenty minutes later, the two V Division officers were in Drew's office.

'Walter, come in and take a seat. You too, Sergeant Bradley. What I want to talk to you about,' Drew said, once all three officers were settled, 'is the German who was floating in the Thames at Putney on the fourth of this month.'

'Hauptmann Konrad Fischer of the Luftwaffe,' said Bradley immediately.

'Very good, Skip,' said Drew. 'Carry on like that and we might even kidnap you for duty in SB.'

'You'll have a fight on your hands, sir,' muttered Hardcastle.

'Working with MI5, we searched every inch of Fischer's body and clothing,' continued Drew, 'and found nothing that would tell us who he was going to see. At least, not in plain English. There was a letter addressed to someone called Ernst Jäger, but we don't know who he is. Presumably, this mysterious Jäger is an Abwehr agent working somewhere in the UK. Like the letter, the papers in his briefcase were in code and have been sent to the Government Cryptography Department, but these things take time and we have to accept that we might never know.'

'Not much that I can do to assist, then, sir,' said Hardcastle.

'Unfortunately, no,' said Drew. 'But as it's not impossible that there might be a connection between this Ernst Jäger and the burglaries and the Ropers' deaths, I thought you should know. Speaking of which, how are you getting on with the Roper murders, Walter?'

'Between you and me, sir, we're not, but we'll get there eventually. However, there is one thing that you can probably help with.' Hardcastle told Drew about the strange encounter that PC Tomlin had had with Keith Shaw, and the subsequent conversation that Hardcastle had had with the man.

'What's your difficulty over that, Walter?'

'Should his employers be told about this extramarital affair? And the fact that he wanted to keep it from the police for some reason.'

Drew pursed his lips as he spent a few seconds mulling over Hardcastle's question. 'I think we'll leave that to MI5, Walter,' he said eventually. 'I suppose it might affect the security checks they do on people like Shaw, but that's their problem.'

'I wonder why we had to go all the way to the Yard, just to be told that,' said Bradley, as they drove back to Putney. 'Surely, Mr Drew could have telephoned you.'

'Did you notice that green telephone on his desk, Jack?'

'Yes, I did. What about it?'

'It's a scrambler and it encodes telephone calls, but the bloke at the other end has to have one, as well. And I don't have one.'

'I got the impression that Mr Drew was not too interested in Keith Shaw's lame excuse for not telling PC Tomlin where he'd been, guv'nor.'

'Well, *I'm* still interested, Jack, and I think we'll set up an observation on the man for a few days and see what happens.'

'Got anyone particular in mind for it?' asked Bradley.

Hardcastle thought about the question for a few moments. 'I'll ask Mr Swain if I can borrow a couple of uniformed officers for a few days. Ideally, a man and a woman.'

'What about Tomlin, guv'nor. He knows what Shaw looks like.'

'Yes, Jack, and Shaw knows what Tomlin looks like.'

Superintendent Geoffrey Swain, the urbane sub-divisional commander, was quite amenable to Hardcastle's request.

'To be honest, Mr Hardcastle, I feel a certain responsibility. Prevention of crime is, after all, as much the job of the Uniform Branch as it is of the CID. And no superintendent cares to have two unsolved murders on his sub-division.'

'Nor does a DDI, sir,' said Hardcastle drily.

'Quite so, quite so.' Swain flicked a piece of fluff from his otherwise immaculate uniform.

Hardcastle began to tell Swain about the matter of Keith Shaw, but was interrupted.

'Yes, I saw the entry in the Occurrence Book, Mr Hardcastle. Strange business. Is Special Branch aware?'

'They give the impression they're not interested, sir, but you can never tell with that lot.'

Swain did not comment on that, but gave Hardcastle a wry smile. 'So, what are you suggesting we should do about it? I believe that this fellow Shaw is in what they call sensitive employment.'

'Yes, sir. He's engaged in the procurement of materiel.'

'That makes his actions seem even more suspicious, in my view,' said Swain. 'You spoke to this paramour of Shaw's, did you?'

'Yes, sir. A Mrs Gillian Flint, wife of a naval commander serving at Portsmouth. I have a feeling, however, that that particular liaison has just come to an abrupt end. Mrs Flint was under the misapprehension that Shaw was unmarried.'

'Until you advised her to the contrary, I take it.'

'Exactly so, sir.'

'You need to be careful, Mr Hardcastle. The commissioner doesn't like police officers having to give evidence in civil proceedings, especially those involving divorce.'

'Of course, sir. However, I came to see you to ask for your assistance. I think it might be a good idea to keep Keith Shaw under observation. Now that his relationship with Mrs Flint is almost certainly at an end, it'll be interesting to see whether he still goes out and, if so, why. You see, I was thinking that, although he undoubtedly visited her, he used it as an alibi in case he was stopped by police. It may be that he went elsewhere for some less romantic reason.'

Swain nodded. 'But when it came to it, he refused to say anything. Anyway, Mr Hardcastle, we can theorize forever. How can I help?'

'A PC and a WPC in plain clothes, sir – preferably from Kingston sub-division – to follow him wherever he goes in the evening. If he goes anywhere.'

'You have no one who could undertake this?'

'I don't have any women detectives, sir, and I thought it might look better if the surveillance was carried out by an officer of each sex. They would look more like a couple.'

'Quite so. Very well, I'll select two officers and send them to you to be briefed.'

TWELVE

P C James Davis and WPC June Taylor, the two officers
selected by Superintendent Swain and briefed by
Hardcastle, started duty that same evening. Davis
was twenty-eight and had nine years' service. June Taylor was
twenty-two and had been a policewoman for just eighteen
months. She was forever being bawled out by her unforgiving
woman sergeant for having her hair touching the collar of her
uniform. It was, therefore, something of a relief to be on duty
in plain clothes so that she could wear her hair the way she
liked it.

Thanks to the introduction of double summer time in
February of that year, it was light until about eleven o'clock.
In Pine Walk, Surbiton, where the Shaws lived, there was
nowhere to hide and it made it a very difficult place to keep
observation in broad daylight without being spotted. Foreseeing
difficulties, Hardcastle drove to the area that afternoon and
saw for himself that there was nowhere from which a discreet
observation could be mounted. However, there was a telephone
kiosk on the corner that gave a view down both Pine Walk
and Chiltern Drive. And that gave Hardcastle an idea, but he
would have to move swiftly.

Driving back into the centre of Kingston, he parked the car
and made his way to the office of Henry Marsh, the area
manager responsible for telephones.

'Yes, Inspector, I can see your problem.' Marsh was
probably nearing sixty years of age, was overweight and grey-
haired. He put the tips of his fingers together and touched his
lips with his two index fingers. 'We're always willing to assist
the police, especially now there's a war on.' He lowered his
hands, linked them together on his desk and leaned forward,
an earnest expression on his face. 'I'll tell you what I can do:
I'll show that kiosk to be out of order and I'll have one of our
canvas shelters erected in front of it. Your chaps could remain

inside the shelter until they needed to move. How would that be?'

'That would be extremely helpful, Mr Marsh, thank you.'

'I'll have to put one of my chaps on site as well, because he'll need to drive the van that takes the shelter equipment up there. He's all right, though; he's one of your special constables.'

It had been the previous Friday night when Shaw had ventured out to his fictitious masonic meeting, and Hardcastle doubted that he would go out again as soon as this evening. However, if Shaw did go out, Hardcastle had taken a gamble on him doing so not long after he returned home from work, and he told the two officers to take up the observation at six o'clock that evening. His gamble paid off and Davis and Taylor saw their target leave his house at half past six.

To the surprise of the two officers, Shaw set off at a fast pace, finally leading them into Kingston town centre, a distance of about a mile and a half. Without a backward glance at any point since leaving his house, he entered the Griffin Hotel, close by the market place.

'Is it all right for us to go into licensed premises while we're on duty, Jim?' As a probationer, June Taylor was mindful that breaching one of the many regulations under which police operated might blight her career.

'Of course it is, June. This is *part* of our duty. It's why we're here.' Davis pushed open the door to allow his colleague to enter first. He crossed to the bar, positioning himself as near to Shaw as he could without raising suspicion. He was in the act of ordering drinks for himself and Taylor when a smartly dressed woman crossed the room from a table in the corner and embraced Shaw.

'Did you get a visit from the police, Gillian?' asked Shaw.

Gillian Flint laughed. 'Yes, I did, darling, and they told me you were married.'

Davis could not remain where he was without arousing suspicion. Reluctantly, he picked up his drinks and crossed to a table where June Taylor was sitting.

'I think we can leave it at that, June. Mr Hardcastle will

be very interested in what I just heard.' Davis repeated the conversation that had taken place between Shaw and Gillian Flint.

'What are they up to, then, Jim? Apart from the obvious.'

'I don't know,' said Davis, 'but I'm sure it's not a straightforward love affair.'

Hardcastle didn't think it was a straightforward love affair, either.

'You and Taylor can return to your ordinary duty, Davis, and thank you both for your efforts. That was a useful piece of information you picked up.'

After Davis's departure, Hardcastle thought about the affair between Keith Shaw and Gillian Flint. Eventually, the next day he decided that it was nothing further to do with him.

And just to confirm it, Hardcastle received a telephone call from Detective Superintendent Aubrey Drew of Special Branch, asking him to call at the Yard.

'I'm sorry to drag you up here again, Walter,' said Drew. 'I think I'd better arrange for you to have a scrambler phone installed. After all, you have got Alan Moore and Company on your patch and some of their employees. And you've got Hawkers, of course. It would save you coming up and down to the Yard whenever I had something sensitive to discuss with you.'

'Thank you, sir. It would save a lot of time.'

'Now then, Shaw and Gillian Flint. I've been authorized to tell you that your two officers were spotted last night.'

Hardcastle was momentarily taken aback by that piece of information. 'But it couldn't have been that they were recognized by either of the targets.'

Drew smiled. 'They weren't. They were spotted by the MI5 watchers who followed the little party all the way from Pine Walk to the Griffin Hotel.'

'Oh, hell!' What little Hardcastle knew of MI5 watchers, they had a reputation for being very professional. Doubtless they would have seen PC Davis and WPC Taylor for what they were – amateurs. 'I thought MI5 weren't interested, sir.'

'Well, it seems they are. After a little gentle persuasion from Mr Canning, mainly involving inter-departmental co-operation, they decided to own up. It seems that Shaw is an MI5 agent and had been tasked to test Gillian Flint who, they believed, was willing to sell secrets that she obtained from her husband, Commander Rollo Flint, stationed at Portsmouth. It turned out, Wally, that Commander Rollo Flint is, in fact, Petty Officer Ronald Flint and knows practically nothing. MI5's interest stemmed from the fact that Gillian Flint lives in an expensive property just off Kingston Hill.'

'Seems to me that almost everyone is working for MI5, sir.'

'Certainly looks that way, Wally. However, they thought that the only way she could have afforded such a property was through spying, but the fact of the matter is that when her parents died, she inherited the house and a substantial sum of money. It is also the case that Petty Officer Flint volunteered for the Navy at the outbreak of war. I think it was just a case of snobbishness that Gillian Flint pretended her husband was a commander.'

'Case closed, then, sir.'

'Reckon so, Wally. But from what your people overheard, it looks very much as though they're continuing their affair.' Drew stood up and shook hands. 'I'll get you a scrambler phone as soon as possible.'

Despite Detective Superintendent Drew's warning, Hardcastle had no intention of keeping the latest information from his assistant.

'Don't that lot ever make background enquiries before they launch an operation, guv'nor?' asked a bemused Bradley.

'It would appear not, Jack.'

'No wonder that Shaw was reluctant to tell the PC where he was going when he was stopped. All he had to do was show him his identity card, but according to the report, he wasn't carrying it. Why Shaw should have refused his name and address, God knows. It doesn't make sense. After all, we visited him last year about his break-in.'

The man in a black dinner jacket, this time without his over-coat, but with his usual white silk scarf and homburg hat, crouched behind a fence close to a gate. Fortunately for him, the gate was immediately opposite the house in which he was interested.

He'd kept a relatively low profile the last few months, waiting for the police's focus to move to other cases, but he still had to be careful this time, and had followed the occupants of the house to the Elite Cinema in the centre of Kingston. The film was *Gone with the Wind* and the man in black knew that it lasted four hours.

It was not that he was averse to murder, but after he had shot and killed the Ropers, he had decided not to risk it, at least for a while. He had made a mistake in losing his glove, added to which it was an indictment on his self-perceived Teutonic perfection and the wrath of the Führer if he ever got to hear of it.

It was now totally dark, thanks to the blackout and the absence of street lighting. Swiftly, he crossed the road, through the side gate of the house and round to the rear. Using his knife to disengage the latch, he opened a window and climbed into the kitchen. Checking the front door and satisfying himself there was no deadlock, he began a search of the house, starting upstairs.

Thirty minutes later, the man in black let out a sigh of disappointment; he had not found what he had been looking for. He took a few items from the mantelshelf in the sitting room and a tiny framed cameo from the wall in the hall, all of which could be secreted in his pockets to make it look like a burglarly, and let himself out of the front door.

He strolled down the road, wishing a patrolling ARP warden 'good night' as he turned the corner.

'Excuse me, sir.' DC Winters, Hardcastle's clerk, entered with a message form in his hand. 'It's from DI Black at Kingston. There was a break-in at Howard Austin's house in Birkenhead Avenue, Kingston, last evening while the Austins were out at the cinema.'

'Ask Sergeant Bradley to come in, John.'

Moments later, Bradley entered the DDI's office. 'Yes, sir, I heard. We've got to catch this cheeky monkey. A possible two murders under his belt and he's just thumbing his nose at us.'

'Whatever else you say about him, he's a clean burglar, Mr Hardcastle.' Howard Austin had remained at home, pending Hardcastle's arrival. 'There was no mess at all.'

'I know you'll have told the first officer to arrive what was taken, Mr Austin, but would you mind telling me?'

Once again, Austin listed the missing items. 'We were particularly annoyed about the cameo, Mr Hardcastle. It's not that it was especially valuable, but Eunice and I bought it on our honeymoon, nearly thirty years ago.'

'Obviously, the advice given about security was not enough, Mr Austin. I'll have another officer survey your property and assess what's required.' In fact, Hardcastle thought that Austin had probably ignored the advice.

'Thank you. That's very good of you, and it'll put Eunice's mind at rest. She hasn't said anything, but I could see she was upset, more about the cameo than anything else.'

'You never know,' said Hardcastle, 'but we might even get that back for Mrs Austin.'

'Why d'you think we were targeted, Mr Hardcastle?'

'For the same reason as the others were. I think the burglar is an enemy agent – or a sympathizer – who is hoping to find some secret files in your house. His method is very similar to the other break-ins involving Moore's employees that occurred over recent months. Furthermore, you have a lot of valuables here that he could have taken. But all he took were a number of comparatively worthless items . . . if you'll forgive me for saying so.'

'No, no, you're quite right, Mr Hardcastle, and that bears out your theory about someone looking for secret papers. But nobody removes anything from the offices. That would be the height of foolishness, apart from resulting in instant dismissal and possible prosecution.'

'But as I queried once before,' put in Bradley, 'does the Abwehr know all that?'

After grabbing a quick lunch in the canteen, Hardcastle and Bradley returned to the DDI's office. Hardcastle settled himself behind his desk and took out his pipe. Filling it slowly and thoughtfully, he remained silent until it was well alight. 'This bastard's running rings round us, Jack,' he said eventually. 'Every beat is filled and yet not a single copper's caught sight of him. He's like a bloody phantom.'

'I suppose we could put every CID officer on the division on to the streets, guv'nor. The burglaries all took place on a Friday between the hours of eight and ten thirty in the evening, and were mainly in the Kingston Hill area. Being in plain clothes, they might stand a better chance of nicking him.'

'It's a good idea on the face of it, but Mariott would never agree to it. Crime enquiries are piling up, and each officer has already got a backlog of cases. To put everyone on the streets with potentially nothing to show for it . . . No, I don't think Mr Marriott would be too pleased about that at all.'

'And nobody's seen our phantom burglar, so we've got no description to go on,' added Bradley moodily.

Hardcastle glanced at his pocket watch, a present from his father on the occasion of the young Hardcastle's sixteenth birthday. All the officers under his command wore wrist-watches, and regarded Walter Hardcastle's use of a pocket watch to be rather old-fashioned. But a few who had known the DDI's father attributed it to parental influence.

'I think we'll have an early night, Jack. Go home and put your feet up.'

Bradley glanced at his watch. It was nigh-on eight o'clock, but in the CID that *was* an early night. But his occasional girlfriend Blanche was playing hard to get lately and that meant an evening spent in his local pub. Alone.

When Hardcastle arrived home, there was a small lorry outside his house. As he felt in his pocket for his door key, the door was opened by a workman.

'Who the hell are you?' demanded Hardcastle.

'We're from the council, guv'nor. We've boarded up your windows and swept up the glass.' The workman lowered his voice. 'If you want the glass replaced, my brother's a glazier and he'll give you a fair price, seeing as how you're a copper an' all.'

'Thanks, I'll bear it in mind,' said Hardcastle, who had no intention of taking advantage of the workman's offer. Individuals who offered a discount to police officers usually wanted something in return, especially if they were ever arrested. And if the workman's brother bore the same shifty countenance as his sibling, it would not be long before his collar was felt.

Muriel Hardcastle appeared from the kitchen. She was wearing an overall and her hair was tied up in a headscarf. There were a few smudges of dirt on her face.

'There's dust everywhere, Wally.' Muriel pushed a lock of hair back under her headscarf.

'What happened exactly, darling?'

'It must have been about seven o'clock, I suppose, when the raid started. They were after Hawkers again. One bomb destroyed a house in Deacon Road and took out all our rear windows.'

'Were any of you hurt? With flying glass, I mean.'

'No, Wally, we were all in the shelter. But that's nothing. The bomb that hit Deacon Road killed the whole Collie family, including Edward's schoolfriend Tim Collie. And his sister and their mother. The man of the family is at sea somewhere with the merchant navy. Won't be a happy homecoming for him.'

'Where are our tribe?'

'In their rooms doing their homework.'

'Good. Knock it off now, Muriel, love, and have a cup of tea. Or something stronger.'

'I could do with a large whisky.' Muriel sank into an armchair and took off her headscarf.

'How's Edward taking the death of his friend?' asked Hardcastle, as he busied himself pouring two substantial measures of Scotch.

'Either it's not sunk in yet or he's just shrugged it off. It seems to me that the kids are more accustomed to death and destruction than we are. I know I was only ten when the last war started, but this one seems different and kids appear to take it in their stride.'

'I was a telegram boy during the last war,' said Hardcastle.

'I can still remember delivering telegrams after the first day of the Battle of the Somme. Almost twenty thousand men were killed that day and nearly forty thousand were wounded. Practically every house in the street I was delivering to got one of those terrible telegrams from the War Office. I remember that the envelopes were specially marked so that we wouldn't ask if there was a reply. Not that we had to; one look at the poor woman's face told you what was in the telegram.'

'You're a cheerful soul at times, Wally Hardcastle,' said Muriel and held out her empty glass for a refill.

THIRTEEN

B y the middle of 1940 the so-called phoney war was well
and truly over. The French had capitulated, the Low
Countries had been overrun and Norway had been
invaded. It seemed that Hitler's determination to dominate the
world was becoming a reality. Britain stood alone, although
the Empire was rallying to her support and there was a greater
variety of foreign uniforms in London than had ever been seen
in the country's long history.

And then the war came to the streets of London and other
major cities. Night after night in that summer of 1940, the
relentless sound of German bombers, the staccato bark of
anti-aircraft guns and the depressing clatter of cascading
brickwork as houses, factories and public buildings fell victim
to the enemy's bombs.

The murders of Frank and Helen Roper remained unsolved,
much to Walter's frustration, but so did many others, and the
growing backlog of cases couldn't be ignored any longer.
Murder victims were not infrequently left in the ruins of
bombed buildings in an attempt by the killer to mislead the
police into thinking that their deaths were the result of an air
raid. Still, the targeting of Howard Austin's home suggested
that the Ropers' murderer hadn't fled the country. And there
was always the possibility that he might slip up again. For
now, all they could do was wait.

Mrs Audrey Kane lived in the next flat to Joyce Butler, whose
'working' name was Kim, and worked at Kingston Hospital,
a short walk from Ravenscroft, a block of flats just off Kingston
Hill. She'd left for work in a rush that morning, but as she
passed Joyce's flat at five o'clock in the afternoon on
Wednesday the thirty-first of July 1940, on her way home, she
noticed that the girl's front door was very slightly ajar.

Mrs Kane was a worldy woman into her late fifties, and

knew that the girl was a prostitute. But she didn't cause any trouble, never giving cause for complaint, and Mrs Kane's maxim was to live and let live.

When Hardcastle appeared, he was greeted by Detective Inspector Kenneth Black, the DI from Kingston, who was the first CID officer to arrive at the scene of the murder.

'A young woman named Joyce Butler, Mrs Joyce Butler, lives here, guv'nor,' said Black. 'At about five o'clock, the victim's next-door neighbour – a Mrs Audrey Kane – on her way home from work, noticed that Mrs Butler's door was slightly ajar. On entering, she called out and, getting no reply, went further in. She found the girl dead on the sitting room floor and suggested that she had probably been struck on the head with a wine bottle which lay broken nearby. There was a lot of blood. Mrs Kane spoke as though she had some nursing experience and reckons she knows a dead body when she sees one.'

'Right. Better have a look. Where's Mrs Kane now?'

'Back in her own flat, guv.'

The constable pushed open the door of Joyce Butler's flat to admit the two senior detectives and Detective Sergeant Jack Bradley.

The sitting room was well-appointed and it was evident that quite a lot of money had been spent on furnishing, curtaining and carpeting. All in all, the flat seemed to have been occupied by a very rich young woman.

'Better have a look at the deceased, Jack,' said Hardcastle.

Joyce Butler was lying on the floor in the room wearing the same clothes she'd presumably worn the previous evening. A broken wine glass and bottle were indeed lying nearby.

Jack disappeared into the bedroom and Hardcastle followed. 'I think that answers the question of what this girl did for a living,' commented Bradley. Items of erotic clothing had been flung around the room. 'She was on the game.'

'That's all we need,' said Hardcastle. 'We might get some fingerprints from the wine bottle and glass, if we're lucky.'

'Looks like a fight that ended in murder if Mrs Kane is right about the cause of death,' commented Hardcastle as he

walked back to the sitting room and bent down to examine
the body, and particularly the head, more closely.

'That was the divisional surgeon's view, guv,' agreed Black,
'but his job was only to certify death.'

'I do know the limitations of divisional surgeons, Ken. I
also know that some of them fancy themselves as forensic
pathologists.'

'I've met one or two, guv. However, I've called Sir Bernard
Spilsbury and he's on his way.' Spilsbury's expertise stretched
back a long way. Twenty-five years ago, he had given evidence
in what became known as the Brides in the Bath case, and in
which his unchallengeable evidence had proved that the death
of George Joseph Smith's wives was a result of vagal inhib-
ition and not drowning, an opinion that resulted in Smith going
to the gallows.

Hardcastle returned to the bedroom and pushed open a door.
Beyond was a luxurious, tiled room that contained a shower
and a washbasin. Above the washbasin was a small mirror-
fronted cabinet containing a number of cosmetics.

'That's an expensive scent, guv'nor,' said Bradley, pointing
to a small bottle of perfume. The label showed the name of a
well-known perfumer. 'I bought it for Blanche last Christmas
and it cost me an arm and a leg.'

'Probably a present from an admirer, Jack, for services
rendered. Might be lucky enough to find a usable fingerprint
on it.'

Hardcastle opened the wardrobe in which there were a few
garments of a garish nature, but all of them expensive, judging
by the labels. 'We'll have a word with this Mrs Kane while
we're waiting for Sir Bernard.'

'I told her you'd want to speak to her,' said DI Black,
and turned to the constable at the door. 'When Sir Bernard
Spilsbury arrives, let Mr Hardcastle know,' he said, before the
two detectives walked the short distance along the balcony to
Mrs Kane's flat.

'Oh, do come along in.' Audrey Kane was a grey-haired,
stout woman with a bright, welcoming smile. She wore a
navy-blue cardigan over her frock. The immediate impression
was of a woman of tireless energy who constantly bustled

about. 'I've just made a pot of tea, my dears. I thought you'd be coming along, sooner or later. Do have a seat while I pour you a cup.' Clearly, she was not one to brook a refusal. In contrast to her neighbour's flat, Mrs Kane's was not as expensively furnished, but was sparklingly clean. Much of the furniture would have been described by Hardcastle's mother, Alice, as 'cheap and cheerful', but it had been well-cared-for.

'I'm sorry if we've kept you from doing something else, Mrs Kane,' began Hardcastle, having introduced himself and Bradley, 'but it was necessary for us to speak to you as soon as possible. I hope you weren't too upset by the sight of the body.'

Audrey Kane laughed, a warm and jovial laugh. 'Good heavens, no, Mr Hardcastle. When you've laid out as many as I have, you aren't put off by the sight of a stiff, I can tell you that, my dear.' She primped her hair and then handed round the tea. 'And as for the number of post-mortems, well . . .'

'It seems you have some nursing experience, Mrs Kane,' suggested Bradley unwisely.

'I'm a state-registered nurse.' Mrs Kane lifted her head slightly and spoke in a tone of voice that implied having 'some nursing experience' was tantamount to an insult to a woman who was entitled to put the letters 'SRN' after her name. 'I'm a sister at Kingston Hospital. I gave up work at St Mary's in Praed Street, Paddington a few years ago to look after my husband. He had the consumption, you know, but when he passed away, I went back to nursing. There's plenty to do now there's a war on.'

'Do you happen to know what time your neighbour's visitor arrived, Mrs Kane?'

'No, that was before I came in, but I saw that her front door was ajar and went in to see if she was all right. But she wasn't.'

'Excuse me, sir.' The uniformed constable tapped lightly on the door and came into the flat. 'Sir Bernard Spilsbury's arrived, sir.'

'If you'll excuse us, Mrs Kane . . .' But before Hardcastle could move, he was interrupted by the appearance of the great forensic pathologist himself, who had followed the PC into Mrs Kane's flat.

'I thought I recognized the name. It's Sister Kane, unless I'm much mistaken.' Spilsbury doffed his hat and then stepped across to shake hands with Mrs Kane. He handed his hat to the constable as though he were a butler.

'Good afternoon, sir. I'm sure you'd like a cup of tea, sir.'

'That would be most welcome, Sister.' Spilsbury turned to Hardcastle. 'Sister Kane was the mortuary nurse at St Mary's for a while, Hardcastle. Got to know some of my cadavers as well as I did.'

'Would you care for a seat, sir?' asked Audrey Kane as she handed him the cup of tea.

'No, I must get on, but before I go, tell me, Sister, what did you make of it?'

'Oh, I'd say she was hit on the head with the wine bottle, without a doubt, sir.'

'That's very helpful.' Spilsbury drank his tea, then gave his cup and saucer to the constable in exchange for his hat. 'It would be very handy if we had a trained nurse on the scene of every murder, Hardcastle.' Spilsbury chuckled at his little jest.

'I'll see if I can arrange it, Sir Bernard,' said Hardcastle, maintaining a deadpan expression.

The four police officers and Spilsbury moved next door to Joyce Butler's flat. The pathologist took off his jacket and leaned over the dead woman's body. Confining himself to looking rather than touching, he made a few notes on the back of an envelope and stood up.

'Sister Kane was right, of course, which is hardly surprising, Hardcastle. I'll let you have a report as soon as I've completed the post-mortem examination.' Spilsbury paused. 'But, of course, you'll be there. Tomorrow morning, say ten o'clock?'

'I'll be there, Sir Bernard. Where would you like the cadaver, sir? Usual place?'

'Yes, the usual place, Hardcastle. St Mary's, Paddington.'

After Spilsbury's departure, Hardcastle brought in the waiting scientists from the forensic science laboratory at Hendon, the photographers and the fingerprint examiner.

The scientific examination of the flat took several hours. There was an abundance of fingerprints and it would take days, weeks even, before a conclusive identification was achieved, but only if those prints matched any filed in the national fingerprint collection held at New Scotland Yard.

One piece of immediately available evidence was a driving licence.

'I found this driver's licence down the back of the settee, sir,' said a detective constable named Barber who was assisting in the search. 'It belongs to a Christopher Farr with an address in Guildford, Surrey and was issued by the Surrey County Council at the beginning of last year.'

Hardcastle took the document and examined it. 'We must trace this Christopher Farr as soon as possible,' he said, 'although if he's in London and ends up in this girl's flat, the chances are that he's now been called up for one of the services and could be anywhere.'

'If he's in the Navy, sir, he could be on the other side of the world by now,' suggested DC John Barber.

'Thank you very much for that helpful observation, Barber. As a reward for your burgeoning detective skills, you can find him. Shouldn't be too difficult; the address is on the driving licence.'

'Yes, sir.' Barber wished that he'd kept his mouth shut.

'There's an army uniform in a cupboard in the bedroom, sir.' Bradley walked into the room holding a battledress blouse. 'If it belongs to the victim's husband, he's a sergeant in the Royal Army Ordnance Corps. His army number's stamped inside.' He turned the collar so that eight large numerals were displayed.

'Should be easy enough to find him, Jack. Get one of the lads on to it.'

At half past eight, Hardcastle decided that there was no more that could be done at the scene for the time being. The cadaver had been removed to St Mary's and the crime scene was sealed and guarded by a uniformed constable.

As they reached the ground floor, the group of detectives met a member of the London Fire Brigade putting a key into the door of a flat.

'What's going on here, then?' asked the fireman, pausing. 'There are coppers all over the place.'

'I'm Divisional Detective Inspector Hardcastle of V Division.

And you are?'

'Leading Fireman Eric Simpson. Who's been murdered? I bet it's that tart at Number Twelve. Joyce Butler.'

'What makes you think that, Mr Simpson?'

'I reckon she's at it. Almost every time I get home, I see some bloke knocking on her door or just leaving. And it's a different bloke each time. It's her hubby I feel sorry for. Poor bastard's in the army while she's having it off with any man willing to oblige. And from what I've seen there's no shortage.'

'You're quite right; Mrs Butler has been murdered, Mr Simpson. Have you any idea where her husband's stationed?'

'My missus was talking to her one time and she said her old man was in the Ordnance Corps down near Dorking somewhere.'

'Have you ever met him?'

'No, otherwise I'd have tipped him off. Mind you, he might know and maybe doesn't give a damn what she gets up to.'

'D'you know if Joyce Butler was in employment?' asked Bradley.

'Yeah, she was an usherette at the Super Cinema in Fife Road.'

'I won't keep you any longer, Mr Simpson,' said Hardcastle, 'but I may need to see you again. This is your flat, is it?' he asked, gesturing at Simpson's front door.

'Yes, that's me. Well, I don't own it, I'm renting it. I've just come off duty. But if I'm on duty – and that seems to be most of the time these days – you'll find me at Kingston fire station.'

FOURTEEN

I t was half past eleven the following day by the time that Hardcastle and Bradley entered the Super Cinema in Fife Road.

'We ain't open yet, love.' A woman was vaccuming the carpet in the foyer, but switched off the vacuum cleaner to make this announcement.

'Is the manager here?' asked Hardcastle, displaying his warrant card.

'Yeah. Up the stairs, love, and it's the door on the left.'

The two detectives mounted the broad staircase and tapped lightly on the door marked 'Manager'.

'Come!' said an imperious voice.

'Pompous bastard,' muttered Bradley, as he pushed open the door, allowing Hardcastle to enter first.

'Good morning,' said Hardcastle. 'I'm—'

'Whatever it is you're selling, I don't want it.' The manager had all the appearances of a fussy little man to whom the trivia of life was important. Probably in his mid-forties and overweight, his top lip was adorned with a pencil-thin moustache. He was already attired in a dinner jacket, ready for the day's performance.

'I'm Divisional Detective Inspector Hardcastle of the Metropolian Police, V Division, Mr . . .?'

The manager scoffed. 'Oh, are you really? I suppose you're selling some sort of burglar alarm, are you? Or some sophisticated security system?'

'And I'm Detective Sergeant Bradley.' Stepping forward, Bradley put his open warrant card within an inch of the manager's face.

The manager leapt to his feet. 'Oh, I'm most terribly sorry, gentlemen,' he said. 'My name's Donald Burton. Please take a seat and tell me what I can do for you. I must apologize for the misunderstanding, but we get so many commercial travellers calling and they'll tell all manner of lies to get past the commissionaire.'

'There was no commissionaire,' said Bradley, further adding to Burton's discomfort. 'We spoke to a lady operating a Hoover.'

'However,' said Hardcastle, 'we've come to talk to you about Joyce Butler.'

'Oh, what's she done now?' asked Burton in a tired voice, as though he was expecting news of yet another transgression.

'You don't sound surprised that we're here to talk to you about her.'

'To be perfectly honest, Inspector, I had to get rid of her. I'd had a number of complaints, mainly from the other members of staff. It seemed that she had a tendency to disappear out of one of the emergency exits before the end of her shift, leaving the other girls to do the clearing up.' Burton paused. 'But why have you come here? What's she done to attract the attention of the police?' He didn't sound surprised.

'She was found dead in her flat yesterday afternoon, Mr Burton. She'd been murdered.'

'Oh, good God!' The colour drained from Burton's face. 'How terrible.' He began to mop at his brow with a large handkerchief.

'Anything you can tell me about her could be useful in tracking down her murderer.' Hardcastle wondered whether Burton's reaction to the news of Joyce Butler's untimely end indicated some closer relationship with the usherette than that of employer and employee.

'It's only just come to my notice,' said Burton, recovering his composure, 'but the girls said that she was man-mad. She was not above talking to patrons and had apparently gone out with a number of them. Her favourite haunt, so I heard, was the Surbiton Assembly Rooms dance hall in Maple Road.'

'Have you ever visited the assembly rooms yourself, Mr Burton?' asked Bradley who, like Hardcastle, was beginning to wonder whether Burton was involved in the death of Joyce Butler.

'Good heavens no!' Burton's response was so adamant as to be almost suspicious.

'Did *you* have an affair with her, given that she was free with her favours, Mr Burton?' asked Bradley, more out of devilment than genuine suspicion.

'Certainly not!' Burton almost managed to puff himself up with rage.

'I think that's all for the moment, Mr Burton,' said Hardcastle, 'but we'll most likely need to see you later on.'

'Of course. Incidentally, any time you want to come in to see a film, I'll leave a free pass at the box office.'

'Thank you, but I doubt we'll have the time.' Hardcastle had a particular loathing of men like Burton who attempted to curry favour with the police with a subtle sort of bribery.

'Bloody sauce,' muttered Bradley, as the pair of detectives left the theatre. 'Did you notice, guv'nor, that he was wearing a ready-made bow tie?'

'It must be something to do with the war,' said Hardcastle. 'What d'you think, Jack? D'you think he could have had anything to do with the woman's murder?'

'No, he's not got the guts to murder anyone. And if he gets called up, he'll swear he's a conscientious objector.'

In any event, Burton's attempt to curry favour was to no avail; a week later the Super Cinema burned down. How it happened was never resolved, but the tragedy was not attributed to enemy action.

Hardcastle and Bradley eventually arrived back at their Putney headquarters. Grabbing a quick lunch of a meat pie, potatoes and peas in the canteen, they set about catching up on anything that might have happened during their absence.

'DC Bleach has traced Joyce Butler's husband, sir,' said Detective Sergeant Gordon Hanley, the officer in charge of the incident room that had been set up to deal with the murder of Joyce Butler. 'He's Sergeant Ron Butler of the Royal Army Ordnance Corps, aged twenty-six, and he's stationed at an ammunition depot just outside Dorking in Surrey.' Hanley slid a piece of paper across Hardcastle's desk. 'All the details are on there, sir.'

'Thanks, Skip.' Hardcastle yawned as he turned to Bradley. 'I suppose we'll get a chance to put our feet up sometime, Jack.' He and Bradley had now been working for two days, with little sleep, and there was still no end in sight. 'Better go and see him.'

'I'll get a car, guv.' Bradley knew that there was no point in suggesting that the Surrey Constabulary should interview the dead woman's husband on behalf of the Metropolitan Police. This was, after all, a murder enquiry and it's never surprising to find, in cases like this one, that the husband very often turns out to be the murderer.

'Get DC Bleach to drive because I don't want you falling asleep at the wheel. In the meantime, I'll ring the military police at Great Scotland Yard and see if I can interest them in this affair. We might just need their help.'

There was an armed sentry at the gates to the Dorking ammunition depot. Having closely examined the warrant cards of Hardcastle and Bradley, he directed them to the guardroom.

A tall man in army battledress was standing at the window, hands behind his back, and turned as the two detectives entered. He was about forty with short black hair and a neatly trimmed moustache. His peaked cap had a scarlet cover and the immaculate creases in his trousers and in the sleeves of his tunic were so sharp that it appeared they might be harmful to the touch. The webbing belt he wore was blancoed white. The bottoms of his trousers hung neatly over his white anklets and his boots were like black glass. Most people would think more than twice before picking a fight with him.

'Mr Hardcastle?' As the soldier turned, the Royal Arms on each of his lower sleeves became visible, as did the MP brassard on his right arm.

'That's me.'

'Regimental Sarn't Major Dick Purdy, Corps of Military Police.' He gripped Hardcastle's hand firmly and then shook hands with Jack Bradley. 'I understand there's a lairy sergeant you're interested in?'

'Yes, and I'd like a room where I can interview him. Is that possible, Mr Purdy?'

'In the army, Mr Hardcastle, everything's possible until it's been proved impossible. And then, we set about proving that the impossible is possible after all. We'll get the whole thing organized by having a word with the conductor.'

'The conductor?' queried Bradley. 'How on earth does a conductor get involved in all this?'

'A conductor, Sarn't Bradley,' said Purdy gravely, as though the detective had just impugned the army that Purdy so admired, 'is a senior warrant officer peculiar to the Royal Army Ordnance Corps. And I do mean peculiar. What he don't know about guns and ammunition and all sorts of other bits and pieces ain't worth knowing.' He glanced at the guard commander, who appeared to be taking an inordinate interest in the arrival of the police and their conversation with the military police RSM. 'And you have heard nothing, Sergeant. You'll be like the three wise monkeys who see no evil, hear no evil and speak no evil all rolled into one. Because I suspect that evil is what we're dealing with here. Got that, have you?'

'Sir,' replied the guard commander.

'If this becomes a topic of conversation in the Sarnts' Mess or, worse still, in the NAAFI canteen, I shall come looking. Understood?' he added, casting a glance at the stickman.

'Sir,' said the guard commander again.

The Conductor of Ordnance was nowhere near as smartly turned out as Purdy. The impression was more like a manager of a large department store who somehow had finished up wearing army uniform, but was not greatly concerned about how it looked. The one thing that would cause anyone to pause before commenting on his turnout was the insignia of the Royal Arms encircled by a laurel wreath, marking him out as one of the most senior warrant officers in the army.

'I'm RSM Purdy of the Military Police.'

The conductor stood up, at the same time eyeing the two police officers suspiciously. 'Trevor Evans, Mr Purdy.'

'These two officers are from the civil police, Mr Evans. Divisional Detective Inspector Hardcastle and Detective Sergeant Bradley.'

'How d'you do, gentlemen. You're not from the Fraud Squad by any chance, are you?'

'No, Mr Evans, we're from the V Division of the Metropolitan Police. Are you expecting the Fraud Squad, then?'

'No, not at all.' The conductor sounded relieved. 'How can I be of assistance?'

'We've been told that Sergeant Ronald Butler is a member of this unit, Mr Evans.'

'Ron Butler? Yes, he is,' said Evans. 'What's he been up to, then?'

'His wife has been murdered,' said Bradley, 'and we have to speak to him.'

'Blimey! When did this happen?'

'Yesterday afternoon, Mr Evans. Her body was found at five o'clock.'

'I'll send for him,' said Evans. 'That'll be a blow for him. He's not long been married.'

'Before you do,' said Purdy, 'these officers would like a room in which to interview him.'

'Of course. I'll get the chief clerk to sort something out.' Evans picked up the phone and dialled a number. 'Staff, it's the conductor. Find a spare room where two police officers can carry out an interview, and then get hold of Sergeant Butler and bring him over here. But don't tell Butler that the police want to talk to him.'

There was a concerned look on Sergeant Butler's face when the chief clerk escorted him into the conductor's office. Butler confirmed that he was twenty-six years of age, and according to his army records had been a soldier only since the outbreak of war. His swift promotion was, according to Conductor Evans, down to his ability to grasp all there was to know about ammunition in order to do the job of an ammunition examiner.

'You wanted to see me, sir.' Butler was a slender figure and smartly turned out. His blond hair was cut very short and he had boyish features that doubtless would last well into middle age.

'These two gentlemen are from the police, Sarn't Butler,'

said Evans, 'and the warrant officer is RSM Purdy of the Military Police.'

This statement caused Butler to appear even more nervous than he had when he entered the office.

'Thank you for your assistance, Mr Evans,' said Purdy. 'We'll take it from here.'

'Show these gentlemen to the room you've allocated to them, Staff,' said Evans to the chief clerk, 'and then you can get back to your duties. Oh, and forget all about seeing the police here.'

The room that the chief clerk had found was airy and spacious. RSM Purdy set about arranging a table and three chairs in a suitable layout to conduct an interview. He placed his own chair a short distance away so that he could hear Hardcastle if there was anything the inspector required. But he knew not to interfere in the interview; that was police business – civil police business.

Hardcastle and Bradley settled themselves opposite Butler. Bradley offered Butler a cigarette and he almost snatched it. His hand was shaking so much that he could hardly keep it still enough to accept a light from Bradley's lighter. RSM Purdy waved a hand of refusal as though the smoking of cigarettes was beneath the dignity of a senior warrant officer.

'I'm afraid I have some bad news for you, Sergeant Butler,' began Hardcastle. Aware that there was no easy way to break devastating news, he went straight to the point. 'Your wife, Joyce, was found murdered in your flat at Ravenscroft at about five o'clock yesterday afternoon.' But the answer that Hardcastle got was not one that he was expecting.

'I'm not surprised, Inspector. In fact, I'm surprised it didn't happen before.'

'Would you care to explain that comment, Sergeant Butler?'

'We got married a year ago, just before the war started. I suppose we got carried away by what was going to happen. I mean, no one seemed to have any idea. Apart from all that, Joyce told me she was pregnant. Well, that was the first lie. She wasn't up the duff at all. All right, we'd had a bit of a tumble from time to time, and I thought maybe it was possible, so I did the decent thing. It was a cheap wedding all round.

It was at a register office, and there was no one to give her away. She said something about her father having cleared off years ago, and the last she heard of her mother, she was hawking her mutton in Shepherd Market. As for the wedding breakfast, that was a meal at Lyons Corner House in the Strand. There weren't any guests; just Joyce and me.'

'When you say the first lie, Sergeant Butler, does that mean there were more?'

'Oh yeah. A few weeks ago, I got a thirty-six-hour pass a bit unexpected like and went home of a Saturday night. She was bloody well in bed with some oik from the Gunners, name of . . .' Butler paused. 'Yeah, got it. Chris Farr. Bombardier Chris Farr. He's stationed at a gunsite in Kensington Gardens. Anyhow, we had a bit of a set-to and I gave him his marching orders.'

'D'you mean you had a fight?' asked Bradley.

'Not likely. That's court-martial stuff for a sergeant to thump a bombardier, and I didn't fancy losing these,' said Butler, tapping the three stripes on his arm, 'just because I'd got a flighty missus.'

'Did your wife say where she'd met this man Farr?'

'After some persuasion, she said she'd met him at a dance at the Surbiton Assembly Rooms in Maple Road, Sergeant Bradley.'

'When you say you used some persuasion, what does that mean exactly?'

Butler paused, but then decided to tell the truth. 'I slapped her around a bit. Nothing serious, mind. Put her over my knee and gave her a bit of a spanking.'

'Were there other men in your wife's life that you knew of then, Sergeant Butler?' asked Hardcastle. 'If we're to find who killed her, we need to know.'

Butler scoffed. 'None that I could identify. But there were odd things that gave the game away. Sexy black underwear I'd not seen before and that she never wore when I was with her. And one time I found a fag end with a cork tip in an ashtray. Well, the missus didn't smoke and I've never smoked cork tips.' He paused thoughtfully for several seconds. 'Come to think of it, I think she was on the game, just like her mother.' Butler paused again.

'This cork-tipped cigarette butt,' persisted Bradley. 'Could it have been left by a woman friend of your wife?'

Butler scoffed. 'I doubt it. She never had any women friends. She was too busy going after something in trousers or, better still, out of 'em.'

'Were you going to divorce her?' Hardcastle asked.

'That was the idea, but there's talk this unit's being moved abroad and, anyway, divorce costs money. I was just going to let her get on with it. She goes her way and I go mine.'

'Does that mean that you've got a girlfriend, Sergeant Butler?'

'Yes, I have, Inspector. Well, d'you blame me?' Butler asked with a boyish grin.

'We'll need her name and address,' said Bradley.

'What for?'

'It's routine,' said Bradley, employing a completely pointless reason that the police always asked and the public never queried.

'Her name's Kate Langley.'

'And her address? Here, put it in there.' Bradley pushed his pocketbook across the table and waited while Butler wrote down the details.

Hardcastle stood up. 'That'll be all for the time being, Sergeant Butler. I'll probably have to see you again, but if you think of anything that might be useful to us, give me a ring at Putney police station. Just ask for me or Detective Sergeant Bradley. It's particularly important if you recall a name.'

Butler just nodded as he walked out of the room. Hardcastle couldn't decide whether he was upset about his wife's death or whether he really was as indifferent as he'd sounded during the interview. Or was he distancing himself from a murder he had actually committed? If he had been telling the truth about his wife's conduct, it sounded like a motive.

'Mr Purdy, there are a few things you could perhaps find out for me. But it mustn't get back to any of them that we've made these enquiries. Firstly, was Butler in barracks last night? And, secondly, does he own a car? And perhaps you'd find out if this Bombardier Farr is actually stationed in Kensington Gardens – again without his knowing.'

'Discretion's my middle name, Mr Hardcastle. Leave it to me. I'll give you a ring as soon as I've got the answers.'

Hardcastle and Bradley got back to Putney at half past five.

'There was a call for you from an RSM Purdy of the Military Police, sir. About ten minutes ago.' Detective Sergeant Hanley, the office manager, handed Hardcastle a message form.

'Jack, come into my office and sit yourself down.' Hardcastle took a bottle of whisky from the bottom drawer of his desk and poured a substantial measure into each of two tumblers. 'Good health,' he said and raised his glass. He picked up the message form that Hanley had given him. 'Ah! According to RSM Purdy, it seems that sergeants are allowed to come and go as they please, provided they're not on duty. He says that as far as is known, Sergeant Butler was in his quarter at Dorking all night. But as the senior ranks have separate rooms, Purdy can't be certain.' Hardcastle looked up, a wry grin on his face. 'Just for good measure, he adds that Butler owns a motorcycle that he keeps at the ammunition depot. As for Bombardier Farr, enquiries are continuing. I don't know about you, Jack, but I've had enough for one day. We'll pack it in and start again tomorrow morning when we've had some sleep.'

'Amen to that, guv'nor,' said Bradley. 'What in particular?'

'This address for Farr that was on the driving licence found at the scene. I think we'll make some enquiries there to see if we can learn something about this Bombardier Farr. You never know, we might be lucky enough to find that he's the killer.'

'That'd be a first, guv.' Bradley laughed cynically. 'Like me winning the football pools.'

FIFTEEN

It was a plain, almost ugly, semi-detached house in one of the roads off Sydenham Road to the south-east of Guildford town centre. It was probably big enough to be shared by two families, but it was evident that none of the occupants enjoyed tending the garden. Weeds thrust their way up between its paving stones and an old bicycle with flat tyres was propped against a side wall.

The woman who answered the door was about fifty, maybe older. It was difficult to tell as she had iron-grey hair dragged back in an unattractive style and wore a shapeless grey frock, the shortness of its sleeves displaying leg-of-mutton arms. She wiped her hands on her apron and, taking the stub of a cigarette out of her mouth, flicked it into next door's front garden. She stared at the two men on the doorstep.

'Yes? What is it? If it's about the rent, you'll have to come back next week.'

'We're police officers, Mrs . . .?' Hardcastle raised his trilby hat.

'Oh Gawd! Has he been killed?'

'I'm sorry, madam,' said Hardcastle. 'Has who been killed?'

'That layabout husband what my daughter Janet got herself wed to.'

'Who are you, then?' asked Bradley.

'Mrs Spurr. Winifred Spurr.'

'Spurr was your daughter's maiden name, then, was it?' persisted Bradley, tiring of the woman's reluctance to part with any information in a straightforward way.

'No, it was Carver. My old man got hisself killed at the end of the last war. He weren't no hero, though. Got hisself run over by an army lorry one night in Cologne, stupid sod. Probably pissed. Anyways, I got married again, after Janet was born.'

'D'you mind if we come in, Mrs Spurr?' suggested Bradley.

'I think your neighbour's taking an interest in our conversation.'

'Huh! Got elephant's ears, that one. Nothing better to do but listen to other people's woes, that's her trouble.' Winifred Spurr led the way into what she called the parlour. It had a colourful carpet with a vaguely Indian design, and a three-piece suite that was probably from a shop that offered hire-purchase terms and made its deliveries in a plain van.

'Can we start again, Mrs Spurr?' said Hardcastle. 'I presume your daughter is Janet Farr, née Carver, and she is married to Christopher Farr, currently serving in His Majesty's Forces.'

'That's right,' said Mrs Spurr, as though that conclusion was obvious.

'Is she at home?'

'If you means is she here, the answer's no.'

'Has she moved, then?'

'No, she's gone down the town to get the rations. Not that there's much in the shops these days. I had to queue for half an hour the other day, just to get a couple of lamb chops.'

'You described Christopher Farr as Janet's layabout husband,' said Hardcastle.

'Well, he is.'

'What makes you think that, Mrs Spurr?'

'I don't think it, I knows it. Always running about after a bit of skirt while his poor wife's sitting at home looking after her two kids.'

'You say you know it. What proof d'you have?'

'I don't have none, but Janet does. Chris is stationed at a gunsite up London somewhere, see, and one night she rings up the unit on account of her not having heard from him for nigh-on a fortnight. But the bloke who answered the phone told our Janet that Bombardier Farr had taken his wife out dancing up the Astoria. Some place up London, so he said. I think it was the Astoria, not that I go up the Smoke if I can avoid it.'

It suddenly occurred to Winifred Spurr to query why the police were here and asking all these questions.

'We're from New Scotland Yard, Mrs Spurr,' began Hardcastle, seeking to impress the woman.

'Oh, my Gawd! She's been done in. My poor Janet's been murdered. And she only went out to get the rations, an' all.'

'Your daughter's alive and well to the best of our knowledge,' said Hardcastle. 'We're merely following up a few leads in a case of ration-book forgery. We have a whole list of names of people who might have been involved, quite innocently, and who have to be checked out.' He decided that it would be unwise to tell Mrs Spurr the real reason for their enquiries. If Christopher Farr turned out to be Joyce Butler's killer, he did not want him forewarned. 'Has your daughter worked in a food shop recently, Mrs Spurr?'

'Good heavens, no.' Winifred Spurr's haughty response sounded like a rebuke, as if Hardcastle had just insulted her. And her daughter. 'My Janet's a hairdresser,' she said.

'In that case, we'll not need to trouble you again, Mrs Spurr. Obviously, the Janet Farr we're interested in is not your daughter.'

'I don't wonder there's a crime wave if this is how you waste your time,' said Winfred Spurr, as she showed the two police officers to the door.

Jack Bradley laughed as he and Hardcastle got into their car. 'What a battleaxe. No wonder Farr doesn't go home often. Fancy having her for a mother-in-law.'

'There are a lot of them about,' commented Hardcastle. 'Fortunately, I get on extremely well with my mother-in-law.'

'What's next, guv'nor?'

'Back to the office, Jack. I'm hoping we'll get some scientific and fingerprint evidence from Joyce Butler's apartment. Then, I think we'll get up to Kensington Gardens. I'm fed up waiting for RSM Purdy to come up with some answers. The longer we wait, the longer that Farr will have time to think up some excuses or even an alibi.'

'Or do a runner, guv'nor.'

The gun emplacement was just inside Queen's Gate of Kensington Gardens, and covered quite a large area. Apart from the Vickers QF 3.7-inch heavy anti-aircraft gun and a direction-finder, there was also a Nissen hut covered completely with sandbags and camouflage netting. There was an eight-foot-high L-shaped pile of sandbags protecting the door to the hut. The whole area was surrounded by barbed wire and guarded by an armed sentry.

As they approached the entrance to the gunsite, Hardcastle and Bradley were stopped by a park keeper who was the epitome of officialdom usually found only in a man dressed in a little brief authority.

'This is a War Department area and is closed to the public,' he announced importantly, as though Hardcastle and Bradley were a couple of tourists bent on having a look around. He held out a hand. 'Identity cards.'

'What about them?' asked Bradley mildly.

'I need to see them.' The park keeper pushed out his chest as though that would add to his authority.

'Divisional Detective Inspector Hardcastle of Scotland Yard.' Hardcastle produced his warrant card, as did Bradley.

'Oh, I'm sorry, gents,' said the park keeper, suddenly deflating in the face of an authority much greater than his own. 'You can't be too careful.'

'You could also try keeping a civil tongue in your head,' said Bradley, as he and Hardcastle passed through the gap in the perimeter. The armed sentry smirked.

As they made their way towards the gun, they were approached by a youthful second lieutenant. He looked, and probably was, about nineteen and had likely been a school prefect a year ago. 'Can I help you, gentlemen?'

Hardcastle introduced himself and Bradley, and again they produced their warrant cards.

'Follow me, gentlemen.' The officer, whose name, he told them, was John Wainwright, led the way to the Nissen hut. The red-backed Bath star on each of his epaulettes appeared to be very new, and he had a habit of frequently striking his right leg with his swagger cane as he walked. 'I've got a bit of this structure partitioned off as an office-cum-bedroom,' he added with a laugh. He shouted for a gunner called Wilkins and told him to find some chairs. Eventually, Gunner Wilkins, who looked old enough to be Wainwright's father, struggled into the office with a couple of fold-up chairs. 'Sorry about all this austerity,' said Wainwright, waving his hand around his cramped quarters as Hardcastle and Bradley sat down. 'We're living rough out here. Wouldn't think it was the centre of London, would you?'

'We're from V Division of the Metropolitan Police,' said Hardcastle, determined to cut short the young officer's monologue about living conditions. 'And we're investigating a murder.'

'Sounds serious,' said Wainwright airily, but there was an element of nervousness behind his strained confidence.

'Murder usually is,' observed Bradley.

'In connection with our enquiries, we would like to speak to Bombardier Christopher Farr, Mr Wainwright.'

'So would I,' said the subaltern, becoming serious for the first time. 'The bugger's gone AWOL'

'When did he go absent?' asked Bradley.

'Two days ago.' Wainwright glanced at a desk calendar. 'That would have been the thirty-first. When the battery sergeant went to rouse the men – we'd received an alert, you see – he found that Farr was adrift. But might I ask why you're interested in him?'

'I don't want you to communicate this to Farr if he returns, Mr Wainwright, but a woman with whom we believe Farr had an affair was found dead last Wednesday afternoon. At five o'clock, in fact. She'd been murdered.'

'Oh God! And you suspect Farr of having killed this woman?'

'Not at all.' Even so, to Hardcastle, it looked very much as though Farr was connected with Joyce Butler's death, but he wasn't going to admit that to Wainwright. 'But we'd rather he didn't know about it until we've had a chance to interview him. In view of what you've told us, though, it's most likely that he'll be in the custody of the Military Police by the time we get to see him.'

'Have you any idea why he should have run?' asked Bradley.

'No idea at all. Occasionally, I would grant him a few hours' leave so that he could visit his wife in Guildford, but he never complained about anything. Neither should he. After all, he might have been in the Middle East with the Eighth Army.

This Kensington Gardens posting is what the troops call a cushy number, but to be frank, I think we stand a better chance of being killed here with nightly bombings, than in one or two of the overseas stations.'

'What does Farr look like?' asked Bradley.

For a moment or two, Wainwright furrowed his forehead in thought. 'About five-nine, I suppose. Auburn hair and a moustache. He's quite well built and was scheduled to take part in the inter-battery boxing competition a few weeks ago, but it was cancelled becaue of the raids every night.'

'One last thing, Mr Wainwright. If Farr turns up of his own volition – and it has happened before – perhaps you'd let me know. I'll give you my telephone number at Putney.'

'Yes, of course.'

'Before we go, we'd like to have a word with the battery sergeant,' said Bradley.

'Oh, is that really necessary, Sergeant?' asked Wainwright sharply, making the mistake of assuming a detective sergeant equated with an army sergeant.

'This is a murder enquiry and we'll talk to anyone we think might assist us,' said Bradley. 'The penalty for obstructing us in the execution of our duty can mean imprisonment.'

'Oh, er, yes. Of course. Sergeant Cassidy is supervising maintenance at the moment. I'll walk over with you.'

'That won't be necessary, Mr Wainwright,' said Hardcastle. 'I'm sure we can find him.'

As Hardcastle and Bradley neared the anti-aircraft gun, Sergeant Cassidy stopped what he was doing and walked across to meet them.

'Mick Cassidy, gents. I'm the battery sergeant, and you're from the police.'

'How did you know that?' asked Bradley, an amused expression on his face. He realized, of course, that Cassidy would have spotted their arrival and promptly interrogated the sentry.

'Because I'm the battery sergeant, I have to know everything. What can I do for you?'

Cassidy was a stocky individual and looked to be about forty-five. The medal ribbons that adorned his tunic testified to service in the Great War, and his pressed uniform would have passed muster for an important parade. Hardcastle guessed that he was probably a regular soldier who had served in the army continuously since 1914.

Hardcastle introduced himself and Bradley. 'We're looking for Bombardier Farr, but we understand from Mr Wainwright that he's adrift.'

'What's that leery little bastard been up to now, apart from having gone over the wall? But something tells me you're not concerned about him going absent.'

As briefly as possible, Hardcastle explained their interest in the missing soldier and his connection with Joyce Butler.

'That's very interesting.' Cassidy pointed to a row of houses on the other side of Kensington Road. 'See the house with the red front door? The basement is ours. It was commandeered when the war started and that's where the lads are billeted.'

'D'you have a quarter over there, too?' asked Bradley.

'No, I've got the other end of the Nissen hut, but I pay a visit from time to time, mainly to see that they're keeping the place in order. However, I paid 'em a surprise visit one night and found that they'd invited a woman in there, and she wasn't wearing too much in the way of clothes.'

'What was that all about, then?'

'I don't think it was a Bible class.' Cassidy laughed. 'Anyway, I threw her out and gave the men a roasting they're unlikely to forget.'

'Did you report it to Mr Wainwright, Sergeant Cassidy?' asked Bradley.

'No, mate.' Cassidy smiled. 'He'd have been talking about court-martials and God knows what else. One of the things you learn in the army is that if you treat the men fairly, and if they're out of order, you give 'em a bloody good bollocking. Start talking about court-martials and you lose their loyalty and that's a bloody dangerous thing to do in wartime. Wainwright's a nice enough kid, but he's still wet behind the ears. He'll learn how to handle men in time, but meanwhile I have to steer him in the right direction.'

'One other thing, Sergeant Cassidy,' Hardcastle asked. 'Did you identify this woman?'

'Oh yes. She was on War Department property and I was

entitled to see her identity card. She was called Joyce Butler
and her old man's a sergeant in the Ordnance Corps. I was
tempted to ring him up and tell him, but then I decided to let
sleeping dogs lie.'

'D'you know who brought her in?'

'Yeah, it was Farr. And because he was a bombardier, I
took him outside and tore him off a strip, rather than do it
in front of the men. After all, he's supposed to be in charge
of that lot, and that includes discipline. Anyway, this time,
he'll get busted down to the rank of gunner for going adrift.
That's for sure.'

Having told Cassidy that they might want to see him
again, the two detectives walked out to where their car was
parked.

'What d'you reckon, guv'nor?' asked Bradley. 'D'you think
that Farr topped our Joyce and then decided to run?'

'Maybe,' said Hardcastle. 'We've deliberately not given
the press anything, though, and unless Farr was the murderer,
he might not know anything about it. No, his running has
probably got something to do with another woman who
he's probably put in the family way.'

'Where do we go from here, then?'

'The Surbiton Assembly Rooms, Jack. But not immediately.
We'll have a run up there this evening. See how the other half
live.'

'They're lucky to have the bloody time,' muttered Bradley.

SIXTEEN

The Surbiton Assembly Rooms had opened in 1890 and by 1910 was showing films until it closed during the Great War. But by the beginning of the Second World War it had become a popular venue for dancing.

'We'll pay to go in, Jack, rather than show out as the law. We can wave our warrant cards about later if we need to.' After a pause, Hardcastle added, 'And don't let me hear you call me "guv'nor".'

Bradley laughed. 'No, guv'nor.'

As it was the first Friday of the month, the day following pay day, most people had money to spend. As a result, the ballroom was comparatively crowded. Among the dancers quite a few of the men, and even some of the women, were in uniform from the military bases in the area. Not only were there British armed forces, and some Empire troops, but a few Free French, Poles and others from mainland Europe who had managed to escape before the unstoppable German army jack-booted its way into their country.

It was not long before a brassy young woman approached Bradley. 'Fancy giving us a whirl, then, good looking?' she asked in a coarse London accent. She was probably in her late twenties and her bleached hair was cut short in a style becoming increasingly popular. Perhaps though, Bradley thought, she works in a factory where long hair was not allowed. Her daringly low-cut top was clearly designed to be the centre of attention, and she wore an excess of make-up.

'Yeah, why not, darling?' Bradley, no mean dancer, seized the girl around the waist and steered her to the centre of the gyrating dancers whose interpretation of the foxtrot would not have met with Victor Silvester's approval.

Following the second dance, Bradley parted company with the girl who was called Ruby Watson, and returned to Hardcastle who was drinking a pint of bitter at the bar.

'Enjoy that, Jack?'

'Not much, no,' said Bradley, attempting unsuccessfully to brush face powder from the lapel of his jacket, 'but I did get some interesting information, although I doubt it'll be of much use. Ruby said she and three of her friends used to meet up here as often as they could with the sole object of getting picked up and spending the night with a man.'

'How come you didn't get propositioned, then, Jack?' Hardcastle ordered a pint of beer for his sergeant and another for himself.

'I did, but I told her it was my night for fire-watching, otherwise I'd have been happy to spend a few hours in the sack with her. So, she gave me her address and said she was looking forward to seeing me again. No chance!'

'But why is any of this interesting, Jack?'

'Because one of this little group was Joyce Butler.'

Hardcastle emitted a short whistle. 'Blimey! You were bloody lucky to have picked her up, Jack.'

'Have you forgotten that it was her who picked me up?'

'So it was,' said Hardcastle, 'but when you look at how many women there are here, why did she pick on you?'

'It's because I'm so devilishly handsome,' said Bradley. 'But what do we do about it, guv?' he asked, as the two of them left the assembly rooms. 'Do we follow it up?'

'Yes, we do, but we must be careful not to put all our eggs in one basket, Jack. As I said earlier, just because Farr has done a runner doesn't necessarily mean that he killed Joyce Butler. The information that Sergeant Cassidy gave us about finding a half-naked Joyce Butler in a room full of the gun crew widens the field. On the other hand, Joyce Butler's killer might not have anything to do with the crew of this gunsite.'

'Would you telephone RSM Purdy of the Military Police, sir?' said DS Hanley, the incident room manager, once they were back at Putney HQ.

Hardcastle and Bradley went into the DDI's office, and Hardcastle made the call. Replacing the receiver, he turned to his sergeant with a grin on his face.

'Farr's been picked up, Jack.'

'Where, guv'nor?'

'In Aldershot, would you believe?'

'Is this bloke mad? Why go to Aldershot? It's the home of the British Army. I'd have thought the obvious thing was to get as far away from there as possible.'

'According to Purdy, a squaddy on the run will often pick somewhere that's full of soldiers, the argument being that he's less likely to be spotted among so many. Unfortunately for Farr, he had a tunic pocket undone and his hands in his pockets.'

Bradley frowned. 'What difference does that make?'

'Apparently, it's a serious offence in the army, and a couple of eagle-eyed young military coppers spotted him and started to report him for being improperly dressed. He was then foolish enough to try to make a run for it and that was that. The two MPs were younger and fitter than Farr.'

'When can we interview him, guv?' Bradley glanced at his wristwatch as if to emphasize that it was getting late.

'Tomorrow morning will be fine, Jack. He's in custody at Aldershot in somewhere called East Cavalry Barracks. Go home and see your girlfriend.'

'Not much chance of that,' muttered Bradley.

'In that case, Jack, there's always Ruby Watson, your dance hall tart.'

Regimental Sergeant Major Dick Purdy was waiting for them in the guardroom of East Cavalry Barracks when Hardcastle and Bradley arrived at midday.

'I'm not here to interfere, Mr Hardcastle,' said Purdy, 'but to offer any assistance I can. Some of these soldiers get very obstructive under the guise of security. D'you want to interview this toerag in his cell or would you prefer to speak to him in an office somewhere?'

'I think an office would be preferable,' said Hardcastle. 'Cells are not really the best places to get the truth out of someone.'

'By the way, Farr appeared before his commanding officer this morning and was reduced to the rank of gunner.'

'That was quick,' said Bradley.

'The army doesn't waste time on them as-run, Sarn't Bradley.'

*   *   *

Gunner Christopher Farr leaped to his feet the moment RSM
Purdy appeared in the doorway, and stood stiffly to attention,
his arms forced down his sides and looking straight ahead. He
was nothing like the description that Second Lieutenant
Wainwright had given them. He was certainly taller than five
foot nine, but was of slender build which, in Hardcastle's view,
made him an unlikely type to take part in boxing competitions.
He had black hair and no moustache. Bradley later described
Farr as a dance hall Romeo and Hardcastle concluded that
Wainwright had mistaken Farr for some other soldier. Although
that was not particularly helpful, Hardcastle ruled out deliberate
prevarication.

'Sit down, Gunner,' snapped Purdy. 'I'm nothing to do with
this interview. This is Detective Inspector Hardcastle of the
Metropolitan Police and his assistant Detective Sergeant
Bradley.' Purdy moved to the back of the room and sat down
some distance from the table behind which Farr was seated.

'Where's your driving licence, Mr Farr?' asked Hardcastle.
It was a question that took Farr completely by surprise.

'Er, my driving licence?'

Hardcastle said nothing, just waited.

'I, er, I don't know offhand.' Farr struggled to come up with
an answer. He wasn't sure why the question had been asked
and why a civil police officer should be asking it.

'I think it must be with my kit.'

The moment the question had been asked, Purdy had
scribbled a note and handed it to Bradley.

'It wasn't with your kit, Mr Farr,' Bradley said. 'When you
went absent, your kit was itemized and put into the quarter-
master's stores. Would you like to try again?'

'I lost it,' Farr finally admitted.

'Where?'

'If I knew that, I wouldn't say it was lost, would I?' replied
Farr, finally showing a bit of spirit. 'Anyway, why have two
busies from the Old Bill come all the way down here to ask
me about a bloody driving licence?'

'How well d'you know Joyce Butler, Mr Farr?' Hardcastle
spoke in a mild tone of voice. He was an expert interrogator,
secure in the knowledge that if he used bullying tactics, he

would get only the answers the suspect thought he wanted him to hear.

'I don't know any Joyce Butler.'

'A night or so before you went absent, Mr Farr, you were responsible for bringing Joyce Butler into the gun crew's quarters where Sergeant Cassidy discovered her in a state of near-nakedness.'

'But I—'

'On one occasion, you escorted her to her flat in Ravenscroft, Kingston Hill, where officers found your driving licence, tucked down the back of a settee.'

'So what? I met her at some dance hall in Surbiton and escorted her home and we had it off on the sofa.'

'On the sofa or in bed?' asked Bradley. 'Where you were discovered by Mrs Butler's husband.'

'So what?' asked Farr for the second time.

'When did this incident occur?'

'I don't know. Must've been about two or three weeks ago, I suppose.'

'Her dead body was found at her flat three days ago, Mr Farr,' said Hardcastle. 'She had been murdered. I am, therefore, arresting you on suspicion of murdering Joyce Butler on or about Wednesday the thirty-first of July 1940. I must caution you now that you're not obliged to say anything unless you wish to do so, but anything you do say will be taken down in writing and may be given in evidence.'

'I never had nothing to do with that.' Farr's face was ashen and he gripped the sides of the table until his knuckles showed white.

Hardcastle turned to Purdy. 'I'd be grateful if you detained Farr here until I send an escort to take him to London, Mr Purdy, probably later today or early tomorrow morning.'

Purdy waited until two regimental policemen arrived and took Farr back to his cell in the guardroom before speaking. 'With all due respect, Mr Hardcastle, Farr is in military custody and I'm not sure that you can just take him away like that.'

'If you care to look at the *Manual of Military Law* in conjunction with the Army Act, Mr Purdy, you will find that the civil authority overrides the military in cases of murder

and other serious offences. Even if they are committed on
military property and in time of war.'

It was half past four that afternoon when Hardcastle was told
that Gunner Christopher Farr had arrived at Cannon Row police
station.

The awesome edifice of New Scotland Yard, built fifty years
previously from Dartmoor stone aptly quarried by convicts
from the nearby prison, was a frightening spectacle for the
innocent, let alone the guilty. Gunner Farr had been unnerved
enough by his interview with the two detectives at Aldershot
and the sight of the Metropolitan Police headquarters had been
sufficient to reduce him to a state of nervous anxiety. His
disposition was not helped as, in common with many others,
he believed the police station to be a part of Scotland Yard.

'We'll go and have a chat with him right now, Jack.'

'D'you think he did it, guv'nor?' asked Bradley as the
two of them arrived at Cannon Row police station, the headquarters of the A or Whitehall Division.

'I don't know, Jack, and I don't like committing myself
until I've got a few more answers.'

'Get someone to bring up Farr and put him in the interview
room, Sergeant, if you please,' said Hardcastle to the station
officer.

'Very good, sir.' The sergeant shouted for the station's duty
gaoler.

Farr had been ordered to change back into khaki battledress
before leaving for London and, judging by his immaculate
turnout, had been inspected by RSM Purdy before being
allowed to depart from Aldershot.

'Smoke if you want to, Mr Farr,' said Hardcastle, as he and
Bradley settled themselves opposite the soldier. He noticed
that Farr smoked cork-tipped cigarettes, but said nothing about
Sergeant Ronald Butler finding a cork-tipped cigarette butt in
an ashtray when he arrived home unexpectedly one evening.

'I didn't have anything to do with Joyce's death,' said Farr
suddenly.

'I'd remind you that you're still under caution, Mr Farr,'
said Bradley. 'That means you don't have to answer any

questions we might ask, unless we wish to clear up an ambiguity.'

'Yeah, I know, but like I said, I went to her place a few times and we had it off. She was a bloody good performer and we were getting on well. I wouldn't have harmed a hair on her head. If anyone done for her, it'd have been her old man. A right nasty bastard was Ron Butler. Mind you, I s'pose that coming home and finding some bloke screwing his missus on the sofa is bound to upset him. But just because he had one more stripe than me, he was chucking his weight about something cruel. There again, I think it was more to scare his missus than me.'

'I take it you were the "some bloke" he found on the sofa well at it,' said Bradley.

'Yeah.' Farr gave a wry smile. 'And it was worth the risk.'

'Did you go back to see Mrs Butler after your set-to with her husband?' asked Hardcastle.

'Nah! Didn't want to chance it, see. But that was for her sake. I could have handled Butler if it'd come to fisticuffs.'

'Are you saying you didn't see Joyce Butler again after that incident with her husband, Mr Farr?'

'Oh no. I kept on seeing her a few times. But not down her place. She had a mate – well three mates – and they looked out for each other. So, we used to meet up at Ruby's flat. Her old man's in the RAF in Malta, poor sod, so there was no chance of him walking in.'

'Ruby who?' asked Bradley, although he was certain he knew the answer.

'Ruby Watson. She's a hairdresser down New Malden way. Got a nice little flat over the shop that the owner of the hairdressers lets her have for next to nothing.'

Bradley thought he knew the reason the owner was so generous, but said nothing.

'Tell me about the evening that Joyce Butler was found in your quarters at the gunsite,' said Hardcastle.

'There's nothing to tell, really.'

'Sergeant Cassidy said that it was you who brought her in.'

'Well, I didn't. But Cassidy's got it in for me. Every chance he gets, he'd have me for something. Typical bloody regular soldier, he is. Resents us what's been called up. As if we wanted to be in his bloody army.'

'If it wasn't you who brought her in, who was it?' asked Bradley.

'No idea,' said Farr. 'I'd just come off duty and when I went across to the billet, she was there. It could've been anyone who brought her in. She was very free with her favours,' he admitted.

'Have you ever had your fingerprints taken, Mr Farr?' asked Bradley suddenly.

'What d'you want to know that for?' Farr sat up, appearing disconcerted by the question and the suddenness with which Bradley had posed it.

'Just answer the question, Mr Farr,' said Bradley.

'You said I don't have to answer a question if I don't want to.' Farr spoke churlishly.

'This has nothing to do with the murder of Joyce Butler, so it's not covered by the caution.'

'I got in a bit of trouble where I was living at the time.' Farr admitted defeat.

'And where was that?'

'Croydon.'

'Look, Farr,' said Bradley, 'we can stay here all night if you want to play games.'

'All right, so I done a bloke up.'

'Explain.'

'It was at a dance hall down Croydon and this bloke was coming on to the girl I was dancing with. I was on a dead cert an' all. So, I told him to clear off, but he wouldn't take no for an answer and grabbed my girl by the arm. So, I chinned him. Well, to cut a long story short, he fell and banged his head on the edge of the bar on his way down, like. Anyway, your lot was called an' I was nicked. But when this bloke was found to have fractured his skull, I got done for GBH with intent. I was lucky in a way, I s'pose, because first off, they were talking about malicious wounding. Even attempted murder. Anyhow, I got a year inside, but a few months later, when the war started, they chucked a whole lot of us out and straight into the army.' Farr gave a cynical laugh. 'I hadn't been in the Kate too long to work out that I'd have been better off staying in chokey.'

Hardcastle stood up and opened the interview room door. 'You can take this prisoner back to his cell.'

'Is that it, then?' asked Farr, as the constable took hold of his arm.

'Not by a long chalk,' said Hardcastle.

'What d'you think, guv'nor?' asked Bradley, once Farr was out of the room.

'Why did you question him about that previous conviction, Jack? We knew that already.'

'I wanted to see how truthful he was.'

'But he must've known we'd have a record.'

'Maybe, but there again, he might not be that clever.'

'You could be right, Jack. But get on to Fingerprint Branch and ask them to compare the prints of Farr that they have on record with the prints found in Joyce Butler's flat. I know he's admitted being there and I know they're doing a comparison check on all the prints, but they might not have got to Farr's yet and a shortcut might help.'

'In hand,' said Bradley. 'I gave them a ring before we came in here to talk to Farr, but they'd already started.'

Included in the strict protocol of the Fingerprint Branch was the requirement that a fingerprint expert had to have at least seven years' experience before he could give fingerprint evidence in court.

Consequently, it was not until the following morning that a Fingerprint Branch officer was able to give Hardcastle the result of his comparison of prints found in the dead woman's flat and those taken from Farr on his conviction.

'Detective Sergeant Furminger, C3 Department, sir.' Furminger was a middle-aged man in a worn, ill-fitting suit. A pair of smeared spectacles were perched on the end of his nose, and one of the tools of his trade, a magnifying glass, was suspended on a cord around his neck. He looked more like an absent-minded professor than a fingerprint expert.

'I hope you've come to tell me that Farr is our man, Skipper.'

'I'm afraid there's no way I can tell you that, guv'nor,' said

Furminger. 'However, one or two of Farr's prints were found around Mrs Butler's flat.'

'He's already admitted having been there,' said Bradley, 'but did you find any on the wine bottle or wine glass?'

'No, sir.'

'Looks like we're back to the beginning, Jack,' said Hardcastle, once Detective Sergeant Furminger had departed.

'I reckon it's got to have been one of the squaddies on that gun battery, sir.'

'If what has been said about her being free with her favours is true, it could have been half the male population of London.'

'What about fingerprinting the whole of the gun crew, guv?'

'I think that's a bit draconian, Jack, and if it is one of them, it would put him on the alert. He could disappear into the wilderness of the Smoke and be lost for ages, if not forever,' said Hardcastle. 'Get on to that Military Police RSM and tell him that he can have Farr back, and ask him if he'd call in and see me.'

SEVENTEEN

'Your Sergeant Bradley told me that you want to talk to me, Mr Hardcastle. I'm sorry I wasn't here sooner, but the paperwork is unbelievable. There are so many squaddies deserting that it takes forever to get it all documented. Anyhow, never mind my woes; what can I do to assist you?'

'I'd be grateful if you could get the dates of birth of all the gun crew for me, Mr Purdy. Sergeant Bradley had suggested fingerprinting them all, but that would alert the murderer if, indeed, he was a member of the gun crew. But if we can have their dates of birth, we can run them through records. If any one of them has a conviction, we can then check with Fingerprint Branch.'

'It wouldn't include Mr Wainwright, of course.'

'It most certainly will,' said Bradley.

'But he's an officer,' protested Purdy.

'If you're suggesting that officers don't commit murder, Mr Purdy,' said Hardcastle, 'I can give you several examples of those who have.'

'I'll arrange to get them immediately,' said Purdy, rather relishing passing on Hardcastle's comment.

'You won't get them from the crew themselves, I hope.'

'I was a policeman in Manchester City for quite a few years before I joined the army, Mr Hardcastle,' said Purdy, as he donned his cap. 'I do know how these things are done.'

On Monday morning, Regimental Sergeant Major Purdy appeared in Hardcastle's office and handed him a list of the gun crew and their dates of birth.

'Thank you, Mr Purdy, that was very quick.'

'Unfortunately, I've not been so fast on my other enquiry, Mr Hardcastle,' said Purdy. 'I've failed to discover who was responsible for taking Mrs Butler into the gun crew's quarters.

Each of those leery bastards said they didn't know who it was and further claimed that she was already there when they arrived. What's more, they said they couldn't remember who else was there when they turned up. When I asked about Mrs Butler's state of undress, some of them said she'd been playing strip poker with a couple of the lads.'

'None of which I believe,' said Hardcastle.

'Nor me, Mr Hardcastle, but I'll get it out of 'em, you mark my words.'

'I think it might be as well, Mr Purdy, if you left any further questioning to me. Thank you for your assistance so far, but I'll be in touch if I need any more help.'

'As you wish, Mr Hardcastle,' said Purdy. 'You know where my office is. Feel free to drop in any time. I happen to have a bottle of duty-free Scotch in my bottom drawer.'

'In that case, I think I might be tempted to find an excuse for paying you a visit, Mr Purdy.'

'I hope so. By the way, the name's Dick.'

'And mine's Wally,' said Hardcastle.

The list of the gun crew's dates of birth had been taken straight to C4 Branch – the Criminal Records Office – at the Yard and the bureau head had authorized a priority search. But the result was disappointing. Apart from Gunner Christopher Farr, none of the crew had a criminal conviction. And their fingerprints would not, therefore, be in the national fingerprint collection, unless they were in the scenes-of-crime section, but Hardcastle thought that unlikely. In any event, they would already have been checked.

'Dammit!' said Hardcastle. 'Now what?'

Hardcastle's question was answered almost immediately by Detective Sergeant Gordon Hanley, in charge of the incident room, tapping on the open door of Hardcastle's office.

'What is it, Skip?'

'A phone call from the station officer downstairs, sir. He's got a caller who has information about the murder of Joyce Butler.'

'Is the caller male or female?'

'It's a woman, sir.'

Hardcastle shouted for Jack Bradley and the two of them went downstairs to the front office.

'She's in the interview room, sir,' said the station officer.

'What's her name, Sergeant?'

The station officer glanced down at the Occurrence Book on his desk. 'Mavis Lavender, sir. She's twenty-three, and her date of birth is the sixth of July 1917. Unmarried. She works at Gamages as a shop assistant, and lives in the company's hostel behind the store.'

'Miss Lavender?' asked Hardcastle, as he and Bradley entered the interview room.

The young blonde woman was sitting sideways-on to the table, her legs crossed. She wore a belted red dress that Hardcastle's mother would undoubtedly have condemned as a 'catalogue dress'. Her lipstick and her fingernails were a bright red, and in place of stockings, she had applied leg make-up. Someone, probably a fellow shopworker, had used a Conté pencil to draw lines on the back of her legs that looked like seams. She wore low wedge-heeled shoes for practical reasons; since the beginning of the blitz, women had often found themselves trudging over rubble and debris from bombed buildings on their way to work, which would have been nigh-on impossible in high heels. Finally, a pillbox hat in a lighter red put the finishing touch to her outfit. Her leather handbag and the brown cardboard box containing her gas mask were on the table.

'Yes, that's me.' Mavis glanced at Bradley and primped the back of her hair.

The two detectives sat down opposite the young woman.

'D'you smoke?' asked Bradley, producing a packet of Kensitas.

'Oh, I don't mind if I do,' said Mavis Lavender in what was often described as a 'telephone voice', and leaned forward so that Bradley could light her cigarette. 'Ta, ever so.'

'I understand that you have something to tell us about Joyce Butler,' began Hardcastle.

'We were friends, the four of us. Me, Joyce, Doris Jackson and Ruby Watson. We used to go dancing together. Mind you,

we weren't always able to meet up on account of having
different jobs. Joyce was an usherette down the Super Cinema
and Doris is a clippie on the number six-oh-four trolleybus
route.'

'Where did you go dancing?' asked Bradley, although he
was sure he knew the answer.

'The Surbiton Assembly Rooms down Kingston way. But
we always looked out for each other. There was one time when
Doris—'

'What exactly is it you want to tell us that you think might
help, Miss Lavender?' Hardcastle knew from experience that
this sort of meandering tale could go on for some time; it was
not the first occasion he had encountered so-called informants
who really had nothing to say when tested.

'Oh, that, yes.' Mavis leaned forward and stubbed out her
cigarette in a tin lid that did service as an ashtray. 'Well, there
was just Joyce, Doris and me at the assembly rooms dance
that night . . .'

'When was this?' asked Bradley, who had his pocketbook
on the table and was making notes.

'Last Tuesday.'

'Are you sure?'

'Yeah. It was my day off from Gamages, see, on account
of me having worked the Saturday before. Anyway, like I said,
me and Joyce and Doris was there having a look at the available talent. Not that there was much of it. Anyway, some bloke
came up and took Joyce off for the quickstep. Very good at
the quickstep, was Joyce. But I s'pose she must've gone off
some place with him because after Doris and me had danced
with a couple of RAF types, we went to the bar where we
always met up if we was separated.' Mavis paused. 'D'you
think I could I have another ciggy?'

Bradley offered his packet and then lit the girl's cigarette.

'We waited at the bar, but Joyce never showed up. We
guessed she must've struck lucky with this guy and had gone
off to find a bed somewhere. Come to think of it, she lived in
an expensive flat down Kingston way, so it wasn't too far.'
Mavis paused as she considered what she had just said. 'I
don't know why she moved down there unless she'd picked

up some sugar daddy. And if the bloke who picked her up was any sort of gent, he'd have taken her home in a taxi. But that would have cost a fortune.'

'What did this man look like, Miss Lavender?' Bradley asked.

Mavis leaned back in her chair and drew on her cigarette, blowing smoke into the air as if this aided recollection. 'Well built,' she said eventually.

'How tall was he?' Bradley could see that extracting useful information from this young woman was going to be difficult.

'Would you mind standing up?' asked Mavis, nodding towards Bradley. 'Yes, about your height,' she said, when he had obliged.

'Moustache, beard, anything like that?'

'No.' Mavis pondered the question a little further. 'I don't think so.'

'If we asked you to sit with a police artist, d'you think you might be able to help him produce a likeness?' suggested Bradley, scratching thoughtfully at his moustache.

'Oh, I don't know about that. I could try, I s'pose.'

'Before we do that,' said Hardcastle, 'I think it might be as well if we interviewed your friend, Miss Doris Jackson. Perhaps you'd give my sergeant her address.'

Mavis took a diary from her handbag and thumbed through it. 'She's got a flat in Fairfield Road in Kingston. She shares it with another clippie called Marion Ferguson.'

'How old is Doris Jackson?'

'About my age, I s'pose. I never thought to ask. Well, one doesn't, does one?' she said, and primped her hair again.

Once Mavis Lavender had left, no doubt to regale the impressionable with a story of how she was helping the police to solve a murder, Detective Sergeant Jack Bradley, who claimed to know about London Transport, very quickly found out when Doris Jackson would be off duty.

'She finished at twelve noon, guv'nor.'

Hardcastle glanced at his pocket watch. 'No time like the present.'

EIGHTEEN

The flat that Doris Jackson shared with Marion Ferguson was on the first floor of a rather old building in Fairfield Road, overlooking the cattle market. The market, normally there most days except Sundays, had become smaller since the outbreak of war. Many of the marketeers were now in the armed forces, and there was some doubt that the market would survive.

The two detectives eventually found Doris Jackson's flat and rang the bell.

'Yeah?' The bottle-blonde woman who answered the door took the cigarette out of her mouth long enough to pose that monosyllabic question, before promptly replacing it. Planting one hand on her hip, she openly examined the two men, her gaze travelling from their heads to their toes and back again. Her grey trousers would definitely have been frowned upon by certain sections of society, as would the V-necked pullover worn without a blouse.

'Miss Doris Jackson?'

Without answering Hardcastle's question, the woman turned and shouted, 'Doris, there's a couple of dishy men at the door asking for you.'

'Who are they?' asked a disembodied voice from somewhere in the flat.

'Who are you?' asked the woman, turning back.

'Divisional Detective Inspector Hardcastle, and Detective Sergeant Bradley.'

'Oh, Christ!' uttered the woman. 'It's the rozzers, Doris. What you been up to?'

'Well, don't leave 'em on the doorstep, Marion, otherwise the neighbours will think we're running a knocking shop. Bring 'em in.'

Turning to address Hardcastle and Bradley, Marion said, 'Come on in. You'll have to take us as you find us. We tend to lounge about once we're off duty.'

The two CID officers were shown into a sitting room. Apart from a pair of stockings hanging from the mantelshelf and held in place by a couple of ornaments, and several copies of *Picturegoer* magazine abandoned on a chair, the room was clean and tidy.

'I'm Doris Jackson.' The young woman could not have been any more than five foot five inches tall, and her brown hair was cut quite short. Barefooted, she was wrapped in a towelling dressing gown that reached her ankles, and looked to be several sizes too large for her. 'Excuse my appearance,' she said, 'but I've just had a bath. You'd be surprised how dirty you get just by being on a trolleybus for eight hours.'

'You should try doing point duty.' Bradley recalled spending eight hours directing traffic in central London and being really dirty from constant exposure to petrol and diesel fumes.

'Have you come about Joyce?' Doris asked, indicating with a wave of the hand that Hardcastle and Bradley should sit down. 'Mavis Lavender told me she was coming to see you.' She suddenly noticed the stockings and snatched them from the mantelshelf. 'Sorry, we weren't expecting visitors.'

'Yes, Mavis Lavender came to see us this morning,' said Hardcastle. 'She told us about a man who befriended Joyce Butler at the Surbiton Assembly Rooms. D'you remember this man? It was the night she was murdered – Tuesday just gone.'

'Not really – I too busy talking to Ruby for most of the night, but I do remember someone she was dancing with the night before. He was quite a big chap and seemed nice enough, what little I saw of him. They went off dancing and that's the last Mavis and me saw of them.'

'Did you actually see them leave, Miss Jackson?'

'No. One minute they were on the dance floor and next minute they'd gone.'

'Did you learn the man's name, by any chance?' asked Bradley.

'No. I think Joyce was afraid that one of us might pinch him. He was more . . . How's best to describe it? He was more grown up, if you know what I mean.'

'Mature?' suggested Bradley.

'That's it. He was a very confident dancer too. You could tell by the way he swept Joyce on to the dance floor. Much

better than these eighteen-year-old kids who think they're
grown up just because they're wearing a uniform. Fumbling
Freddies, I call 'em. Hands everywhere and hoping to get their
end away before they get killed, I suppose.' Doris's philosophy
of life was far beyond her years. 'Poor little buggers.'

'Would you know him if you saw him again, Miss Jackson?'
asked Hardcastle.

'I sure would,' said Doris. 'D'you think it was him who
killed Joyce?'

'That I don't know, but I'd certainly like to speak to him
about the events of that evening. Should you see him again,
let me know. But whatever you do, don't approach him.'
Hardcastle turned to the other woman. 'Were you at the
assembly rooms dance hall that night, Miss . . .?'

'Marion Ferguson, and no, you won't catch me going
anywhere near that sort of place. I have enough trouble dealing
with amateur Don Juans when I'm at work. Mind you, there's
one or two bus drivers who've received my knee in their
crutch, and that dampened their ardour, I can tell you.'

Hardcastle sat down behind his desk and took out his pipe. 'I
suppose it's a lead of sorts, Jack, but we've got no description
of the man who took her home, apart from his being mature,
and we don't even know that he was the one who *did* take her
home. For all we know it could have been some other bloke.'

'Now we know that Joyce was a professional tom, it widens
the list of suspects, guv'nor, but no way we can prove that
any of them was responsible for Joyce Butler's death,' said
Bradley, stating the obvious.

Ignoring Bradley's truism, Hardcastle suddenly flicked
his fingers. 'The fireman!'

'Fireman? What fireman?' Bradley failed to follow his
chief's line of thinking, albeit momentarily. 'Ah, the bloke in
the ground-floor flat at Ravenscroft.'

'That's him. Leading Fireman Eric Simpson of Kingston
fire station. I wonder if he's on duty at the moment.'

'I'll find out,' said Bradley. Five minutes later, he was back.
'Yes, guv'nor, he's there.'

*   *   *

'There's somewhere over here where we can talk, gents,' said Simpson. 'But if we get a shout, I'll have to leave you. Unless you want to come with us,' he added with a wry grin. He led them across the main area and behind a couple of fire appliances to a small room.

'The night after Joyce Butler was murdered, you'd just come off duty.'

'That's right.' Simpson took out a packet of cigarettes and offered them. Bradley accepted, but Hardcastle, a pipe smoker, declined.

'Is it all right to smoke in here?' asked Bradley.

'Yeah, sure. If the place catches fire, we know how to put it out. We've done the course.' Simpson chuckled at the thought. 'Mind you, there'd be an enquiry. And an enquiry means paperwork. Lots of it.'

'I know what you mean.' Hardcastle had suffered a mountain of paperwork when, as a sergeant, a Flying Squad typewriter for which he had signed had gone missing.

'The night of the murder,' said Bradley, opening his pocketbook, 'you told us that every time you saw Joyce Butler, she was on the arm of a different bloke. And from what you'd seen, there's no shortage.'

'Absolutely right,' said Simpson.

'Did you ever see a man who's been described to us as mature and, the witness said, was quite a big chap?'

'Can't say I have,' said Simpson thoughtfully. 'Mind you, most of the men she had with her were mature. I don't know why they weren't in uniform. I suppose they might have been and changed into civvies to go dancing.'

'Did you ever go to the Surbiton Assembly Rooms?' asked Bradley.

'No,' said Simpson. 'Passed it a few times on our way to a shout, but we were more often going in the opposite direction. Towards Hawkers.'

'I'll give you my telephone number, Mr Simpson,' said Hardcastle, 'and if you do think of anything, perhaps you'd give me or Sergeant Bradley a ring.'

Just as Hardcastle and Bradley were about to leave, an air-raid siren sounded from the roof of Kingston police station.

'Any minute now the bells will go down,' said Simpson, using a hand to cup his ear in pantomimic anticipation. Sure enough, seconds later the alarm sounded in the fire station and suddenly the area was alive with firemen, in ordered chaos, rushing to the appliances. 'They're after Hawkers again,' he said.

On Tuesday the sixth of August 1940, just seven days after the murder of Joyce Butler, Police Constable Albert Stringer, a fifty-seven-year-old police pensioner who had been recalled to service at the outbreak of war, was patrolling Charing Cross Road. Although it was still light, he was walking at less than the four miles an hour laid down in the regulations for beat duty men. But it was a speed that suited Stringer, a man who never rushed at anything. One of his strengths, and a strength particularly suited to police duty, was his temperament. Before taking any action that might be considered rash or unwise, he would consider the situation carefully. And he did so now.

There had been an air raid the previous day when a shop premises had been destroyed and buildings on either side had been badly damaged. Superficial damage, mainly broken windows, had been done to several other nearby structures and 'Business as Usual' signs had appeared in those shop windows that were still intact.

Stringer occasionally sought out insecure premises and other unusual matters that required police attention. At nine thirty, just half an hour before he was due to go off duty, he glanced into the rubble-strewn shop, and spotted the body of a woman in the ruins.

It was not unusual to find dead or injured members of the public in the aftermath of an air raid, but not twenty-four hours later. A body as open to view as this one would be sent straight to the mortuary by the heavy rescue squad, whose members would have remained at the bomb site until they were satisfied that there were no more victims buried. Furthermore, the body had not been there an hour ago, the last time Stringer had walked this part of his beat. On closer examination, he noted that the victim was quite a young woman, probably in her early twenties. Ducking under the barriers erected by the local authority, he knelt down, removed his steel helmet, and felt for a pulse, but to no avail. One thing was certain – she had not been killed by a bomb; she had been strangled. For a moment or two, he tugged thoughtfully at his greying beard.

Going to a nearby telephone box – still in working order despite the best efforts of the Luftwaffe – he called Kingston police station and told the duty officer what he had found. He returned to the body and within minutes a black Wolseley police car drew up and Detective Inspector Bob French alighted, accompanied by Detective Sergeant Bernard Turner.

'What have you got here, then, Stringer?'

Succinctly, and with his customary care, Stringer explained, once again, the circumstances under which he had come across the dead woman.

'And you said this body wasn't here an hour ago?' asked French.

'That's correct, sir.'

'Searched it, have you?'

'No, sir. I thought it better to wait for you.'

'Good man.' French glanced at his sergeant. 'See what you can find, Bernie.'

'Her handbag's still here, guv'nor,' said Turner, extracting it from where it had been partly concealed by the body. He opened it and examined the contents. 'There's a bit of cash here, guv, and her identity card says she's Mavis Lavender and her address is shown as Gamages' hostel. Gamages is a department store at Holborn Circus.'

'I do know where Gamages is, Bernie,' said French wearily. 'Robbery wasn't the motive, then.' He removed his trilby hat and scratched his head. 'Better send for the duty pathologist, I suppose. Get on the blower, Bernie, and organize it, will you? And call out the DDI.'

It had just gone eleven o'clock when Walter Hardcastle heard the telephone ringing. Cursing beneath his breath, he padded downstairs in his bare feet.

'Hardcastle,' he said as he answered the phone.

'It's DS Turner, sir.' Turner went on to explain briefly about the body that PC Stringer had found in the ruins of a shop in Charing Cross Road. The moment Turner mentioned the name of Mavis Lavender, Hardcastle was wide awake. By the time he had finished the call, his wife, Muriel, was standing at the top of the stairs wrapped in her dressing gown.

'Have you got to go out, love?'

'Afraid so. Another dead body.' Hardcastle sighed.

'I'll make you a cup of tea while you're getting dressed.'

Hardcastle telephoned DS Bradley and told him about the murder of Mavis Lavender.

'I'm on my way, guv'nor.'

Hardcastle was met by Detective Inspector Bob French and Detective Sergeants Bernie Turner and Jack Bradley, Hardcastle's own assistant, at the bombed-out shop where Mavis Lavender's dead body had been found.

'I reckon you'll be able to shed more light on this topping than I will, guv'nor,' said French.

'Possibly, Bob,' said Hardcastle guardedly, and briefly explained about the murder of Joyce Butler and his interview with Mavis Lavender the previous morning. 'It looks to me as though whoever murdered Joyce Butler was afraid that Mavis Lavender had seen him pick up Joyce at the Surbiton Assembly Rooms and was worried that she'd identify him to us.'

'There's not much point in murdering her *after* she'd identified him to us,' suggested Bradley.

'Maybe so, but it would certainly stop her giving evidence at a trial, Jack.' Hardcastle wondered whether the hope of a distant trial was being too optimistic, given the present paucity of evidence.

It was just after midnight when Dr Francis Camps arrived. A distinguished pathologist, Camps had been instrumental in bringing a number of murderers to justice.

His examination of the body was quick and thorough and, having made a few notes, he asked DI French to arrange the removal of the body to Kingston hospital where he would carry out a post-mortem examination.

It was when the ambulance crew were lifting the body that

Detective Sergeant Bradley spotted something shiny that had been beneath the woman's body.

'This looks interesting, guv.' Bradley picked up the object that had caught his eye; it was a small gold-coloured badge consisting of a facsimile bullet bearing a pair of wings.

'What on earth is that, Jack?' Hardcastle asked.

'I haven't a clue, guv. Whatever it is, it might, with any luck, belong to her killer.'

'Take possession of it as an exhibit, Jack,' said Hardcastle. 'God knows what it is, but obviously we need to find out quickly.'

'That's two of their group who've been murdered now, guv'nor,' said Bradley. 'D'you think we should put a guard on the other two: Ruby Watson and Doris Jackson?'

'I was just thinking that, Jack, but there's a difficulty with Doris Jackson: she's a bus conductress.'

'Perhaps a woman officer in plain clothes,' suggested Bradley, 'but we'd have to clear it with the transport authority, otherwise it will cost a fortune if our girl has to pay for eight or so hours on a bus every day.'

'I'm not underestimating our women officers, Jack, but I'd rather we put a male officer on that duty, because I think if this bloke goes for Doris, he's more likely to do it in public when he can make his escape. And we'd need a very fit young officer to chase him and still have enough strength left to put a hammer-lock-and-bar on him when he catches him. But I think we should use a WPC to look after Ruby Watson as she's a hairdresser. At least, that's what she told you when she picked you up at the Surbiton dance.' Hardcastle shot an amused glance at his sergeant. 'Or perhaps you'd like to take up the job yourself, seeing that you got on so well with her.'

'I'll pass on that one, guv'nor, if it's all the same to you.'

'We'll use a WPC, Jack. Having a man hanging around in a ladies' hairdressing salon would look a bit suspicious.'

Their conversation was interrupted by the wailing of the air-raid siren. 'Here we go again,' said Bradley, as the first heavy throb of Dornier bomber engines was heard overhead.

* * *

George Large, the superintendent in charge of the Fulwell bus
depot from which Doris Jackson worked, was eager to assist
the police. As befitted his name, George Large was a big man,
his waistcoat straining at its buttons. His white shirt had a
detachable celluloid collar that appeared to be a size too small
and his striped necktie was neatly tied.

'She's one of our best conductresses,' he said. 'I wouldn't
want to lose her. So, anything I can do to help the boys in
blue, just say the word.'

'If you can give me details of her schedule,' said Hardcastle,
'that'll be a start. Would it be all right with you if my man
collected Miss Jackson from her home address and took her
to work from there?'

'Of course it would, Inspector.'

'In that case, I'll telephone his name to you as soon as I
get back to Putney and I'll tell him to introduce himself to
Miss Jackson when he arrives. That just leaves the question
of cost.'

The superintendent waved his hand dismissively. 'Good
heavens, don't worry about that. After all, you're looking after
one of our girls. We haven't had policemen on board since
the days of the General Strike fourteen years ago. If he speaks
to me when he gets here on Thursday afternoon, I'll issue him
with a pass, just in case a jumper gets aboard.'

'A jumper, Mr Large?' queried Bradley.

'An inspector, Sergeant. They board buses at various places
to check that fares have been paid.' Large paused and grinned.
'And to make sure the conductor's not on the fiddle.'

'You said Thursday afternoon, Mr Large.' Hardcastle took
out his pipe, rubbed the bowl on his sleeve and filled it with
tobacco. He offered the pouch to Large. 'Do you?' he asked.

'Thank you. That's very kind.' Large took a pipe from his
inside pocket and began to fill it. 'Doris is off tomorrow,' he
said, between puffs as he got his pipe well alight. 'She's next
on duty at one o'clock on Thursday afternoon.'

'You mentioned the General Strike just now, Mr Large,'
said Bradley. 'I take it you were involved in that.'

Large bristled. 'I was management, even back then,' he said.
'We didn't go on strike. When you've spent three years driving

a bus on the Western Front, you have a different view of what's important and what isn't.'

'You were one of those drivers who took their buses over there, were you?'

'I was indeed. We were the old London General Omnibus Company in those days, but we were drafted into the Army Service Corps. The King gave the corps the "Royal" prefix after the war was over. What's more, the King decreed that every year a representative of London Transport should attend the Armistice Day service in Whitehall.' Large paused, looking into the middle distance as though recalling those shell-torn days of the Great War. 'Still, I mustn't keep you gentleman by telling you my war stories,' he said, briefly touching his Royal Army Service Corps tie.

From the bus depot, Hardcastle and Bradley made their way to New Malden High Street. In the centre of the parade of shops they found the Salon de Jules, ladies' hair stylists, a four-chair establishment of which, at that time, only one chair was occupied. The client was being attended to by a man who, Hardcastle presumed, was Jules himself. He had a silly little moustache that made him appear more Italian than French, and a spotted bow tie.

The hairdresser paused, scissors in one hand and comb in the other, both held high in the air in a theatrical gesture. 'We do not cut the 'airs of gentlemens, m'sieur,' he exclaimed in a pantomime French accent.

'I should hope not,' said Bradley. 'We're police officers.'

'Oh Gawd!' Suddenly Jules's pseudo accent disappeared and was replaced by pure Cockney. 'Linda, love,' he shouted, in the direction of a door at the rear of the salon, 'come and take over while I talk to these gentlemen.'

A slender blonde emerged from the back room of the salon, shot what she obviously believed to be a sexy glance at Bradley, and picked up the scissors and comb that Jules had just abandoned. Without a word, she began to cut the customer's hair.

'Better come in the back room, guv'nor,' said Jules, and led the way into a tiny office.

'Is your name really Jules?' asked Hardcastle.

'Good God, no. That's for the punters. I'm Charlie Perks. Now, what's this all about?'

'It's about Mrs Ruby Watson,' said Bradley.

'*Mrs* Watson. D'you mean she's married?'

'The fact that she's called *Mrs* Watson might be a clue, Mr Perks. And yes, she's married and her husband's in the Royal Air Force, serving in Malta, poor devil.'

'But your relationship with Mrs Watson,' said Hardcastle, taking a guess that there was one, 'is not why we're here.'

'Oh!' Perks sounded very relieved.

'We are concerned about Mrs Watson's safety.' Hardcastle went on to explain about the murders of Joyce Butler and Mavis Lavender. 'As a result of those killings and the fact the two dead women, Mrs Butler and Miss Lavender, were close friends, we fear that Mrs Watson may become a target.'

'Oh, my Gawd! D'you mean he might come here and murder us?'

'We've no idea,' said Bradley, rather enjoying the sight of the panic-stricken pseudo French hairdresser, 'but just to make sure, we intend to place a woman police officer in here. If you have no objection, that is.'

'No, no, not at all,' said Perks hurriedly, sounding immensely relieved.

'Is Ruby here?' asked Hardcastle.

'Not at the moment. She just popped out to get a pint of milk.'

But at that moment, the door of the office opened and Ruby Watson entered. She saw Bradley and did a double-take. 'What you doing 'ere?' she asked, placing the milk on a table.

But before Bradley was able to answer, Perks said, 'They're from the police, Ruby love.'

'What's up, then?'

Bradley explained to Ruby Watson about the murders and the fear that she might be at risk. Then, he explained the precautions they intended to take.

'D'you know, I had an idea you was a copper, Jack,' said Ruby, 'when you started asking all them questions when we was dancing down the assembly rooms. But you never took me up on me offer, did you? That surprised me because I've known a few coppers in me time and they're a randy lot.'

'I've been very busy, Ruby. You know how it is.'

'I hope you're going to pick out a good-looking copper to take care of me, Jack. I s'pose it ain't no good asking for you, is it?'

'No, like I said, Ruby, I'm busy. And it won't be a man either. We've got a woman officer lined up to look after you.'

'What good's that? I need a tough he-man guarding me.'

'Don't worry about that, Ruby. The woman we've got in mind is very good at unarmed combat.'

Ruby pouted. 'Well, that's a bit of a let-down, I must say.'

NINETEEN

Hardcastle had called in a favour from the sub-divisional inspector in charge of the Cannon Row police station area. The result was that Woman Police Constable Eve Sullivan was assigned to protect Ruby Watson.

'That should ruin her love life,' commented Bradley drily.

'Whose? Ruby's or Miss Sullivan's?'

Bradley laughed. 'You've got no soul, guv'nor. Have you lined up someone to accompany Doris Jackson, yet?'

'Yes. I spoke to a mate of mine at West End Central and he's given me a PC by the name of Craig. He said that he's a good bloke who's accustomed to working in plain clothes.'

'I hope he's a trolleybus enthusiast,' said Bradley.

'I don't know about that, but he represents the Metropolitan Police at athletics, so he should be a match for any villain who takes it on his dancers.'

'How very apt,' commented Bradley.

On the day following Mavis Lavender's murder, Jack Bradley spent an hour studying the brass object that he had found beneath the dead woman's body. But being no nearer discovering what it meant, he decided to take his problem to the Imperial War Museum in Lambeth, South London, where he was introduced to the curator that dealt with insignia, a man called John Ward. Ward was an elderly man, studious in appearance, who peered at Bradley through heavy horn-rimmed spectacles.

'I'm surprised to find that you're still open, Mr Ward,' said Bradley, once introductions had been effected.

'We're closing next month for the duration of the war, Sergeant Bradley. We had hoped to remain open, but it's been pointed out to us that our name might lead the Luftwaffe to believe that we're some sort of military installation masquerading as a museum. On top of that, the army has claimed back some of our exhibits.' Ward shook his head. 'We must be in a parlous state if the army is relying on museum pieces to fight the *Wehrmacht*. However, what can I do for you?'

Bradley handed over the brass item that he had found under the body of Mavis Lavender. 'I wondered if you could identify that for me, Mr Ward.'

'Royal Air Force brass air gunner's badge, Sergeant Bradley,' said Ward, returning it after a brief examination. 'Discontinued in 1939 in favour of the "AG" cloth half brevet. The one you found is certainly not worn today. Without encroaching on your expertise, and in view of its virtual redundancy, is it possible that the badge has nothing to do with your body and may have been there longer than the deceased?'

'We think that's doubtful, Mr Ward. Thank you for your assistance.' Bradley decided not to explain to the curator the first steps taken by the police at the scene of a crime.

The next obvious place to go was the Air Ministry in Kingsway. There was an armed soldier at the door to Adastral House who referred Bradley to a flight sergeant manning a desk just inside. He, too, was armed.

'Can I help you, sir?' asked the flight sergeant.

Bradley produced his warrant card and explained that he was investigationg a murder in Kingston upon Thames, and needed the help of the RAF.

'I think your best bet is to have a word with an RAF police officer, Sarge. Just one moment.' Picking up his telephone, the flight sergeant dialled a number and explained about Bradley's enquiry. 'Someone will be down shortly,' he said, as he replaced the receiver.

A young officer descended the stairs and approached Bradley with his hand outstretched. 'Detective Sergeant Bradley? I'm Flight Lieutenant Martin Peters, Special Investigation Branch. Come up to my office.'

Peters invited Bradley to take a seat in the tiny office and sent for coffee.

'Now, Sergeant Bradley, how can we help?'

Bradley produced the brass insignia and placed it on Peters' desk. 'I found this under the body of a young woman on a bomb site in Charing Cross Road. She had been murdered. The Imperial War Museum told me that it's an air gunner's insignia, but its use was discontinued in 1939.'

'Quite right,' said Peters. 'How were you hoping that we might help you?'

'Ideally, we'd like to trace anyone who's lost this, Flight Lieutenant, but I realize it's a tall order.'

'Damn right it is.' For a few moments, Peters swivelled his chair from side to side. 'Sergeant Bradley, there are over a million men and women in the Royal Air Force, a substantial number of them aircrew. And of the aircrew many are air gunners, one of the most vulnerable members of the crew, especially the tail gunner. With the best will in the world, you are asking me to solve a problem that is nigh-on impossible to solve.' Martin Peters paused for a moment. 'Another thing, if the squadron commander caught any of his gunners wearing the old insignia, he'd get a flea in his ear.'

'Oh well,' said Bradley, as he stood up, 'it was worth a try.'

'There is just one thing that might be worth trying, Sergeant Bradley. The Free Polish airmen wear RAF uniform, but could still be using the old insignia.' Peters returned to his desk and scribbled a name and address on a slip of paper. 'This is the Polish military police officer that we liaise with. When were you thinking of going?'

Bradley glanced at his watch. 'I've got time now, if they can see me today.'

'Good. I'll give them a ring and let them know you're coming. RAF Uxbridge is high security, now that it's the HQ of Eleven Group. I'm sure the Polish military police will help, if they can. I've always found the Poles very helpful.' He chuckled. 'In more ways than one.'

Even though Flight Lieutenant Peters had told RAF Uxbridge that Bradley was coming, a telephone call was not enough to meet the stringent security precautions prevailing. He was asked for his warrant card at least three times before he was shown into an office in Hillingdon House.

'I'm Detective Sergeant Jack Bradley, Murder Squad, and I'm looking for . . .' He pulled out the piece of paper given to him by the RAF officer at Adastral House. 'Yes, a Captain Kasia Sikora.'

The shapely woman who stood up from behind her desk was not in uniform. She was probably in her mid-thirties with shoulder-length black hair. She laughed.

'You've found her.'

'But you're a woman.'

The woman laughed again. 'I can tell you're a detective, Sergeant Bradley.'

'I'm terribly sorry, ma'am.' Being unfamiliar with Polish names, Bradley had expected to find that Captain Kasia Sikora was a man, but that the Polish military police captain was an attractive woman who laughed at him had momentarily flustered him.

'Martin Peters telephoned to say you were coming to see me, Sergeant Bradley,' said Sikora in flawless English. She shook hands with a firm grip. 'Please sit down. Can I persuade you to a glass of vodka? I won't tell anyone you're drinking on duty if you don't tell anyone I'm drinking on duty.' She laughed infectiously.

'You've persuaded me,' said Bradley.

Opening a small cupboard next to her desk, Captain Sikora produced a bottle of vodka and two shot glasses into each of which she poured a measure almost to the top. She pushed one glass across her desk towards Bradley. '*Okrzyki,*' she said, downing the contents of her glass in one swallow.

'Toast!' said Bradley, assuming that is what she had said, and he too emptied his glass. 'Ye gods!' he exclaimed, grasping his throat as he went red in the face.

'You like?' asked Sikora, laughing.

'It should come with a fire extinguisher,' Bradley was able to say, once he finished choking.

'That's proper vodka. I make it myself, not like the stuff you buy here in the shops.'

'You can't buy it in the shops any more.'

'Well, down to business, eh?' said Sikora, becoming suddenly professional.

'I don't know whether you can help me or not, Captain Sikora,' he began.

'Please call me Kasia,' suggested Sikora.

'I'm Jack,' said Bradley, and went on to explain about the murder of Mavis Lavender. Finally, he placed the air gunner insignia on the captain's desk.

Sikora picked it up, examining it closely. 'To my knowledge, Jack, there are two squadrons that still use this insignia. At least, they did. Leave it with me and I'll make some enquiries. If it happens to be one of our people, you realize that we have the right to try him or her by court martial.'

'Are you sure about that, Kasia?'

'Oh yes. It is your Allied Forces Act that says so. However, we are getting ahead of ourselves. It might have nothing to do with any of our personnel.'

'I'll leave it in your capable hands, then, Kasia.' And with that, Bradley had to be content.

'We should have lunch sometime, Jack.' Sikora shook hands, this time holding on to Bradley's hand a little longer than when they had met.

'Good idea,' said Bradley, wondering how he could get out of it without offending this charming Polish lady.

The first twelve days of the police watch on Ruby Watson and Doris Jackson were uneventful. WPC Eve Sullivan had read every one of the out-of-date magazines in the hairdressing salon while keeping a watchful eye on Ruby Watson and every customer who had entered the salon, aware that an attacker could as easily be a woman as a man. She had drunk countless cups of tea and refused the offer of a free hair styling from 'Jules'.

By the end of the thirteenth day, Hardcastle began to believe that he had made a mistake in thinking that either woman was in danger or, worse still, that the murders of Mavis Lavender and Joyce Butler were unconnected. There was also the possibility that the officers on the protection duty were becoming so accustomed to their task that they would be less vigilant. It was a recognized failing for which the officers could not be blamed. However, Hardcastle decided to keep them on the detail rather than introducing reliefs as being the lesser of two risks.

But on the fifteenth day there came a breakthrough.

Doris Jackson was on the early shift on bus route number 46 from Victoria to Alperton. She had told her driver, Douglas Grant, known as Dougie, why she had a police escort. Grant was a thirty-year-old who laboured under the misapprehension that driving a bus was a reserved occupation, an illusion of which he was to be disabused very soon, despite his splay-footed gait that he believed would afford him an exemption from service.

Doris was standing on the platform and had just rung the bell to indicate to the driver that it was safe to pull away from the bus stop when she saw a familiar face.

'Don,' said Doris excitedly to her escorting policeman, PC Don Craig, 'that's him, just crossing the road.' She pointed at a man hurrying from behind the bus to the opposite side of the road.

Craig was seated on the bench seat just inside the bus and immediately leaped to his feet.

'Stop the bus, Doris.'

Doris Jackson rang the bell three times, the recognized signal for an emergency stop. Craig jumped from the bus and began to follow the suspect.

Dougie Grant dismounted from his cab and walked round to the platform. 'What's up, girl?' he asked, expecting to have a troublesome passenger pointed out to him.

Doris Jackson quickly explained, in almost a whisper, what PC Craig was doing.

'I can't keep the bus hanging about while he makes up his mind whether he's going to come back or not,' complained Grant. 'I've got a schedule to keep to.'

'You'll do as I tell you, Dougie Grant. I'm the conductor and, as such, I'm legally in charge of the bus, so go back to your cab and have a sandwich or something until I tell you to go.'

'I hope you know what you're doing,' muttered Grant bad-temperedly, and strolled back to his cab. He did not like being put in his place, especially by a woman.

Don Craig was back minutes later. 'We can carry on now, Doris.' There was an element of bitterness in his voice.

'What happened, Don?'

'I lost the bugger. It was almost as if he sensed I was following him and suddenly disappeared. He must've gone into one of the houses because I can't see where else he could've gone. You're certain it was him, Doris?'

'I'm absolutely positive, Don.' Doris rang the bell and the bus finally moved off.

DCI Hardcastle was not pleased that Craig had lost the suspect, but had to admit that it did sometimes happen, even to the most experienced surveillance officer. Nevertheless, on the plus side, Doris Jackson was adamant that she had recognized the man who she had seen dancing with Joyce Butler the evening before the woman's murder.

'Working on the basis that villains are creatures of habit, Jack, we'll mount an operation at the Surbiton Assembly Rooms. We'll take Doris Jackson there and hope that she spots this man. If she doesn't, we'll just keep on until he shows up.'

'Just the two of us, guv'nor?' asked Bradley.

'Not bloody likely, Jack. He might've given Craig the slip, but he's not going to get away from us. We'll draft in half a dozen men just to make sure that we get him in the net. And I think we'll take Ruby Watson, too.'

The following Friday evening seemed to be the obvious time to mount an observation at the Surbiton Assembly Rooms. Hardcastle held a briefing at the Yard before the selected officers set off.

'Having considered the matter, rather than six men, I have selected three male officers and three female ones. This will enable you to pair up on the dance floor and give the impression of being in a relationship.' There was an outburst of laughter as the officers deliberately misconstrued what Hardcastle had said. 'All right, all right. The reason, if you haven't worked it out already, is that I don't want any of you dancing with someone else at a time when you're most needed. To that end, you will keep an eye on either me or DS Bradley and work on our signal if you are needed. Have each of you got your flute?'

There were a few mumbles of agreement and one or two displayed a police whistle.

'If there is what used to be called a hue and cry, blow your whistle; it will disconcert anyone trying to escape and alert everyone else that there is a fleeing felon.' Hardcastle paused. 'I hope.'

Doris Jackson and Ruby Watson had put on their finery. Ruby had obviously had her hair dyed again that very day – no doubt free of charge if she was paying her rent to 'Jules' in kind – and was wearing even more make-up than when they had first seen her. In both cases the girls were attired in what could only be described as posh frocks, designed to show off their figures to advantage.

PC Don Craig and WPC Eve Sullivan were also among the team of watchers, mainly because Doris and Ruby respectively knew and trusted them, and because Craig had also seen the suspect.

However, plans rarely worked as anticipated when it came to making an arrest. The suspect inadvertently gave himself up. With all the bravado of a self-perceived ladies' man, he walked straight up to Ruby Watson and asked her for a dance. But that was as far as he got.

'It's him!' shrieked Doris Jackson, who was standing beside Hardcastle, and pointed an accusing finger.

Unsurprisingly, the man had heard her above the noise of the twenty-two-piece dance band, and the accompanying vocalist who was competing with the tenor saxophonist as she tried to make heard the words of 'We'll Meet Again'. Spinning on his heel, the man ran into the centre of the whirlpool of dancers, and made for an emergency exit on the far side of the hall. Furious men and their womenfolk were pushed out of the way. Several lost their balance and hit the floor, and one slipped on a hitherto undisturbed patch of French chalk. One woman tripped and fell headlong, tearing her precious stockings as she did so and uttering a very unladylike oath. Her irate partner gave chase after the fleeing suspect, but Jack Bradley, who had placed himself near the exit some time previously, intercepted the wanted man, neatly tripping him.

As he fell to the ground, several of Hardcastle's team descended on him and yanked him to his feet. By this time, Hardcastle had reached them.

'Sergeant Michael Cassidy, I am arresting you on suspicion of murdering Joyce Butler on or about Wednesday the thirty-first of July 1940.'

'Is this some sort of joke?' demanded Cassidy, but the police put his rhetorical question down to his overweening personality.

Cassidy was escorted to Cannon Row police station where his fingerprints were taken. On the express orders of Detective Superintendent Fred Cherrill, priority was given to comparing Cassidy's fingerprints with those found on the broken wine bottle and the wine glass found in Joyce Butler's flat.

In the meantime, even though he would rather have awaited the result of the fingerprint examination, Hardcastle decided to question the suspect.

'You were seen dancing with Joyce Butler in the Surbiton Assembly Rooms the night before her murder. When did you first meet her, Cassidy?'

'It wasn't a meeting, like it was a date. It was when I decided to do a snap inspection of the billets and found her playing strip poker with the gun crew. But I told you that already.'

'What would you say if I told you that several members of the gun crew are prepared to testify that it was you who brought Joyce Butler into the billet and that you were taking an active part in the fun and games?'

'They're a load of lying bloody toads, that lot. Look, I'm a disciplinarian and if they can say anything to screw me, they'll bloody well do it. It happens all the time in this man's army. But that's all lies.'

'Seven years is the going rate for perjury, Cassidy. D'you think those men are likely to risk that to save your neck?' suggested Jack Bradley.

The phrase that Bradley had used reminded Cassidy that if he was convicted of murder, he would face the death penalty. He remained silent, and resolved that he would say as little as possible from then on. He knew about the police and their propensity for 'stitching you up' if they couldn't find anyone else.

'Have you ever been in trouble with the police before, Cassidy?' asked Hardcastle.

'No,' said Cassidy, and smirked. 'But then, you'd know that, wouldn't you?'

'And you were in the last lot,' said Bradley, nodding towards the three Great War medal ribbons on Cassidy's tunic. Somewhat irreverently, they were referred to as Pip, Squeak and Wilfred after the cartoon characters appearing in the *Daily Mirror.*

'So?'

'Where did you serve?'

'Wipers.'

If Cassidy thought Bradley wouldn't know where that was, he was wrong. Geoffrey Bradley, Jack's father, had served in the Salient for part of the war and Jack knew that the small city of Ypres was known throughout the army as Wipers.

'What did you do between the wars?' asked Hardcastle.

'What did I do? I was in the army.'

'So, you've been a soldier since 1914.'

'Yes.'

'Are you married?'

'No.'

Hardcastle decided to leave it there. There would have to be further enquiries made of the army because he had come to the conclusion that Cassidy was an inveterate liar coupled with the leery attitude of the old soldier. All of which added up to the fact that he was not too intelligent.

Cassidy was kept in custody at the police station overnight pending further enquiries.

Detective Sergeant Bradley began making his enquiries the next morning. He walked down Whitehall to the military police office at Great Scotland Yard and sought out Regimental Sergeant Major Richard Purdy.

'Dick, I'm in need of some help.' Bradley explained about the arrest of Cassidy on suspicion of murdering Joyce Butler. 'He told us that he had been in the army continuously from 1914. Is there any way of checking that quickly?'

'I should be able to get the answer right now.' Purdy reached for the telephone and gave the operator an extension number. 'War Office,' he mouthed to Bradley, while he was waiting. Once connected, he asked the relevant questions about Sergeant Michael Cassidy of the Royal Artillery. Ten minutes later, Purdy had the answer. 'No, he wasn't, Jack,' he said, and replaced the receiver.

'That doesn't surprise me, Dick.'

'He was stationed in France for the whole of the last war, and took his discharge there in 1919. My mate at the War Box believes he stayed in France until just before the German invasion in the present war. At which point, he came back to Blighty a bit bloody sharply and joined up again.'

'I wonder why he told us he'd been in the army all the time. Perhaps he's got something to hide.'

Bradley, being possessed of what is known as a copper's nose, intended to pursue Cassidy's inexplicable lie, and made his way to the office that dealt with matters that had been circulated by the International Criminal Police Commission in the St Cloud area of Paris before the war started.

The detective sergeant in the ICPC office, who introduced himself as Nick Starkey, sucked through his teeth when Bradley outlined his problem. He started where all policemen start, by asking for Cassidy's date of birth. Moving across to a filing cabinet, he eventually extracted a docket and returned to his desk. He lit a cigarette and spent a few minutes thumbing through the contents of the file.

'In the circumstances, Jack, this amounts to so much waste paper, because this guy Cassidy is wanted by the French police on a charge of murder committed in April 1939. Apparently, he fled to the UK immediately afterwards, but there are now hundreds of jack-booted Huns marching all over France. There's no way the courts are going to consent to extradition just to see him handed over to the Gestapo.'

'We could try him here,' said Bradley. 'A British subject can be tried at the Old Bailey for a crime committed anywhere in the world.'

'Yes, I know. But in this case there's a snag, Jack,' said Starkey wearily. 'Cassidy was born in Dublin in the Republic of Ireland. Consequently, my old mate, no court in the UK has jurisdiction to try a foreign national for a crime committed in France. Anyway, all the evidence will be in France and can't be got at. And I very much doubt that the Irish government would be interested enough to seek his extradition from the UK. So, Cassidy will have to wait until the war's over before we can send him to the guillotine. Assuming we win, that is, which is not looking too hopeful right now.'

'Mind you don't get snapped up by the Ministry of Propaganda, Nick. You'd be an instant success. By the way, does your file tell you who Cassidy murdered?'

'Yes, a French national, Marianne Cassidy, née Lebreton, his wife.'

When Bradley reported back to Hardcastle, he was surprised by his response.

'That's all very interesting, Jack, but it turns out that Cassidy is not our man.'

'*Not our man, guv'nor?*' Bradley could not hide his disbelief. That a man wanted for murder in France had not committed another murder in London was beyond his comprehension.

'Cassidy's fingerprints aren't a match, Jack. I got the report an hour ago. What's more, there is no fingerprint evidence that he was ever in Joyce Butler's flat.'

'So, we start all over again?'

'Unfortunately yes, but it's in the nature of a policeman's lot.'

'So, Cassidy's suspected of murdering his wife and there's not a damned thing we can do about it.' Bradley was appalled; to a policeman it didn't seem right that a murderer was free to walk about the streets of London because the law couldn't touch him.

The science of fingerprints is an involved business. The fingerprints in the national collection, which is held at New Scotland Yard, are classified into the four main categories: arches, loops, whorls and composites.

Once a scene-of-crime fingerprint is classified into one of the groups, an officer begins the torturous task of comparing them with the collection. This physical examination is time-consuming and requires an expertise only achieved after many years. Once an identification is made, the result is taken to a senior officer who examines the prints and, if he is satisfied, confirms that there are sufficient points of similarity to be able to confirm that they are, in fact, identical.

There were many fingerprints lifted from the scene of Joyce Butler's murder and priority was given to those on the wine bottle and the wine glass. However, those prints were not in the national collection.

Furthermore, the International Criminal Police Commission in Paris had been taken over by an odious SS general called Reinhard Heydrich and he had promptly transferred the office to Berlin. Almost overnight, it had become ineffective as one after another of the free nations withdrew its support. Consequently, any hope of identifying a fingerprint taken by a foreign police force was stillborn.

Hardcastle was becoming frustrated at the lack of progress in the murders of Joyce Butler and Mavis Lavender. Every avenue he pursued seemed to come to a dead end.

'We'll begin again, Jack, and interview some of the original witnesses a second time. There's Sir Bernard Spilsbury's colleague, Sister Audrey Kane, and there's the leading fireman. What's his name?'

'Eric Simpson, sir.'

'Of course. While we're at it, we might as well talk to Simpson's wife as well. According to her husband, she had several conversations with Joyce Butler and more or less described her as a tart.'

'When d'you want to start, guv'nor?'

'We'll make Sister Kane this afternoon's job, Jack. I wonder if she's on the phone.'

'Probably,' said Bradley. 'A senior nurse might be called in at any moment, given the pounding that the Luftwaffe is giving London at the moment. I'll find out.' He was back in Hardcastle's office a few minutes later. 'She's at home, guv, and she said she'll put the kettle on.'

TWENTY

It was two o'clock that afternoon when Hardcastle and Bradley arrived at Sister Kane's Coram Street flat. Since their last visit, a bomb had taken out a building opposite, leaving a gap like a missing tooth. The buildings on either side had been shored up with great timber baulks.

'Come in, my dears,' she said warmly. 'I'll just make the tea and I've got some cake, too. Then we can get down to business. Excuse the state of the windows, but last night's bomb took out all the glass. For once, the council came round promptly and boarded them up.'

Audrey Kane disappeared into the kitchen and they could hear her singing one of the popular wartime songs – 'We're Going to Hang Out the Washing on the Siegfried Line' – as she bustled about. Minutes later she was back in the sitting room with a tray of tea.

'Now, my dears, how can I help you?' She poured out the tea and handed it round, followed by a large wedge of home-made jam sponge.

'I wondered if you had thought of anything else that might help us, Mrs Kane,' Hardcastle began. 'To be perfectly honest, we seem to have reached a dead end.'

'I can't really think of anything, my dear. Like I said, I noticed that Mrs Butler's door was slightly ajar, so I went in to see what had happened. And that, as you know, is when I found the poor girl.'

'After we'd talked to you,' said Bradley, 'we spoke to Mr Simpson.'

'Oh, the fireman downstairs.' There was a slight edge of disdain to Audrey Kane's voice.

'I get the impression that you don't like him very much, Mrs Kane,' Bradley continued. 'He told us that his wife had spoken to Joyce Butler and she'd formed the opinion that the woman was a tart.'

'He told you his wife said that?' A look of amazement crossed Audrey Kane's face. 'He hasn't got a wife, my dear, he's a widower. He told me that the only time I spoke to him. Oh! And he kept going on about his time in America and how it was bigger and better than anything in this country.'

'Is there anything else that you can think of, Mrs Kane?' asked Bradley.

'Not at the moment, my dear.' Audrey Kane's face took on a thoughtful expression. 'If anything comes to mind, I'll give you or Mr Hardcastle a ring, Mr Bradley.'

'Thanks for your help, Mrs Kane, and the tea,' said Hardcastle as he and Bradley took their leave. 'The cake was beautiful.'

'Are you going speak to Simpson now, guv'nor?' asked Bradley, as they passed the door to the fireman's flat.

'No, I think we'll make some enquiries of the United States Embassy first. For all we know, Mrs Kane might have misunderstood what Simpson said to her, or he may just have been boasting. Or even making it all up just to shut up someone he saw as a nosey woman.'

The United States Embassy was in Grosvenor Square in London's Mayfair district. America was a neutral country, although they helped the United Kingdom surreptitiously with materiel of various kinds.

Because of this neutrality, and the fact that their diplomatic mission was in the centre of a warring nation, extra precautions had been taken and it was some time before Hardcastle and Bradley were admitted to the office of the legal attaché.

Despite his diplomatic cover title of legal attaché, Willis Lamenski was an FBI agent and had been stationed at the embassy since 1937.

'I suppose you just stopped by because you want something, Walter.' Lamenski grinned as he shook hands with Hardcastle and then Bradley. 'Howdy, Jack.'

Hardcastle outlined what little the police had learned about Leading Fireman Eric Simpson. 'It's a bit of a long shot, Willis, but we're hoping that he's got a record of some sort in the States. Is there any way you can find out?'

Lamenski's secretary appeared silently with a tray of coffee which she placed on a table before leaving just as quietly as she had entered.

'I'll do what I can, Walter,' said Lamenski, a little uncertainly, 'although records Stateside tend to be spread out. But if it was something serious and was investigated by the Bureau, or if we were asked for assistance, it might turn up. Leave it with me.'

'Thanks, Willis.' Hardcastle knew that was the best he could hope for, but he also knew that Lamenski would do his very best to assist his 'limey' friends.

It took twenty-four hours.

'Walter, I have something for you about Simpson,' said Willis Lamenski. 'If you dropped by it would save me from trying to explain over the phone.'

'I don't know how you did it, Willis, but Jack and I will be round to the embassy straight away.'

Half an hour later, having ensured that they were admitted without delay, Lamenski, Hardcastle and Bradley were seated in the FBI agent's office.

'This man is a Brit, Walter, but he was in the New York Fire Department for six years.'

'How did he get into the FDNY, Willis? I thought you had to be a US citizen.'

'Because he had been in the British Army in the last war,' replied Lamenski, 'he was exempted all the usual entry qualifications such as the requirement to be an American citizen. However, in 1926, he was caught taking a sixteen-year-old girl across a state line. The girl openly admitted that she frequently had sexual intercourse with Simpson. That, of course, is a federal offence contrary to the Mann Act. He was lucky to get away with doing just six months in the slammer, something to do with his war record, I guess, but he was deported back to the United Kingdom in 1927.'

'That's terrific, Willis,' said Hardcastle. 'Thanks very much.' He paused. 'I don't suppose you've got a copy of his fingerprints?'

'Now the man wants miracles!' Lamenski spread his hands in a parody of amazement at the request. Then he laughed.

'Right here, Walter.' The agent handed over an envelope. 'D'you reckon he's your guy?'

Hardcastle and Bradley stood up and shook hands with Lamenski. 'I'll tell you in about twenty-four hours, Willis.'

'That long, huh?' Lamenski laughed, and showed them out.

'Got him!' announced Hardcastle triumphantly, and handed Detective Superintendent Cherrill's report to Bradley. 'Simpson's fingerprints are a positive match for those on the wine bottle and the wine glass.'

'How are we going to handle this, guv'nor?' asked Bradley.

'We're going to nick him, of course, Jack, but I don't want to forewarn him. First of all, we'll find out whether he's at work or at home. What was the name of that smart young DC who was with us when we searched Joyce Butler's place?'

'Barber, John Barber.'

'Get hold of him and tell him to find out when Simpson will be at home. Without making himself obvious.'

As it happened, Barber was even more resourceful than Hardcastle had believed. He called on Mrs Audrey Kane who, he discovered, was one of those people policemen love. She habitually monitored the comings and goings of the residents and was able to tell Barber that Simpson was at home. Barber asked if he might use her telephone and promptly informed Hardcastle of Simpson's current whereabouts. It was five o'clock that same evening.

'Well done, Barber. Did you happen to ask Mrs Kane if there was any way out of his flat other than through the front door?'

'I did, sir. All the flats are the same, and the front door's the only way in and out.'

'Thank you, Barber. Stay there until Sergeant Bradley and I arrive to make the arrest.'

'I've been expecting you, Mr Hardcastle.' Eric Simpson had a resigned expression on his face. 'As a matter of fact, I've been wanting to get it off my chest.'

'Get what off your chest?' asked Hardcastle.

'I did it. I killed Joyce.'

'Eric Simpson, I'm arresting you on suspicion of murdering Joyce Butler on or about Wednesday the thirty-first of July 1940. You're not obliged to say anything, but anything you do say will be taken down in writing and may be given in evidence.'

Simpson was placed in the back seat of the police car between Hardcastle and Bradley, and Barber drove them the short distance to Gray's Inn Road police station.

Having negotiated the sandbagged entrance, Hardcastle explained to the station officer the circumstances of Simpson being brought to the station. The fireman was then taken to an interview room.

'I would remind you that you are still under caution, Mr Simpson,' said Hardcastle.

'I don't care about that. I just want to tell you what happened.'

'Go ahead, then.'

'I met Joyce at the Surbiton Assembly Rooms on the Tuesday. I'd seen her before, of course, because she lives in the same block of flats on the floor above mine in Coram Street, but then you know that, don't you?'

'This was the thirtieth of July, when you met, was it?'

'Probably. I'm not very good at dates. Anyway, I saw Joyce standing at the bar with her mates and I asked her for a dance. She agreed straight away. We had a couple of dances and I escorted her back to the bar and bought her a drink. She talked a lot about it being a dangerous job in the fire brigade with all these bombs dropping.'

'Take it a bit slower, if you can, Mr Simpson,' said Bradley. 'I'm writing all this down.'

'Sorry. We had another couple of dances and a few more drinks and then she said she ought to be going. I offered to walk her home, what with the blitz and everything. I don't like the idea of a girl going home alone. Anyway, we lived in the same block as each other.'

'Yes, go on.' Bradley looked up from his note-taking and stared briefly at Simpson. He found it difficult to reconcile Simpson's apparent earlier concern for the safety of a woman whom he later murdered. But then the minds of murderers have remained a mystery even to some psychiatrists.

'When we got back to her place, we shared a bottle of wine and I thought I was on a promise. I got a bottle of Scotch from my place and she downed two or three of those. We laughed and joked for a while, but then, quite suddenly, she turned nasty on me. I don't know what caused her sudden change of mood. Perhaps it was the whisky. Come to think of it, she did say that she wasn't used to it.'

'What happened next?'

'She said I was too old and that she didn't sleep with old men. She started shouting at me to "get the hell out of my flat". Then, she began punching me and calling me names and threatening to tell her husband and the police that I'd tried to rape her. As I said just now, I think it was the whisky talking. She went really wild, and at one stage, she picked up a carving knife and came towards me. I grabbed the wine bottle and hit her over the head with it. It was self-defence.'

Hardcastle glanced at Bradley, who nodded. Hardcastle wanted to make certain that his sergeant had recorded that last telling statement.

'We know it was your fingerprints on the bottle and the wine glass, that's why we arrested you.'

'How did you know that?' Simpson looked genuinely surprised, an expression that immediately changed to one of annoyance.

'The Americans told us that you'd been convicted of taking a sixteen-year-old girl across a state line for purposes of prostitution. That, as you know, is a federal offence. You were imprisoned for six months and then deported. The FBI sent us a copy of your fingerprints.'

'They'd no right to tell you that,' protested Simpson.

Hardcastle smiled. 'I can see you don't know much about co-operation between the law enforcement agencies of the free world, Simpson. Of course, if you'd been convicted of an offence in any of the countries now overrun by the Germans, you might have got away with it.'

'When we saw you the night after the murder,' said Bradley, 'you were just opening the door to your flat and you said you'd just come off duty. That's not true, is it?'

'No. I was going to run. To get as far away as I could. But when I got out in the street, there were police everywhere, so I went back and that's when I met you.'

Hardcastle crossed the room and opened the door. 'Take this prisoner back to his cell, please, Constable,' he said to the waiting policeman.

'What d'you think, Jack?' asked Hardcastle, once they were alone.

'According to Sir Bernard Spilsbury, guv'nor, Joyce Butler was struck from behind with the bottle, so that rules out self-defence, as does the later strangulation. He's just trying to avoid the rope in the hope that the jury would accept a plea of manslaughter.'

'Not a chance,' said Hardcastle. 'Now comes the hard part: the report for the Director of Public Prosecutions.'

'Oyez! Oyez! Oyez! All those having business with this court of oyer and terminer and general gaol delivery, pray draw near. God Save the King.' Having delivered the time-honoured opening of an assize court, the Old Bailey usher resumed his seat, his moment of glory over.

Eric Simpson appeared in the dock, flanked by two prison officers. He now appeared older and less confident of himself than when Hardcastle and Bradley had first seen him on the night of the murder.

The clerk of the court, a silver-haired man, emaciated to a greater extent than food rationing would seem to be responsible for, coughed and picked up a sheet of paper. 'Eric Simpson,' he began in a strained voice, 'you are charged in that on or about Tuesday, the thirtieth of July in the year of Our Lord one thousand, nine hundred and forty, you did murder Joyce Butler. Against the Peace. How say you upon this indictment: guilty or not guilty?'

'Not guilty, My Lord.' Simpson had wanted to plead guilty, but his counsel advised him that this particular judge would not accept such a plea, believing the prosecution should prove their case beyond all reasonable doubt in cases of murder.

'Bring in the jury,' said the judge, but before proceedings began, he addressed the court with a cautionary instruction that had become customary since the outbreak of war. 'Ladies and gentleman, in the event of the air-raid warning being sounded during these proceedings, I shall immediately suspend them and you will be escorted to the comparative safety of the cells beneath the court. The ladies and gentlemen of the jury will be kept in separate accommodation by the jury bailiff. I would further caution persons involved as witnesses in these proceedings not to discuss the case as this may well be perceived as a contempt of court.'

Once the jury had been sworn in, in this case five elderly men and seven women, the proceedings, at last, began.

'Very well, Mr Attorney.'

'May it please, My Lord.' Sir Donald Somervell rose to his feet and introduced his junior and the counsel comprising the defence team. 'This a fairly straightforward case, My Lord.' He began his opening speech for the prosecution by outlining the circumstances surrounding the murder of Joyce Butler. 'Mrs Butler's husband is serving in the army somewhere in southern England.' It had become the custom not to reveal the exact location of armed forces units, even in proceedings before the court, unless it was absolutely necessary. 'It is alleged that she and the accused met at the Surbiton Assembly Rooms on the evening of Tuesday, the thirtieth of July this year. She invited him to her home at Ravenscroft flats, Kingston Hill, where they indulged in a large number of alcoholic drinks consisting of wine and of whisky. Separately, of course, My Lord.' The attorney smiled at his little joke. 'It is further alleged that the moment the accused suggested sexual intercourse, Mrs Butler flew into a rage, the outcome of which was an argument that culminated in the accused murdering her. I call my first witness: Divisional Detective Inspector Walter Hardcastle of V Division, New Scotland Yard.'

There was never much of a problem when police were examined by prosecuting counsel and Hardcastle was merely required to confirm what the attorney had outlined in his opening address. The real test came when the leading defence barrister, an eminent King's Counsel, Andrew Sangster, stood up to cross-examine.

His first action was to hitch his gown back on to his shoulder, although there was no need for theatrics with his reputation at the bar.

'When did you first meet the accused, Eric Simpson, Divisional Detective Inspector?'

'At about eight thirty in the evening of Wednesday the thirty-first of July this year, sir.'

'What were the circumstances, Divisional Detective Inspector?' Sangster asked, turning back to Hardcastle.

Hardcastle explained his meeting with Simpson and how he had claimed to have just come off duty.

'But he hadn't, had he?' Sangster was doing his best to prove that Hardcastle was not a very good investigator.

Overall, the trial went much as the Attorney General had predicted. Evidence was given over a period of three days. But Andrew Sangster was unable to find any cracks in the strong evidence that pointed indisputably to Simpson's guilt.

Finally, the jury took a period of three hours to bring in a verdict of guilty.

'Eric Simpson, have you anything to say before sentence of death is passed upon you?' asked the clerk of the court.

'No, sir,' replied an impassive Simpson.

The judge donned the black cap. 'Eric Simpson, you stand convicted of murder. The sentence of the law upon you is that you be taken to a lawful prison and thence to a place of execution. That you be there hanged by the neck until you are dead and that your body be buried within the precincts of the prison in which you shall have last been confined before your execution, and may the Lord have mercy on your soul.'

The judge's chaplain, a thin man of suitably melancholy appearance, added the single word 'Amen'.

Simpson did not react in any way, but when the judge ordered him to be taken down, he merely turned on his heel and descended the steps to the cells.

The customary three Sundays had not passed before the air raid occurred. One of the two escorting prison officers on death watch in the condemned cell holding Eric Simpson was playing chess with him.

At thirteen minutes to four, when the occupants of the cell were awaiting afternoon tea, all three were killed instantly when a bomb fell, destroying that corner of the prison.

'He who lives by the sword shall die by the sword,' said Bradley laconically when he heard the news.

Ironically, it was on the same day that Bradley received a telephone call from Captain Kasia Sikora of the Free Polish Army's military police.

'Jack, we found that Corporal Wojtek Baros was the airman who lost his air gunner insignia. When he was interviewed, he stated that he had met Mavis Lavender at the Astoria dance hall in Charing Cross Road and was escorting her to her home when she suddenly started screaming abuse at him, saying that she did not intend to sleep with "a damned foreigner". She began to fight with him, and at some point, he lost his insignia. He admitted losing his temper and strangling her on a bomb site in Charing Cross Road and leaving her body there. The court martial is here at Uxbridge at ten o'clock tomorrow morning.'

'Will the proceedings be in Polish, Kasia?'

There was a throaty laugh from Captain Sikora. 'No, in Chinese.'

'Sorry,' said Bradley. 'Silly question. Is there a need for me to be there, officially, I mean?'

'Yes, please. The court may wish to question you. There will be an interpreter, of course.'

At nine o'clock the following morning Bradley made his way to RAF Uxbridge. A Royal Air Force police corporal met him at the entrance and examined his warrant card carefully.

'You're here for the Polish court martial, Sergeant Bradley.' It was not so much a question as a statement of fact.

'That's correct.'

'Righto, Sarge, I'll show you the way, otherwise you'll get lost.'

Captain Kasia Sikora was waiting for Bradley when eventually he was delivered to the door to the courtroom. But he did not immediately recognize her. Her long black hair was in a French roll and she was wearing uniform, including the square cap peculiar to the Polish Army, with a belted tunic fastened to the neck. Her skirt overlapped the top of her knee-length black boots.

'Hello, Jack.'

'Good heavens, Kasia, that's a very attractive outfit,' said Bradley, and immediately regretted it.

But Kasia Sikora just smiled. 'The trial is inquisitorial, Jack.' Although she spoke perfect English, she had a bit of trouble with that word, but so, thought Jack, do a lot of people for whom English is their first language. 'Unlike your court-martials or your courts system in general.'

'Are you a lawyer, as well as being a military policeman, Kasia?'

'Yes, I am, but in case you haven't noticed, I am a police-woman not a policeman.' Sikora smiled mockingly at him. 'I would have thought you'd have worked that out by now. Shall we go in? The court is about to convene.'

Bradley wondered why it was that every time he made a comment, Sikora responded in such a way as to make him look foolish. And that provoked a question.

'If you don't mind me asking, Kasia, are you married?'

'Not any more, Jack. My husband was killed when the Germans bombed Warsaw on the first of September last year. Fortunately, there were no children.' She turned abruptly on her heel and pulled open the door to the courtroom.

Despite Sikora having told Bradley that the trial would be inquisitorial, he was surprised at how few people there were in the spartan courtroom.

'That's the accused.' Sikora nodded in the direction of a man of about thirty seated at a table with a military policeman on either side of him. 'That's Wojtek Baros, and he's a corporal in our air force. He lost the air gunner's badge that you found under the body of Mavis Lavender. And this is Lieutenant Tomek Golubski, your interpreter,' she added, as a young man in uniform walked towards them.

'I'm pleased to meet you, Sergeant Bradley,' said Golubski, and shook hands.

'Ah, here we go,' said Sikora, as a thin, stooped figure entered the courtroom from a door at the rear. 'Colonel

Aleksander Filipek, president of the court.' Bradley reckoned
he must be at least seventy.

A table had been set aside for Bradley, Sikora and Lieutenant
Golubski. There was a smartly attired young officer on one
side of the court. 'He presents the prosecution case against the
accused,' whispered Sikora.

The proceedings were very short. Colonel Filipek
signalled to the prosecutor to begin.

'The prosecuting officer has just said that Corporal Wojtek
Baros admits having lost his air gunner's badge at a bomb site
in Charing Cross Road on Tuesday the sixth of August this
year and that he further admits having murdered Miss Mavis
Lavender on the same date.'

'So, what happens now?' asked Bradley.

Golubski held up a finger of silence as the president stood
up, to be followed by everyone in the courtroom. Colonel
Filipek's announcement was short and appeared to come as
no surprise to the assembled military.

Lieutenant Golubski leaned towards Bradley. 'That was the
sentence, Sergeant Bradley. Corporal Baros will be executed
by firing squad tomorrow morning. And that is the end of the
proceedings.'

Colonel Filipek nodded to the court and went out through
the door from which he had entered less than thirty minutes
previously.

'Come up to my office, Jack,' said Sikora. 'I think we
deserve a vodka after that, don't you?' And without awaiting
a reply, she set off, leaving Bradley no alternative but to follow.

'You didn't really need me at this court martial, did you,
Kasia?' Bradley waited until they were seated in the military
policewoman's office before making the accusation.

'No. Baros had confessed to the murder and there was
nothing else to be done, but to pass sentence.'

'In that case, why did you want me here?'

Sikora smiled. 'One way or another, I was determined to
take you out to lunch, Jack.' She was quite brazen about her
deception. 'I've booked a table at the Polish Hearth Club,
which is a favourite of mine. Now, if you wait a moment, I'll
change out of uniform.' She downed her vodka at a gulp and

disappeared through a door leading to a private room.

Ten minutes later, she was back, now attired in a grey two-piece suit with her black hair once again worn loose and her make-up discreetly applied.

'Are you ready, or do you want another vodka?'

'No thanks, Kasia. One is quite enough.'

'Good. In that case, we'll go.' Sikora picked up her handbag and led the way down to the guardroom where a British military police car was waiting. 'The usual place, please, Charlie.'

'Yes, ma'am.' The British military police corporal saluted, laughed and opened the rear door of the car. These two obviously knew each other well, and Bradley wondered just how well. On the other hand, she may have taken so many men to her favourite restaurant that her driver knew instinctively where she intended to go.

Sikora led the way into the bar at the elegant premises of the club in Princes Gate. 'Vodka, Jack?'

'I'll have a Scotch and water if I may. If they have any.' Whisky was becoming increasingly difficult to obtain since war broke out, but the Polish Hearth Club did not seem to be suffering a shortage. 'Here, let me pay, Kasia.' Bradley began to take out his wallet, but Sikora put her hand over his.

'You're not a member, and only members are allowed to buy drinks or pay for meals.'

And that meant that Kasia Sikora had manoeuvred Bradley into a position where courtesy demanded that he would have to return the woman's hospitality at some future date. And that, he decided, was exactly what she had intended all along, but he surprised himself by realizing that he did not really mind.

Nevertheless, the Polish military police captain was proving to be a complex personality, maintaining a light-hearted conversation over lunch even though she had witnessed a man being sentenced to death only an hour or so previously.

TWENTY-ONE

'**E**xcuse me, sir.' Winters, the DDI's clerk, hovered in the doorway, clutching a sheaf of papers, a week later. 'Well, come in, man. What is it?'

'I've been looking at the crime book regarding these break-ins, sir,' Winters began nervously.

'And . . .?' Hardcastle needed no reminding of his failure to apprehend the man he suspected of being Helen and Frank Roper's killer.

'They all took place on a Friday between the hours of eight and ten thirty in the evening, and were mainly in the Kingston Hill area, but one or two isolated incidents were in Surbiton and the centre of Kingston.'

'I'm aware, Winters. What are you suggesting?' Hardcastle suddenly took an interest and thought of DAC Marriott's advice to listen to one's subordinates. They may have thought of something that hadn't crossed your mind, he'd said, although he already had an inkling where this was going.

'Well, sir, I've made a chart of sorts showing details of each of the burglaries.' Winters handed over his sheaf of papers. 'If we were to put as many police officers as possible into those areas, or perhaps just the Kingston Hill area, on Fridays between those hours, we might just catch the Ropers' killer.'

'Good work, Winters, but we considered that some time ago. However . . .' It occured to Hardcastle that things were different now. Back then, the backlog of cases was almost overwhelming. Things had certainly improved in the last few weeks. Hardcastle stood up. 'I'll see what can be done. In the meantime, don't mention this to anyone else.'

'No, sir.' Winters was delighted that the DDI had complimented him on his suggestion, even if it had already been thought of by someone else. It was the first time he had been commended for anything.

From his own office, Hardcastle went straight to Superintendent Swain's office.

'Spare a moment, sir?'

'Yes, Mr Hardcastle, come in.'

Hardcastle spent the next few minutes explaining the plan and the background to it.

Swain spent some time studying Winters' chart. 'This will almost cover the entire sub-division,' he mused, and looked up. 'I'll speak to the sub-divisional inspector at Kingston, Mr Hardcastle, and tell him to rearrange his late turn relief from two to ten to, say, five p.m. to one a.m., and the early turn can stay on for the extra three hours. The night duty will overlap so we can use them as well. I'll also arrange for other sub-divisions to provide as many men as they can. Presumably, Mr Hardcastle, you'll be putting out some CID officers.'

'Every man I've got, sir.'

At four p.m. on the evening of Friday the thirteenth of September, all the officers who had been assigned to the operation to catch the burglar, and suspected murderer, the previous two Fridays with no success were gathered again in the yard at the rear of Kingston police station. DDI Hardcastle explained once more exactly what he hoped they would achieve and reminded them not to take any chances as their quarry was very likely to be armed. He had obtained authority for several officers to carry firearms, but emphasized they were only to be used if they or a colleague was in mortal danger.

Hardcastle decided, however, that he would not accompany the officers. It was, in his view, a job for the uniformed inspectors who were far more accustomed to this type of operation than he was. Instead, he would remain at Kingston police station.

He wasn't too optimistic about their chances of success. There had been no noticeable activity or break-ins from their mark since he'd targeted the Austins, and they'd had no luck the previous two Fridays. But if Hardcastle had learnt anything about this man, it was that he was knew how to bide his time, even give the impression that he'd left the country, before striking.

By half past eleven, Kingston was once again swathed in the pitch-black darkness of the rigorously enforced blackout. The air-raid siren had sounded thirty minutes previously. The sound of heavy bombers seeking out, but more often missing, strategic targets was constant. Searchlight beams criss-crossed the night sky, occasionally illuminating the barrage balloons that hovered like ghostly giant whales.

Because of the encompassing obscurity at ground level, the man in black, alert though he may have been, did not see any of the policemen who had been drafted into the area. But they were there, almost invisible in their dark-blue uniforms and their blue steel helmets.

The man made his way slowly along the street, unable to see such objects as lamp posts or postboxes, despite the white bands painted around them, until he was almost on top of them. As usual, he was attired in a dinner jacket, a homburg hat and a pair of unlined leather gloves. His customary white silk scarf was slung carelessly around his neck, but as the weather was still quite warm, there was no need for the overcoat he had worn during the winter months.

Although the air raid had been going on for some time and the night was punctuated by the occasional explosion, the man in black was unperturbed; he took the view that he could as easily be killed in his own home as out here on the street.

One minute later, he was almost proved right, and he became aware of the unique whistling of a falling bomb as the Doppler effect was created by its rapid velocity. Seconds later, there was an explosion in the next street that momentarily illuminated the sky, followed by the crash of falling masonry. But in that brief flash, Police Constable Max Dodge, standing beneath a tree, was sharp enough to see the man in black on the opposite pavement. And observant enough to notice that he was wearing a glove on his left hand even though it was a very warm night.

'Excuse me, sir,' said Dodge, walking towards the man, at the same time shining his lantern on him.

The man in black did not hesitate. In readiness, he had already removed the glove from his right hand and was holding his pistol low on the right side of his body. As the policeman came closer, the man in black fired. At the last minute, Dodge threw himself sideways and, thanks to the impenetrable darkness, the bullet went wide. Dodge pulled out his whistle and blew three short blasts. Moments later, police officers appeared from everywhere, their lanterns criss-crossing each other, and deliberately shouting to disorientate the suspect as they descended upon him. Curtains were pulled aside in nearby houses and some lights came on, causing one police officer to shout, 'Put that bloody light out.' It was a pointless request in view of the light created by the policemen themselves.

All this sudden activity, and the sight of blue uniforms in the torchlight, disconcerted the man in black sufficiently to enable Dodge to dive at the man's legs in a classic rugby tackle and bring him to the ground. Grasping the wrist that held the pistol, the officer repeatedly smashed it on the ground until the man in black relinquished his hold.

Kneeling on the man's chest, Dodge said, 'You're nicked, chummy.'

It was just after midnight when the duty inspector entered the DDI's office.

'I'm Inspector Carson, sir, night-duty patrolling officer here. I thought you'd wish to know that a beat-duty PC was shot at earlier this evening during the operation to apprehend our burglar.'

'Was the officer injured?'

'No, sir. The gunman missed, thank God. It was PC 481V Dodge, sir, and he arrested his attacker with the assistance of other officers.'

'Has the prisoner been identified?'

By way of an answer, Carson handed Hardcastle the arrested man's national identity card. 'He's being held in the cells here, sir.'

'Has DS Bradley come back into the station, Mr Carson?' asked Hardcastle, as he returned the identity card to the inspector. 'I know he was out on the ground, earlier on.'

'Yes, sir. He's having a cup of tea in the canteen.'

'Ask him to see me as soon as he can, please.'

A few minutes later, Bradley appeared in Hardcastle's office.

'Did Mr Carson fill you in, Jack?'

'Yes, sir, he did. Bit of a surprise.'

'Is Superintendent Swain at the station?'

'I'm told he came in about an hour ago, once the bombing started to get a bit heavy. There have been several incidents on the division and a close call at Hawkers. But they only managed to knock down the gates.'

'Mr Carson told me about that, but no injuries there, I understand.'

'No, sir.'

'Jack, would you ask Mr Swain if he'd be willing to sign a written order to search under the Official Secrets Act? You know the circumstances if he needs further explanation. Once you've done that, meet me at the premises and bring a couple of constables and a woman officer with you.'

By the time Detective Sergeant Bradley and the accompanying officers arrived at the arrested man's house with Superintendent Swain's written order to search, it was two o'clock in the morning. The siren indicating the 'All Clear' had been sounded from Kingston police station an hour earlier and it was hoped that the rest of the night would be quiet. The London docks were getting another pasting and a dull red glow in the eastern sky made a mockery of the blackout.

Hardcastle rapped continuously on the lion's-head knocker for a good three or four minutes before the curtain was pulled back. A woman peered around the edge of the half-open door.

'What on earth is it?' she demanded.

'Police.' Hardcastle held his warrant card open and shone his torch on it.

The woman retreated into the hall and did not seem at all surprised when the DDI was followed by Detective Sergeant Bradley, two uniformed constables and a woman police sergeant.

'It's about your husband, Charles, Mrs Cavanaugh,' said Hardcastle.

'I'm not Mrs Cavanaugh,' said the woman.

'When I came here last autumn, Mr Cavanaugh introduced you as his wife. You were playing the piano.' Now that the door was closed, the curtain back in place and the hall light switched on, Hardcastle recognized the woman, but now she was wearing black silk pyjamas and had taken time to apply make-up and brush her long blonde hair. 'Why didn't you contradict him when that's what he said at the time?'

'Mrs Cavanaugh can't play the piano,' replied the woman unconvincingly.

'Who are you, then?'

'I'm Mrs Cavanaugh's companion, Anna Tobin.' She used both hands to sweep her blonde hair back over her ears.

'I think you'd better fetch Mrs Cavanaugh down here, Mrs Tobin. It is *Mrs* Tobin, is it?'

'No.' Anna Tobin raised her head slightly. 'It's *Miss* Tobin.'

'We'll be in the sitting room, Miss Tobin.'

Without questioning this instruction, Anna Tobin turned and mounted the staircase.

Hardcastle nodded to the woman police sergeant who followed Tobin upstairs in case she attempted to destroy some important evidence.

About five minutes later, a woman entered the room where Hardcastle had previously interrupted a musical soiree. She was tall – perhaps a couple of inches under six foot – and painfully thin. She clutched a cotton dressing gown around herself as if to disguise her slender frame, but succeeded only in emphasizing it. Her flaxen hair was long enough to fall several inches below her shoulders.

'I'm Eve Cavanaugh. You wanted to see me?' Although the woman's English was good, her voice bore the trace of an accent, but she had spoken too few words for Hardcastle to identify it.

Having introduced himself and Bradley, Hardcastle said, 'Your husband was arrested late last evening for attempting to murder a policeman, Mrs Cavanaugh.'

'Oh, that is not good.' Eve Cavanaugh suddenly sat down in an armchair, her knees clamped tightly together. 'Where was this, please?'

'In Richmond Road.'

'What was he doing there?'

'I was about to ask you the same question, Mrs Cavanaugh.'

The woman shrugged her bony shoulders. 'I don't know. He went out often for a walk in the evenings.'

'*Wo wurder dein Mann geboren?*' Bradley spoke suddenly and in rapid, impeccable German, surprising Hardcastle almost as much as he surprised Mrs Cavanaugh.

Eve Cavanaugh replied immediately. '*Mein Mann wurde in Frankfurt geboren.*' It was probably the surprise of being addressed in her native tongue that caught her wrong-footed and caused her to revert to her own language.

'*Und Sie?*'

'*In Frankfurt auch.*'

'Would you like to let me into the secret, Jack?' Hardcastle spoke quietly in an aside.

'Yes, sir. I asked Mrs Cavanaugh where her husband was born, and she told me it was Frankfurt. Then I asked her where she was born and she said she was born in Frankfurt as well.'

'Mrs Cavanaugh,' said Hardcastle, 'I have an order to search these premises.'

'But why? Why should you want to search my house?'

'Because you are German and so is your husband. And that means you are enemy aliens.' The DDI's statement was uncompromising and lacking in sympathy, but the country was at war and, doubtless, several civilians on his division had been killed in the air raid that night.

'Then do as you wish.' Eve Cavanaugh spoke in resigned tones, as though nothing else could possibly happen to her following the arrest of her husband and the authorities now knowing that she and her husband were German. It was noticeable, too, that her accent had become more pronounced, probably as a result of the stress caused by the arrival of the police and the news they bore.

Hardcastle deputed the woman sergeant to stay with the two women and to report any conversation between them. He hoped that Anna Tobin didn't speak German, but if she did, he told the sergeant to tell them to talk in English. Taking one of the constables with him, he told Jack Bradley to take the other one.

In the study, Hardcastle found a British passport in the name of Charles Cavanaugh. It had been issued in 1938 and showed his place of birth to have been Chepstow in Monmouthshire. This was clearly a false document; his wife had just told Detective Sergeant Jack Bradley that her husband had been born in Frankfurt.

Minutes later, Bradley joined Hardcastle in the study. 'I reckon this is the mate of the one we found at the Ropers' house, guv'nor,' he said, displaying a glove in an evidence bag. 'God knows why he didn't destroy it, but I'll send it off to the lab; they might find something that confirms it. My constable came across a room that looks as though Cavanaugh used it as a storeroom for his proceeds from burglaries. One interesting item was a brass table bell that he claimed had been stolen when his house was burgled. Personally, sir, I don't think his house was broken into at all. I reckon that the story about the bell was just a cover story designed to move suspicion away from him. Incidentally, we also found a small cameo which, no doubt, will please Mrs Austin.'

'If Charles Cavanaugh is an enemy agent, Jack, it beggars belief that he deliberately embarked on a series of burglaries, including staging his own, that in the end put him at greater risk of being arrested. Whtatever information he was after, it must be extremely valuable to the Abwehr. No doubt something secret to do with Moore's important contribution to the war effort. He doesn't seem to have found it, however. I think it's time we handed this lot over to the relevant department.' Hardcastle moved across to the telephone on Cavanaugh's desk and dialled Whitehall 1212, one of the most famous telephone numbers in Britain.

'Scotland Yard,' said the voice of the operator immediately.

'Special Branch, please.' Hardcastle waited until he was speaking to the duty officer. 'This is DDI Hardcastle of V Division. Be so good as to get Detective Superintendent Drew to telephone me at this number urgently.' He reeled off the number that was printed in the centre of the dial.

'But it's nearly three o'clock in the morning, sir,' the duty officer protested.

'I'm perfectly aware of the time, Inspector,' said Hardcastle. 'I've been on duty since God knows when arresting people,

so don't waste any more of my time.' He replaced the receiver
and turned to Bradley with a smile on his face. 'My father
would love to have been in on that conversation, Jack.'

Minutes later, Aubrey Drew returned Hardcastle's call.
'What is it, Wally?'

Hardcastle explained, as succinctly as possible, what had
occurred since the arrest of Charles Cavanaugh and what
had been found in the man's house.

'Good work, Wally,' said Drew. 'I'll be there later this
morning with my team. In the meantime, would you be so
good as to take Mrs Cavanaugh and Miss Tobin into custody
and lodge them at Kingston police station. And, perhaps, I
could rely on you to deal with the stolen property.'

'Yes, sir. I'll get one of my detective inspectors to return
it, when he has a spare moment.' Hardcastle was not pleased
that the donkey work should be passed down to him, but
managed to keep the sarcasm out of his voice. 'What about
the murder of the Ropers, sir? I'm sure that once the pistol
that was in Charles Cavanaugh's possession has been tested
by ballistics, it will prove to be the one that killed them.'

'I hope you're right, Wally,' said Drew. 'Or are you thinking
that his wife was a co-conspirator in the matter of espionage?
If it turns out that she was active in supporting her husband,
she'll probably hang anyway.'

'No, sir, I'm just thinking of getting a double murder off
my books.'

'Ah, I see. Well, Wally, that would seem to be a matter for
DAC Marriott. Perhaps you'd better have a word with him.'

The dawn was rising in the eastern sky by the time that
Hardcastle and Bradley got back to Putney police station.

'Sit down, Jack.' Hardcastle opened the bottom drawer of
his desk and took out a bottle of whisky and two glasses.
Pouring three fingers of Scotch into each glass, he pushed one
across to his sergeant. 'Where on earth did you learn to speak
fluent German, Jack?'

'My mother is Swiss, sir. She was born Mia Beck in Davos,
a German-speaking part of Switzerland. My father, Geoffrey,
was a keen skier and he went there in 1907 and met my mother

who was a waitress in one of the restaurants.' Bradley took a sip of his whisky. 'He brought her back to England and they married the same year. What you might call a whirlwind romance, I suppose. I was born two years later. As a result, I was brought up in a bilingual household.'

Hardcastle laughed. 'I should keep that to yourself, Jack, otherwise MI5 or Special Branch or some other arcane organization will poach you.'

It was six weeks later that Hardcastle received a call from Detective Superintendent Drew of Special Branch asking him to go to the Yard.

'I'm sorry you're still waiting for your scrambler telephone, Wally,' said Drew, when Hardcastle arrived at Scotland Yard.

'I suppose I'm fairly low on the list of priorities, sir.'

'It would seem so, Wally. However, I'll get on to them and gee them up. Now, to get down to business. As you were instrumental in arresting the Cavanaughs and Anna Tobin, I've been authorized to tell you the outcome,' Drew began. 'It turned out that Anna Tobin was indeed British, and was a member of Sir Oswald Mosley's British Union of Fascists. We'd had her under surveillance for a while, but then discontinued it. She was not considered to be anything more than a pawn, and her only interest in the BUF would seem to have been to sleep with as many of its members as possible.' Drew chuckled. 'Male or female. However, we have proof that she actively supported Cavanaugh in his attempts to acquire material from Moore's to pass to the Abwehr, although there's nothing to suggest he found what he was looking for. They were tight-lipped, of course. We were right, though. There was an enemy agent working at Moore's, but at the Kingston plant.'

'It seems very strange that Eve Cavanaugh should have been sent over here, given her accent.'

'I'm coming to that, Wally. We've discovered that Cavanaugh's real name is Ernst Jäger and he was a major in the Abwehr. His British passport was a very clever forgery presumably manufactured by the German government. Eve Cavanaugh's passport was a similar forgery and showed her to have been born in Halifax. The Yorkshire one, not the Canadian one,' he added.

'Unfortunately, we didn't know she was here,' continued Drew, making a rare admission of fallibility. 'God alone knows why she came, but she wouldn't have had any problems with the Immigration Service, given that she had a pukka British passport. Perhaps she didn't trust her husband and Anna Tobin to behave themselves, not that it made any difference. Incidentally, Hauptmann Konrad Fischer, whose body your people found in the Thames, was on his way to a meeting with Cavanaugh – or Jäger, I should say. The Government Cryptography Department managed to crack the code written in the letter and the papers in his briefcase, which turned out to be very useful and enabled us to make three more arrests.'

'Cavanaugh certainly gave the appearance of being the real thing,' said Hardcastle. 'What I was going to ask, sir, is why did he pretend that Anna Tobin was his wife?'

'Quite simply because his wife spoke with a German accent and, presumably, it was considered wise to keep her away from anybody who was English. It probably came as a blow when Eve turned up on his doorstep. And we've no idea how she found out where he was.'

'But surely to God, the Abwehr would have kept a watch on Eve, and yet she slipped away, presumably under the noses of the Gestapo.'

Aubrey Drew smiled. 'Despite the reputation the Germans seem to have acquired for super efficiency, Wally, they do sometimes make glaring errors. The Scottish police recently arrested a German agent who had just come ashore from a German submarine. His trousers were soaking wet and he had a small case in which the constable found a large German sausage. Well, you can't buy one of those in this country for love or money. All of which proves that the super-efficient Nazi regime sometimes makes mistakes.'

'What's going to happen to that little trio, then, sir?'

'It's happened,' said Drew in a matter-of-fact tone. 'Because Cavanaugh was a German officer, he had the privilege of being executed by firing squad at the Tower of London two weeks ago. His wife and Anna Tobin were each sentenced to ten years penal servitude. Rather lenient, I thought.'

'I reckon that clears up the murders of Frank and Helen Roper, then,' said Hardcastle. 'Our ballistics people confirmed that the Luger pistol Cavanaugh fired at PC Dodge was the weapon used to murder the Ropers.'

'Cavanaugh admitted murdering the Ropers, Wally,' said Drew. 'It seemed to the interrogating officer that it was almost a matter of Prussian pride that he'd done so.'

A detective constable knocked and entered. 'Excuse me, sir. Mr Hardcastle's clerk telephoned just now. He had taken a message from Mr Marriott's clerk to the effect that if Mr Hardcastle is still here, he's to see Mr Marriott as soon as possible.'

'Could be your move to A Division, Wally,' said Drew, winking.

'Or Special Branch, sir,' retorted Hardcastle.

Hardcastle stood up and left Drew's office to find out exactly what Marriott had in store for him.

GLOSSARY

AFS: auxiliary fire service.

AIR MINISTRY: department of government responsible for the Royal Air Force, later incorporated into the Ministry of Defence as MOD (Air).

ARP: air-raid precautions. Part of the Civil Defence organization. Among other tasks, air-raid wardens checked that the blackout regulations were observed, and assisted at bomb scenes.

AWOL: absent without leave.

BAG CARRIER: an officer, usually a sergeant, deputed to assist the senior investigating officer in a murder or other serious enquiry.

BAILIWICK: area of responsibility.

BEF: British Expeditionary Force in France and Flanders.

BELL, on the: using the bell on a police car as a warning to afford it precedence.

BLITZ: name given to the intensive raids on London by the Luftwaffe. (A shortening of the German word *blitzkrieg*: lightning war.)

BOMBARDIER: one rank below sergeant in the Royal Artillery, equal to a corporal in other regiments (except the Household Cavalry).

CHARLADY: a cleaning woman.

CHOKEY: a prison (ex Hindi).

CID: Criminal Investigation Department.

CMP: Corps of Military Police.

COLLAR, to feel a: to make an arrest.

DABS: fingerprints.

DAC: deputy assistant commissioner.

DANCERS, to take it on one's: to run or to escape.

DC: detective constable.

DCI: detective chief inspector.

DDI: divisional detective inspector.

D NOTICE: a government notice issued to news editors requiring them not to publish certain information for reasons of national security.

DUFF, up the: pregnant.

FEEL A COLLAR, to: to make an arrest.

FIREWATCHING: employees of large premises were required, by roster, to spend the night on duty to tackle incendiary bombs before they took hold.

GAMAGES: a London department store (now closed).

GBH: grievous bodily harm.

GREAT SCOTLAND YARD: location of an army recruiting office and a military police detachment. Not to be confused with New Scotland Yard, half a mile away in Whitehall.

GUNNERS, The: an informal term for the Royal Artillery. In the singular, the lowest rank of a member of that regiment (equivalent to a private soldier in some other regiments).

GUV or GUV'NOR: informal alternative to 'sir'.

HAMMER-LOCK-AND-BAR: a hold used by police when arresting a fractious prisoner.

HANDLEY Tommy: a popular wartime comedian responsible for ITMA (qv).

HAWKING HER MUTTON: leading a life of prostitution.

ITMA: an acronym for *It's That Man Again*, a popular radio show starring Tommy Handley, aired between 1939 and 1949 when Handley died.

KATE, IN THE: Cockney rhyming slang. Kate Carney – in the army.

KNOCKING SHOP: a brothel.

NICKED: arrested or stolen.

OCCURRENCE BOOK: handwritten record of *every* incident occurring in a police sub-division.

OLD BAILEY: Central Criminal Court in a street called Old Bailey.

PC: police constable.

PICCADILLY WINDOW: a monocle.

PICKFORDS: a large furniture removals company.

POLICE GAZETTE: official nationwide publication listing wanted person, etc. Now superseded by the Police National Computer (PNC).

PREVIOUS: prior convictions.

RAF: Royal Air Force.

REDCAPS: the Corps of Military Police.

RP: regimental police, not to be confused with the Corps of Military Police.

RSM: regimental sergeant major (a senior army warrant officer).

SHILLING: a pre-decimal coin equivalent to 5p.

SKIP *or* SKIPPER: an informal police alternative to detective-sergeant, station-sergeant, clerk-sergeant and sergeant.

SMOKE, The: London.

SQUADDY: a rank-and-file soldier. Plural: **SQUADDIES**.

SRN: state-registered nurse.

SYLVESTER, Victor: famous British bandleader of the 1940s who led a 'strict tempo' dance band and had his own radio programme.

TAPE(S): the chevron(s) indicating a non-commissioned officer's rank.

TERRITORIAL ARMY *or* TA: a volunteer force locally organized to provide a reserve of trained manpower that can be mobilised in the event of an emergency.

TUMBLE, a: sexual intercourse.

UXB: unexploded bomb.

WAR OFFICE: Department of State overseeing the army. (Now a part of the Ministry of Defence as MOD Army.)

WDC: woman detective constable.

***WEHRMACHT*:** German army.

WIPERS: Army slang for Ypres in Belgium, scene of several fierce Great War battles.

WPC: woman police constable.